AND THEN MY LIFE HAPPENED

ANA MURBY

ISBN 978-0-578-34816-2 (Paperback)
ISBN 978-0-578-34817-9 (Digital)

First Edition

Branded Gen, Inc.
2900 N Government Way #313, Coeur d'Alene, ID 83815
Brand People. Brand Products. Brand Industries.
www.brandedgen.com

Chapter One

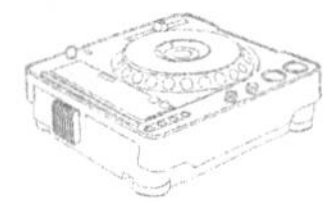

"DJ MADDOX!" THE CROWD chanted with a huge roar of excitement. DJ Maddox, a young man in his early thirties, paced back and forth behind a curtain, feeling hesitant. No, that wasn't the right word; anxious was a better word. For a while now, he'd had this deep feeling of anxiety and emptiness whenever he was about to go on stage. He kept it to himself of course. He didn't want anyone to know that a well-known celebrity such as himself wasn't living his best life. No, he couldn't let that news make the headlines. That would ruin him.

He paced like a madman behind the curtain, clenching his glass of vodka so tightly he could have crushed it. He wanted to drop the glass to the ground, the shattering sound echoing in his ears as he escaped this tormenting feeling that the walls were closing in on him. He felt like he was suffocating.

With each shout from the crowd, his heart pounded harder, and his labored breathing intensified. A few tears streamed down his tortured face as he drummed his fingers on his glass. He saw a groupie for a fellow DJ approaching him with a grin, so he composed himself, drank his vodka in one gulp, and then slammed the glass down onto a nearby table before putting on a fake smile and jogging onto the stage.

"Another lit show, Maddox!" one of his female groupies said, wrapping her arms around his waist and kissing his cheek.

DJ Maddox sighed. "Thanks."

She walked away toward a nearby room, leaving DJ Maddox alone with his dark thoughts. *You could do it, you know. You could do it right now. You know you want to anyway, so why are you waiting?* his thoughts screamed at him. He saw a table with some unopened beers on it and grabbed one. He popped off the top and drank half the beer in one gulp before letting out another long sigh, this one followed by a few unexpected tears. Seconds later some of his friends came walking toward him, smoking, drinking, and laughing, so again he composed himself.

They ushered him into a room with adoring fans and groupies, most of whom were women all too willing to give themselves to these men. This was not unusual behavior for DJ Maddox. He was a very handsome man, full of irresistible charm, and whenever the women found out about his job, they were putty in his hands.

Once in the room, he finished his first beer and then reached for a bottle of rum sitting on a table. He started drinking it and mingling, smiling on the outside but screaming on the inside, fighting the dark voices that tormented his thoughts all day, every day.

DJ Maddox lay in his bed, wide awake, the sun shining on his face and a woman's arm draped over his bare chest. He looked at her and noticed she was one of the women who had thrown herself at him after his show last night. He groaned, grabbing at his head—another hangover. He wiggled his way out of the bed without waking her up and put on a shirt and pants before heading out to his balcony.

He stood out in the humid August morning air and listened to the hustle and bustle of Manhattan below his thirteen-story building. He took a deep, labored breath; closed his eyes; and shed some tears. These tears weren't the result of someone having a bad day, week, or even month. No, these tears were formed from years of pain stuffed down so far you couldn't see the beginning of it anymore.

He took in another deep breath, held it for a few agonizing seconds, and then let it out slowly, wiping his eyes again after more tears formed. He climbed onto the wooden table on the balcony and stood there for a second before shakily moving forward onto the ledge.

He looked down at the ant-sized cars and people below, breathing heavily while the tears rolled down his cheeks like a faucet turned on full blast. *Come on. Do it! You know you want to!* His thoughts screamed at him like a heckler. He closed his eyes tightly, lifted his foot like he was going to walk forward, and then shook his head, opening his eyes and weeping bitterly. *No, I can't.* He slowly stepped back onto the wooden table, crying and whispering, "I can't do it," over and over again as he got back down on the balcony floor.

He heard the woman calling his name from the penthouse, so he quickly wiped his eyes with his shirt, cleared his throat, and tried to calm down the best he could before turning around with a fake smile ready on his face.

"There you are. I was searching all over for you." She started, hugging him with a grimace. "Wow, you look awful. You must have had more to drink than I did last night, and

I was hammered before your show even started." The woman cackled, unaware of anything that had just happened.

DJ Maddox chuckled awkwardly. "Yeah, I am definitely hungover. I think I am going to try to get some more sleep."

She kissed his cheek. "That's fine. I need to go to work now anyway. I will see you at your concert tonight."

"Tonight?" he said, confused.

She snickered. "Wow, you are hammered. Yeah, it's Sunday. Tonight is your final show for the Kick-Off to the End of Summer Festival."

DJ Maddox nodded slowly as she walked out the door. He turned back toward the balcony and sighed heavily. As he began to hyperventilate, he ran into the kitchen, rummaging through his cupboards until he found what he was looking for: a bottle of vodka.

He took the top off and downed half of it before gasping for air. He started to cry bitter tears again while screaming out in angst, hoping his neighbors wouldn't try to come check on him; he wanted to be left alone right now. He finished the bottle in another gulp and made a decision. He walked to the bedroom, packed a bag, and headed out the front door with intent.

"Michael, have you seen DJ Maddox? He needs to be on stage in five minutes," his agent asked one of Maddox's best friends and fellow DJs who was walking by.

"Nope, sorry. I haven't seen him since last night. We got pretty hammered, so maybe he's still asleep," he said, walking off with a chuckle.

DJ Maddox's agent sneered then grabbed his phone and dialed his number angrily. It went straight to voicemail—again.

He grunted. "Maddox, you drunk idiot, Chuck here again. Not sure where you are, but you should be here. Your set starts in four minutes." He hung up and took another lap around the area to search for him.

DJ Maddox pulled his street bike into a parking spot rather quickly, kicking up some sand on the ground. He stepped off of his bike and, taking off his helmet, left it on his bike. He ran his hands through his raven-colored hair a few times, trying to make it look decent before heading toward the motel lobby. He walked in, heard the chime of the bell over the door, and jumped.

The young motel clerk watched this newcomer closely. He had a five o'clock shadow and was wearing a sweatshirt, tank top, sweatpants, sandals, sunglasses, and a backpack on his back. He definitely didn't look familiar to her and seemed overdressed for a hot August day. He approached the front desk with a smirk.

"Good afternoon. Welcome to the Hampton Jewel Motel. My name is Vanessa. Did you need to check in?" she asked, staring at him intently with her soft brown eyes.

"Yeah, I didn't make a reservation. This was kind of a last-minute trip. Is there a room available?" he asked, hopeful.

She nodded. "Yes, we have one room available."

"Good, I will take it." He spoke curtly.

"For how many nights?" she asked, getting some paperwork from a filing cabinet behind her.

"Do I have to answer that right now?" he asked. "I'm not sure yet."

Vanessa smiled. "That's fine. Please fill this out for me." She handed him a reservation slip.

"Do I need to fill this out?" he asked.

"Yes, it's for our records. You aren't running away from the law, are you?" she asked in a joking tone.

He shook his head. "No, I'm just trying to keep a low profile. I don't want people to know I am here."

"Why? Are you famous or something?" she joked again.

Maddox looked at her, surprised. "Actually, yes, I am."

"Oh, really? Are you an actor, musician, or something else?" she asked, intrigued.

"I'm a DJ...DJ Maddox," he said arrogantly, waiting for her to be impressed, but all she did was stare at him with an awkward smile. She genuinely didn't know who he was. He frowned and shrugged. "Don't worry about it. I'll use my real name; not many people know me by that name anyway." He started filling out the form.

"I'm sorry. I don't know who you are. I haven't listened to a lot of music lately. I have a friend who listens to techno music. Maybe I can ask her if she knows who you are," Vanessa suggested.

"No! I'm here to get away from people who know me Don't say anything to anyone, okay?" he begged, handing her the paper roughly.

Vanessa was taken aback by his rough tone but kept her composure. "Of course. Enjoy your stay, Mr. Maddox." She handed him his key.

"Just called me Brody please. I don't know why I put my last name on there anyway since people know it," he murmured as he walked outside.

Brody dropped his bag on the floor at the motel room door and flopped onto the bed face first. He breathed into the sheets softly for a few seconds before rolling over and sitting up. He grabbed his phone and turned it on. After several minutes of various notifications, his phone was quiet.

He only spent a few minutes scrolling through the texts from his agent, a few of his friends, and some random girls he had hooked up with and apparently given his phone number to in the past. They were all trying to figure out where he was. He dropped the phone on the bed with a groan, pulled a bottle of rum from his bag, and started drinking.

He was halfway done with the bottle when his phone rang several more times. He kept shutting the calls off, but they kept coming. More texts too—all from his agent—and they weren't very nice ones either. He finished his bottle of rum, tossed the empty bottle on the bed, and grabbed his phone. He had finally had enough of the intrusion. He muttered a few choice words as he shut his phone down, deciding to keep it that way until further notice. He tossed the phone back onto the bed next to his empty bottle and sighed with relief.

"Hello again, Mr. Mad—I mean Brody. How is the room? Is it to your liking?" Vanessa asked with a genuine smile as he walked into the office again.

He stuck his hands into his jacket pockets and shrugged. "Yeah, it's fine I guess. It's not like the usual places I stay in. They have a more expensive style, but it will do. Is there a place around here where I can eat?"

"Of course. There are many places on the boardwalk. Most of it is seafood, so I hope you like that," Vanessa said.

"Any place you would recommend specifically?" he asked, sounding annoyed.

"I personally enjoy Rocky's Clam Shack. It's not too far from here, walking distance actually. If you go out these doors and to the right, it's five doors down from here. Use my name when you order; Rocky will give you a discount," she advised him with a smile.

Brody chortled disrespectfully. "Money isn't a problem for me. I don't need a discount. I'm famous, remember?"

Vanessa nodded. "Of course, I understand." She went back to her paperwork silently.

He could tell he had probably offended her, but he didn't care too much right now—he was starving. "Thanks for the suggestion," he said as he walked out the door quickly.

Brody stepped up to the door of the Clam Shack as an elderly couple was coming out. He saw many people crowded inside and realized he could be recognized at any moment. He grabbed his sunglasses and put them on before walking inside. Once inside, he felt like all eyes were on him; that was usually how it was when he walked into a room. He took a deep breath and made his way to the counter to order, trying not to look as suspicious as he felt. He willed himself to be less paranoid so as not to draw attention to himself.

"What can I get you?" Rocky, a middle-aged man, asked with a toothy grin.

Brody looked at the menu and realized he was hungrier than he thought. "I will take the clam fritters, a basket of fried shrimp, the fish and chips, and a chocolate banana shake."

"Sure thing. What's the name?"

Brody paused before answering. He wasn't going to give his real name, so he thought fast: "Dave." Rocky nodded and wrote the name down on the slip before he handed it to his cook. Brody paid for his food and walked away to find a seat.

He sat at a table near a window and stared out at the people walking by; they all seemed so happy and carefree. He wondered what that was like. He hadn't been carefree in years. He frowned, thinking about all his troubles. He went back up to the counter to order a beer and then back to his seat to wait again, popping off the cap of the beer with his keys. He downed more than half of it in one gulp.

"Dave, your order is up," Rocky called loudly. Brody stood up and grabbed his food, his mouth watering and his stomach roaring as he carried the tray back to his seat. He sat down and dug into his food like a ravenous beast.

Brody started back to the motel in a food coma and saw Vanessa locking the office door before heading to her car. She spotted him walking toward his room and smiled warmly, waving. "How was dinner?" she called out to him, walking toward him. Brody was surprised that her bubbly tone wasn't grating on his nerves as it was before; he assumed it was because he was no longer hangry.

"It was amazing, I haven't eaten that good in a long time. Thanks again for the suggestion, um, I'm sorry...what is your name again?" Brody asked.

"It's Vanessa. I'm glad you liked the food. Rocky's is my favorite place to eat at on the boardwalk. Are you going to check out the boardwalk now? There's no place like it," Vanessa suggested with a grin.

Brody saw a group of teens walking by. "I don't think so. It's too crowded right now, plus I'm tired. I'm going to try to sleep."

"Okay then, but before you leave, you should check out the boardwalk. It's a wonderful place—one of my favorite places in all the world."

Brody cackled unintentionally. "In the world, huh? You must not get out much. I've been all over the world, and I can say with confidence, there are many more spectacular places around the world than a boardwalk. No offense."

"I agree. There are many other places that have their charms too. I guess when you are born here, you kind of grow attached to it more than other people," Vanessa said with a friendly smile.

Brody tried to stifle a yawn.

"Well, have a good night, Brody," Vanessa said, waving and starting back to her car.

Brody watched her walking away and smirked. *She isn't bad to look at, coming or going*. He walked into his motel room while coming up with a plan to try to woo her.

Chapter Two

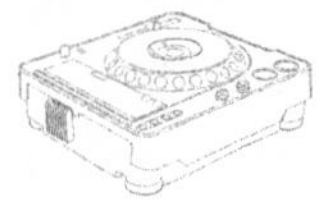

Brody lay in bed, arms sprawled out and begrudgingly wide awake. He looked at the alarm clock on the nightstand next to him—8:30 at night. He had been lying in bed for about two hours and hadn't slept at all. He couldn't believe it; he was so exhausted. But why was he surprised he couldn't sleep? In his line of business, he needed to be a night owl. He was so used to it by now that sleeping during the night was only a pipe-dream. He groaned, rolled over, and closed his eyes again, tossing and turning all night until finally falling asleep close to four in the morning.

"Good morning, Brody. How did you sleep?" Vanessa greeted him as he came into the office wearing the same thing he had worn the day before. He seemed even less in the mood to chat this morning than he did yesterday afternoon.

"I didn't sleep. Where can I get some pancakes?"

"There aren't many places open right now on the boardwalk. You will have to go into town to find a place to eat." Vanessa answered.

Brody rubbed his eyes and yawned. "Okay, do you happen to have a list of the restaurants around here?"

Vanessa bent down under her desk and rifled through some papers before standing back up and handing him a few brochures. "Feel free to check these flyers out. They have menus on them, so you can get a better idea of what you want," Vanessa suggested. Brody leaned over the counter and started looking through the flyers. Vanessa caught a whiff of him; he wreaked of alcohol, but she didn't let on that she noticed it as she went back to her paperwork.

He skimmed through the brochures but was more interested in checking Vanessa out. In fact, that was his whole idea for coming in here anyway. He didn't care where he ate breakfast; he rarely ate breakfast anyway. He just wanted to see this girl again. Something about her captivated him, and it wasn't just her face. Maybe it was how she kept a calm and respectful tone even when he was rude to her.

He stole a glance of her, unnoticed. She was probably about his age, maybe a little younger. She smelled like peaches and cream and was rather attractive from the profile he was staring at. He opened the second brochure and pretended to read this one too but stole another glance at her instead.

He saw the intense look on her face as she wrote in a thick notebook, pushing her long, wavy brown hair behind her ears whenever it fell into her face. He pushed the brochures toward her with a smirk. "Did you already eat?" he asked, leaning against the counter coolly.

Vanessa looked up at him. "I'm sorry…what?"

"Do you want to join me for breakfast? My treat," Brody offered boldly.

Vanessa smiled, flattered. "That's very nice of you, but I can't." She looked back down at her paperwork.

Brody looked at her with a proud grin. "Is it the bike? We can take your car if you're uncomfortable on a motorcycle."

Vanessa looked up at him and smirked. "That's not it."

"Is it the sleeve tattoos and gauges? I may look a little rough around the edges, but many girls find that I am as cuddly as a teddy bear," Brody persisted.

Vanessa was impressed by his overconfident spirit and snickered. "I can't go because I am on the clock, and I already ate breakfast."

Brody smiled flirtatiously. "So if you weren't on the clock and if you hadn't eaten breakfast, then you would have gone out with me? Is that what you are saying?"

Vanessa started to blush uncontrollably at the awkward situation she found herself in.

She was about to answer him, but he cut her off. "You don't have to answer. I think I like not knowing your answer more. It gives me something to think about until the next time I ask you out," he said, winking at her before walking out the door. Vanessa went back to her paperwork, chuckling.

"When does your shift start, Kate?" Vanessa asked her best friend as they ate lunch in the motel office during Vanessa's lunch break.

"I need to be at the arcade in half an hour. Did you know that Doug decided to do half off games at the arcade for all of August?" Kate said, not sounding excited about it.

"That seems like a nice promotion. Why don't you seem happy about it?" Vanessa asked.

Kate groaned. "It means the place will be overrun with loud kids. My head already hurts by the end of the night on a normal day because of the noise. Now it will be worse."

Vanessa grimaced "When is he starting this promotion?"

"He started it yesterday since it was the first day of August. He said he wanted the kids to enjoy their last month of summer, but I think he just wants more money," Kate said. Vanessa nudged her playfully.

Kate snickered. "I'm kidding. Doug is a good boss. He loves making people happy. He said he plans to do this promotion every August if it works out this time. Tomorrow is your day off, right? Are you going to come to the beach with Daniel and me?" Kate asked.

Vanessa shrugged. "I told my mom I would go shopping with her. She is still looking for the perfect birthday gift for my dad."

"Okay, well, just message me if you do plan to meet us so we know to look for you. I want to see you as much as I can before you leave," Kate told her.

Vanessa nodded and hugged her. "Of course."

"Okay, time for me to go. Love you. Have I told you how happy I am that you are home?" Kate asked with a grin.

"Only every time I come home for the summer," Vanessa said with a chuckle.

"Well, it's true every time I say it. I miss you so much; you have no idea," Kate responded, walking out the door and bumping into Brody unexpectedly. Her eyes widened, and her mouth gaped open in shock. Vanessa walked out the door quickly after seeing Kate start to freak out.

"Oh my goodness, you are DJ Ma–" Vanessa covered her friend's mouth and whispered to her about his desire to stay unannounced. Kate nodded and collected herself. "I am a huge fan." Kate took hold of his hand and shook it for the both of them. Brody looked around frantically.

"Brody, this is my friend Kate. I mentioned her to you yesterday, remember?" Vanessa chimed in.

Brody finally breathed. "Oh, I see…hi, Kate."

Kate giggled like the starstruck fan she was. "I have so many things I want to talk with you about, but I don't have time right now. Please don't leave Hampton Beach until I get a chance to talk to you again."

Brody shrugged. "I have no plans to leave anytime soon."

Kate nodded. "Cool, and your secret is safe with me. I won't tell anyone you are here. I don't think they would believe me even if I did." She walked off excitedly.

Vanessa chuckled. "That was hilarious. She was not expecting that. I'm sure it made her day."

Brody grunted. "Are you sure she won't tell anyone anything?"

"Maybe just my brother; she's dating him. She has been my best friend since middle school. You can trust her to be true to her word. Did you get your pancakes?" Vanessa asked.

"Yes, I did. I am going to try to rest now. I'm not sure if you have some sort of cleaning service here, but please do not let them disturb me. I am a very clean person, so I won't need it for the duration of my stay."

Vanessa nodded. "Okay, I will make sure the cleaning crew knows that." She went back inside as the office phone rang. Brody walked quickly back to his room.

Chapter Three

BRODY WOKE UP FEELING less than refreshed, which was ironic considering he had managed to fall asleep Monday afternoon and stayed asleep until Tuesday morning. He took all the empty alcohol bottles from the previous day off his bed and threw them into the already overflowing trashcan next to the TV. He grabbed his phone instinctively but grimaced and put the phone back in his bag. He could feel his hangover pounding now and made his way to the shower.

After he was more presentable, he started toward the office, determined to get Vanessa to go out with him today. He noticed a new face behind the desk once he walked inside. An elderly man was standing there looking through some files. Brody quickly fumbled around for his sunglasses in his pocket. He knew it was probably a stretch that this old man knew who he was, but he wasn't going to take any chances. He walked up to the man nonchalantly, clearing his throat to get his attention.

The man looked up. "Good morning, sir. Welcome to the Hampton Jewel. Are you already checked in?" the elderly man asked nicely.

"Yes, I'm good.... What happened to that Vanessa girl who works here?" Brody asked.

"Oh, Vanessa doesn't work here. She was just filling in for me while I was out of town for a few days. She works down at Rocky's Clam Shack."

Brody nodded slowly. "Thanks for the information." He walked outside and stood there for a few seconds, looking around. It was still morning, so he assumed that Rocky's wasn't open yet. He pulled his sweatshirt hood over his head and walked cautiously down the boardwalk.

"Thank you again for coming with me to find Dad's birthday gift. I think he is really going to like this one," Vanessa's mom said with a grin.

"Mom, Dad always likes every gift you give him," Vanessa reassured her.

"I know he does, sweetie. I just like to top myself every year. It's a personal challenge for me. So what are you doing for the rest of the day? Are you spending it with Daniel and Kate at the beach?" her mother asked. "Yeah, I guess so. You know I don't like swimming that much. I'll just sit under the umbrella and read a book," Vanessa said in between bites of her lobster roll.

Brody walked by Rocky's and caught a glimpse of Vanessa and a woman laughing at a table. He walked in and went right up to the table, sunglasses still on.

Vanessa looked up and smiled. "Oh hey, Brody, how are you?"

"I was going to stop by and see you in the motel lobby this morning, but you weren't there. The old man told me you don't actually work there," Brody said in a short tone, like he was upset she hadn't mentioned it to him, herself.

"Yes, that's right. I was just helping Fred out while he was in town for a business thing. I work here actually. Today is my day off, so if I weren't here eating, you wouldn't have found me here either," Vanessa explained innocently.

"Sweetie, who is this?" Vanessa's mom whispered, looking confused.

"Oh, I'm sorry, Mom. This is Brody. He's staying at the motel."

Her mother looked at him and held her hand out. "Hi, I'm Grace, Vanessa's mom. Nice to meet you, Brody. That is a very masculine name.... How long have you been a friend of Vanessa's?"

Brody shook her hand, grinning with self-importance. "We just met the other day."

"Why don't you join us? I'll buy you something to eat. What will you have?" Grace spoke in a mothering tone.

He looked at Vanessa smugly. "I guess you didn't tell her who I was." He turned to her mother and chuckled. "Thanks for the offer, ma'am, but I can buy my own food. I have plenty of money."

Grace stood to her feet slowly. "Brody, don't deny me the chance at some joy. Giving is my passion. I insist. What will you have?"

"I will take the clam fritters please," he said simply. Grace smiled and walked away.

Brody sat down next to Vanessa and let out a sigh. "I haven't said the word 'please' to anyone in ages. She is scary with that soft but stern tone."

Vanessa chuckled, trying again to ignore the overwhelming stench of alcohol on his breath. "Yeah, she takes her giving very seriously. Like she said, it's a passion of hers." Brody took his sunglasses off to rub his eyes, revealing how bloodshot they were. She tried not to let on that she had noticed as he put them back on.

Vanessa started to eat her lobster roll again, and Brody slyly admired her features once more while she ate. She was classically beautiful, unlike the girls he was used to being around; he called them "manufactured girls." Those women wore tons of makeup, so it was hard to tell what they really looked like. Vanessa didn't wear any makeup, or if she did, it wasn't noticeable.

He smiled to himself as he watched her quietly eating her lobster roll with poise. He also noticed she didn't dress like all the girls he was used to being around. She dressed conservatively, leaving everything to the imagination. He found it oddly intriguing.

He leaned back in his chair and cleared his throat. "So when are you going to let me take you out?" He stretched his arm out behind Vanessa's chair.

Vanessa chuckled nervously. "What makes you think I want to go out with you?"

"Most women do. They like my job. I guess it's an aphrodisiac to them," he explained, grinning at her.

She couldn't see his eyes through the sunglasses, but she assumed they matched the arrogance in his smile.

Vanessa took a sip of her iced tea. "So you assume I am 'just like all the girls,' huh? Easily amused by your profession? Remember, I didn't know who you were."

Brody chuckled in disbelief. "Your friend is a huge fan of mine. I'm sure she's made you listen to my stuff before, and I'm sure she talks about me. I bet you knew about me more than you let on. I think you were playing hard to get, and I like that."

Vanessa blushed uncontrollably again. His flirtatious

personality was hard to resist. "We haven't seen much of each other in the last several years, so she hasn't had a chance to mention you or your music to me. She has had me listen to some techno music before, but I'm not a fan. No offense to your line of work." Vanessa said.

"None taken. I know it's not for everyone. What kind of music do you like listening to?" he asked, scooting closer to her. Vanessa's mother came back to the table with his meal just then, so he moved back to where he was originally, much to Vanessa's relief.

"Thank you for the meal," Brody said respectfully.

"You are most welcome. So what are you in town for?" Grace asked.

"I am here strictly for pleasure," Brody said, biting into a clam fritter and then realizing how that must have sounded. His face went blank. Grace looked at him with a quizzical eyebrow.

"I didn't mean that the way it sounded. I just meant I'm not working or anything. I am strictly here to rest and clear my mind," Brody reiterated, embarrassed. Vanessa laughed to herself.

"Oh, I see. I thought you meant you were here to fornicate," Grace said with a smirk.

Vanessa laughed loudly as Brody choked on his food, taken aback by what she had said. "Fornicate? No, ma'am. I don't plan to do any of that anytime soon. I have had my fill of that recently…I mean…I am going to stop talking now and eat." Brody fumbled over his sentence, blushing uncontrollably. Vanessa was enjoying this moment so much, laughing so hard she was no longer making any sound. Brody found it very cute but at the same time annoying because it was aimed at him. He didn't want to be the butt of someone's joke, but boy, did he like the sound of her laugh, even if it was at his expense.

Grace giggled. "I am just messing with you, kiddo. You seem a little rigid. I was trying to loosen you up. Thank you for being a good sport, Brody."

"My mom's other passion is making people laugh," Vanessa piped up after collecting herself. Brody simply nodded and continued eating quietly.

"Sweetie, I need to head out and finish the preparations for your father's birthday party tomorrow. Brody, feel free to join us. There's no reason for you to be alone the whole time you're. I enjoy meeting new people, so I hope you will come," Grace said, hugging her daughter and tousling Brody's hair before leaving.

"I like your mom. She's bold and funny, even if she used me as the butt of her joke," he commented, fixing his hair.

"I'm glad you were a good sport. My mom doesn't mean any harm when she picks on people. She is a very friendly soul. The party is going to be at six o'clock tomorrow evening; I will take you if you want to go. Be in front of the motel office at five."

Brody nodded and started eating again. "You didn't answer my question yet. What kind of music you like to listen to?" Brody asked again, wiping his face with a napkin.

"I don't really have time to listen to music," Vanessa responded quickly.

Brody could tell she didn't want to elaborate, so he changed subjects. "You know, this could be considered our first date."

Vanessa smirked. "I don't think so. My mom doesn't usually buy the meals when I'm on a date."

Brody nodded, chuckling. "Okay, you got me there. So you *do* date."

"What? You thought I was hidden under a rock or something? I have been out with a few people in my lifetime," Vanessa said with a grin.

Brody inadvertently chuckled at her expense. "Only a few? I can't even count how many girls I have been with." He cleared his throat and instantly regretted what he had said when he saw how Vanessa reacted to the comment. It got awkwardly silent as Brody looked around and saw a huge group of people coming into the restaurant.

"Do you want to get out of here?" Vanessa asked after some time.

Brody nodded. "Yeah, but hold on. I wanna grab a beer. Do you want one?" Vanessa shook her head. He jumped from his seat and went to order one As Vanessa waited for him outside. He started sipping the beer as he walked out the door.

"Come with me. I'm heading to the beach to meet up with Kate and my brother. Don't worry. We have a secluded area we usually hang out in, not too many people around." Brody looked uneasy but followed her anyway. They walked the boardwalk silently for a few minutes.

"This boardwalk is interesting. I can see why you like it. I walked it earlier and bought a sweatshirt and sweatpants," Brody commented, sipping his beer. Vanessa didn't respond. "I'm sorry for what I said earlier, about the women. I don't know why I said that," Brody apologized, letting his guard down a little.

"So it's not true?" Vanessa asked.

"Oh, it's true, but I didn't need to go bragging about it like I'm proud of it," Brody responded candidly.

"So you aren't proud of it?" Vanessa remarked, intrigued.

"I was at some point in time, but I don't think I am anymore," Brody told her, taking another sip of his beer. Vanessa glanced at him and saw a glimpse into a vulnerable part of him that he tried not to show her but just couldn't help it. They walked in silence again.

Brody went back to his self-important demeanor suddenly and smirked. "So would you let me take you on a real date?"

"You don't give up easily, do you?" Vanessa asked, sounding slightly annoyed.

"Not when it is something I really want," Brody said, finishing his beer.

"I'm a Christian," Vanessa told him offhandedly.

Brody shrugged. "So? I've been with a few women who were Christians. I don't discriminate."

Vanessa sighed heavily. "Yeah, I don't really have time for a commitment right now."

"Whoa, I didn't say a commitment; I said a date. You don't have time to go out with me just once?" he protested. Vanessa didn't respond, but her face said a lot. "Never mind. Forget I asked. I didn't mean to pressure you," Brody apologized sincerely, trying to drain out any remnants of beer from his bottle before throwing it away in a nearby trashcan.

"I grew up believing that dating is meant for the purpose of finding a spouse one day, and I am not looking for that right now," Vanessa explained finally.

"Wow, that is deep…and so not how I have been viewing dating," Brody confessed with an awkward chuckle.

"Why are you here in Hampton Beach? You aren't here just to hit on me, are you?" Vanessa asked jokingly as they stepped onto the sand.

Brody snickered. "Very funny. No, you were not on my list of accomplishments when I got here, but the fact that you are rejecting me like you are is making you more and more irresistible," he confessed.

Vanessa was flattered by the compliment but didn't want to show it, so she kept the focus on him. "So why are you really here?" Vanessa waved at Kate and her brother in the distance while waiting for him to respond. Brody saw Kate's eyes widen as she leaned over to Vanessa's brother and whispered something to him. Brody swallowed a lump in his throat and looked at Vanessa, concerned. She smiled. "Everything will be okay. Just try to have fun."

Brody could feel his heart pounding in his chest, and his palms were getting sweaty. He took a deep breath and nodded slowly. "Can I get back to you with my answer? I'm not ready to answer such a big question."

Vanessa wanted to laugh. After all, it wasn't a huge question. It shouldn't have been tough to answer, but she could see his demeanor changing as she got another glimpse of vulnerability from him. She nodded. "Of course." As they got closer to her brother and Kate, Vanessa decided to try to keep the conversations light today, for Brody's sake.

Chapter Four

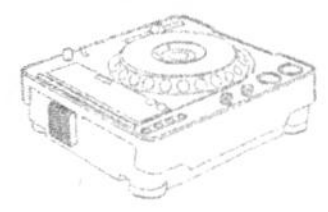

"Hey guys," Vanessa said, hugging her brother and Kate. They sat down under the tent.

"Who is this?" Daniel turned to face Brody, hand stretched out.

"I'm Brody," he said simply.

"Nice to meet you Brody. I'm Vanessa's twin brother, Daniel, and yes, I will answer your question—I am the oldest twin," Daniel said with a straight face.

Brody chuckled awkwardly because Vanessa and Daniel looked very different. Daniel had a much darker skin tone than Vanessa, and in his mind, there was no way they were twins even though they did look to be the same age.

Vanessa groaned. "Daniel, no one ever believes that."

"They aren't meant to believe it. Everyone knows we aren't twins; it's pretty obvious. It's just a joke to lighten the mood," Daniel explained to Brody, patting him on the back.

"Hi again Brody," Kate said in a giggly voice.

Brody smiled nervously. "Hi, Kate."

Daniel cleared his throat. "I am also Kate's boyfriend, Brody."

Vanessa slapped her brother playfully on the shoulder. "Daniel, leave him alone. You are always picking on people."

"It's not picking; I'm trying to loosen him up. He looks scared," Daniel protested.

Kate grunted. "He's trying to stay anonymous, Daniel. Of course he will be scared being around a lot of people. Let's just relax and have some fun."

"How did it go shopping for Dad?" Daniel asked, grabbing a bottle of water from the ice chest.

"She found a nice gift," Vanessa answered.

"So, Brody, what brings you to Hampton Beach? Have you been here before?" Daniel asked.

"I haven't been here before. It just seemed like a nice place to check out, I guess. I'm here getting clarity," Brody said.

"Clarity on what?" Daniel prodded innocently.

"Daniel, leave him alone. He wants to keep his business private, sweetie," Kate piped up, kissing him on the cheek.

Two hours later, Kate got called into work, so Daniel drove her. As Vanessa was about to walk away, she looked at Brody. He was staring at the ocean pensively. Vanessa watched him silently, wondering what was going on.

"Are you ready to go, or do you wanna stay longer?" Vanessa asked softly.

Brody turned around and smiled warmly. "I'm going to stay here a little longer. The waves lapping on the shore and the salty sea air are so peaceful."

Vanessa walked closer to him and laid a gentle hand on his shoulder. "Is everything okay? Do you want me to leave you alone?"

"No, I think I need you to stay," he said, his voice wavering. Vanessa nodded and turned to face the ocean too. They didn't say a word for several minutes. They just stood there listening to the waves.

"I think I'm depressed," Brody started haphazardly, glancing at Vanessa before looking back at the ocean. "I think I have been for the last four years, maybe five years." Brody let his tears fall now. "I get anxiety attacks before each of my shows. I can't breathe, my heart pounds and feels heavy, and I have been doing a whole lot of random crying too."

"And the drinking? Did that start five years ago too?" Vanessa asked with a serious look on her face. Brody gave her a sidelong glance before turning back to the ocean once more. "I didn't think you noticed that. No, I was doing that and some drugs too as soon I broke into the music scene, but after a year and a half of drugs, I quit that. All the alcohol is probably because of this though. Usually I'm drunk when I'm on stage; I'm a functional drunk apparently. I drink so much because then I don't have to feel all this inner turmoil." Brody looked at Vanessa, expecting to see judgement on her face but found what looked like compassion.

"You aren't happy?" Vanessa asked.

Brody snickered. "You know, you would think I would be; after all, I have my dream career. I have a ton of money, fans, and girls, and I travel the globe. Shouldn't I be happier than I am?"

She took a breath and searched for the right thing to say to him. "The problem with happiness is that it's fleeting; it's based on circumstances. You need joy if you want something constant."

"How do I get joy?" Brody asked.

Vanessa smiled. "I know how to find joy, but I don't know if you will like the answer."

"Try me," Brody said.

"You find joy in Christ...only in Christ," Vanessa told him.

Brody chortled. "Is that a fact?"

Vanessa shrugged. "Like I said, you probably wouldn't like the answer, but it's true." They turned back toward the ocean and stared at it quietly.

"Sorry for dumping all that on you, but you asked me earlier what brought me here, so I told you," Brody explained after some time.

"Why here? Why didn't you find a place closer to you to lie low?" Vanessa asked.

"I'm well known in New York, where I'm from. I couldn't find a place there to lie low without someone finding me. As for coming here, I don't know why I am here exactly. It might sound funny, but I felt like I was told by an inner voice to come here. Does that make any sense?" Brody confessed.

Vanessa grinned. "It makes sense to me. God is my inner voice—maybe it was him talking to you." Brody chuckled in disbelief. "Thank you for your honesty, Brody. I really appreciate you opening up to me like you did. I need to go now though. I have a Bible study at my church that I need to speak at today. Will you be okay if I leave you?" Vanessa asked, still concerned.

Brody nodded vehemently. "Oh yeah, I am better now that I told you all that. Go ahead—if you got places to be, I don't want to keep you. I'm going to head back to the motel and just rest. Today took a lot out of me."

They started toward the boardwalk and parted ways at the grass near the parking lot where Vanessa was parked. Vanessa watched as Brody walked away, his head downcast and hands in his pockets.

She felt a nudge in her heart to go back to Brody. She

sighed. *Lord, now? I have Bible study.* She started walking toward her car, but the feeling wouldn't go away; in fact, it intensified. She sighed once more. *God, I know your timing is always perfect, but this doesn't seem perfect to me.* Vanessa walked a few steps forward and grabbed the door handle before she stopped and heard God speak strongly to her: *Go now!* "Okay, Lord, I'm going," Vanessa said out loud, turning back toward the boardwalk. She didn't see him anywhere, which confused her. She knew he wasn't that fast.

Suddenly she saw him head out of a store with a brown paper bag. She watched as he opened it and put it to his lips. She shook her head and went back to her car quickly. She got in, drove to the motel, and waited outside his door for him to show up.

After ten minutes, he finally came into view, still drinking from the brown paper bag. Vanessa tried to stay calm as he approached her with a shocked look on his face.

"Hey, I wasn't expecting to see you here. I thought you had somewhere to go."

"Yeah, I did, but it seems God had other plans for me. What do you have there, Brody?" Vanessa asked softly.

"It's gin. You want some?" he asked with a chuckle.

Vanessa snorted. "No thanks. Why are you drinking again? Didn't you say you have an excessive drinking problem?" Brody shrugged and finished the bottle before leaning over Vanessa's shoulder to open the motel door. She stepped aside and walked in after him.

She looked around the room with a disgusted look on her face. The room reeked of alcohol and looked like a tornado of alcoholic drinks had blown through there. There were bottles strewn all over the floor and bed and overflowing in trash cans.

Vanessa looked at Brody, disappointed. "What is all this? Please tell me this isn't just from today!"

Brody finished off the bottle in the brown bag and tossed it on the ground. "Nope, this is from the few days I have been here." Vanessa was pleased to know it wasn't all from today but was still disappointed in how much he had drunk.

"I could drink this much in one day, though, if I wanted to," he remarked, sitting on the bed.

Vanessa sighed heavily. "That's not healthy, Brody."

He shrugged.

"So why are you here?"

"I don't know," Vanessa said, looking around.

Brody chortled. "Okay…" They were silent as Vanessa watched Brody grab a half-empty bottle of beer from the dresser and start drinking it.

"I felt God calling me to come back to you. Do you know why he would have told me to do that?" Vanessa said after a few minutes.

He shook his head, putting the now empty beer bottle back on the TV stand. "I'm going to take a shower now. Do you want to join me?" Brody asked crassly. Vanessa looked away in disgust. He hung his head. "Sorry. That was the alcohol talking." Brody grabbed some clothes from the dresser and started toward the bathroom.

Vanessa sat on the bed awkwardly, praying. "God, why am I here?" Vanessa asked in a whisper.

Suddenly she heard a thud in the shower and raced to the door. It was locked, so she knocked on the door. "Brody, everything okay?" No answer. She knocked again…still no answer. Her heart started pounding as she used her weight to try to unsuccessfully break down the door. She looked around the room frantically for something to get the door open and then remembered she had a paper clip in her car. She raced outside, grabbed it, and raced back into the room and to the bathroom door, praying for Brody.

She finally got the door open to the steam room. She saw blood under the shower curtain and gasped as she opened it and saw Brody lying on the ground. He was just staring at the wall, the water falling on his naked body, his wrists covered in blood. She grabbed a towel and laid it on him then knelt down and slapped him gently in the face. "Brody…Brody, talk to me. What happened?"

He started to laugh eerily. "I tried to kill myself. I got further along in the process this time."

"This time? You mean you have done this before?" Vanessa asked, turning the shower off and wiping water out of her face. She grabbed a couple washcloths and wrapped them tightly around his wrists.

"I gotta call the police. I think you are bleeding too much, Brody," Vanessa said, scared.

Brody's eyes widened, and he shook his head vehemently. "Don't you dare! I don't need the press figuring this out. It will ruin me!"

Vanessa started to weep. "Then what am I supposed to do?"

Brody chuckled. "Let me finish the job."

Vanessa's eyes narrowed. "I will do no such thing!" She snapped out of her emotions and went into action. She had been trained for this type of situation, so she willed herself to focus now.

She took the washcloths off and saw that the cuts were still bleeding. She needed to stop the bleeding so she could assess the damage. She wrapped the cloths around his wrists again with some rubber bands she had found in her car. "Do you have any alcohol in here you haven't drunk yet?" Vanessa asked quickly.

Brody snickered. "You can try to find something."

Vanessa got up and raced around the room, finally finding a little vodka in a bottle. It would do for now. She went back to the bathroom and knelt down. She took the cloths off and saw the cuts were still bleeding. She started to weep again as she opened the bottle and poured what was left over the cuts the best she could.

Brody winced. "That hurts! What a waste of alcohol." Vanessa ignored his comments and continued to work quickly, wiping away her tears and getting some blood on her face.

She rinsed out the washcloths and then wrapped his wrists again before heading to the closet to get the bathrobe that was hanging in there. She went back to the bathroom and did her best to put it on him, and then she lifted him up, her adrenaline being the main reason she could move him at all because Brody was becoming deadweight now. She flopped him onto the bed and then grabbed her phone to call her mom. She explained that there was a huge situation, and her mom needed to bring her sewing and First Aid kits to the motel as soon as possible.

Vanessa sat on the bed next to Brody, anxiously waiting for the arrival of her mom. She tried to keep Brody conscious as she waited. "Brody, can you hear me?" she asked.

He groaned. "Yeah, please stop talking. I'm trying to sleep."

"No, Brody, you can't sleep right now. I need you awake." She noticed the blood was starting to soak the washcloths, and she started to weep again as she looked up at the ceiling. *Lord, I can't go through this again. Please protect him*, Vanessa prayed silently. Moments later, she heard her mom knocking quietly on the door. Vanessa raced to the door, opened it, pulled her mom in, and pushed her to the bed where Brody was sprawled out, his eyes shut now.

Vanessa leaned over him and slapped his face again gently. "Brody, wake up!" He opened his eyes, and she sighed with relief.

"What happened here, sweetie?" Grace asked, sitting on the bed. Vanessa tried to explain through her tears while insisting that Brody refused to go to the hospital for fear of the bad publicity. Finally Grace patted Vanessa on the shoulder. "Just follow my directions, and we will be okay. Come on. Let's take these washcloths off and see what we are dealing with."

Grace removed them and handed them to Vanessa to rinse off. Grace grabbed some rubbing alcohol and a clean washcloth and told Brody to bite down on it. She poured the alcohol on the wounds, and muffled obscenities could be heard as he winced in pain. She started to examine the cuts and smiled at Vanessa. "They aren't that deep. That's good. I will keep pouring alcohol on his wounds a few more times, and he should be done bleeding enough to start stitching him up." Vanessa smiled and nodded.

After half an hour of agonizing stress for Vanessa, her mom finished stitching Brody up. She cleaned up her stuff while Vanessa grabbed the soiled clothes and packed them in a bag before taking them to her car. Once they were finished, Vanessa hugged her mom tightly. "Thank you for helping me, Mom. He didn't want the police or any medical people here," Vanessa confessed.

"It's a good thing I was trained in First Aid, huh?" Grace said.

Vanessa nodded. "Will he be okay?" Vanessa asked.

"His wrists will be fine, yes, but judging from the state of this place, it seems he is in more trouble than cuts on his wrists," Grace observed, looking around the room.

"He has a drinking problem. I'm going to help him get over that though," Vanessa replied.

Grace laid her hand on her daughter's shoulder and looked at her seriously. "Does he want that?"

Vanessa swallowed a lump in her throat and got choked up. "I hope so."

Vanessa said goodbye to her mom and then looked around the room once more before heading to her car to get a trash bag from the trunk. She went back into the room and started to clean up.

Chapter Five

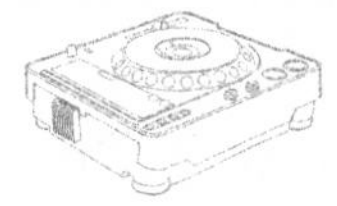

Vanessa started to yawn as she tried to keep her eyes open while sitting in the desk chair, staring at Brody. The morning rays of sunlight started to sneak in through the cracks in the shades. She yawned again before grabbing her cellphone off the desk to call into work.

"Hey, Rocky, it's Vanessa. I hate to do this, but I can't come in today. Something important came up that I need to take care of. Honestly, it could take at least a week to take care of. Do you mind keeping me off the schedule the rest of the week? If it's not too much trouble..." Vanessa whispered, looking at Brody. He was still sound asleep.

"That's not a problem, Vanessa. I understand your life's work. I am always prepared for when you can't come in. Take all the time you need. I wish you luck with whatever it is," Rocky said, hanging up.

Vanessa put her phone back on the table and thanked God she had such an understanding boss. She turned around to face Brody again and wondered if she should wake him, but he looked so peaceful—or dead. Now she panicked and raced to him. She listened closely for a breath and heard a few. She sighed with relief and went back to her chair. Her eyes started to get heavy as she willed herself to stay awake.

An hour later, Brody touched her shoulder, and she shot up, eyes wide, startled. She looked at Brody. "Hi. Sorry, I must have fallen asleep." She stood up and stretched.

Brody looked at her with his bloodshot eyes. "Did you sleep here?"

"Sleep? No, I didn't sleep. Well, I mean, I just fell asleep now, but I didn't sleep last night. I did stay here all night though," Vanessa answered, stifling a yawn.

Brody furrowed his brow. "Why?"

"I wanted to keep an eye on you," Vanessa answered with a smile.

Brody didn't respond. Instead, he looked around the room, surprised by the state of it. He looked back at Vanessa. "Did you clean the room last night too?" She nodded proudly. He chuckled, started toward the bathroom, and shut the door behind him.

"What are you doing?" Vanessa asked quickly.

"I'm taking a leak. Is that okay with you?" Brody snapped. Vanessa didn't respond. Seconds later, he came out of the bathroom and frowned. "Sorry, I wasn't trying to sound rude. Why am I wearing a bathrobe?"

Vanessa furrowed her brow. "You don't remember what happened last night?"

Brody chuckled. "Oh, I remember everything. I told you; I'm a functional drunk."

"Then you shouldn't wonder why you are in the robe, right?" Vanessa questioned. The room was silent. "I stayed because I was concerned for your safety, Brody," Vanessa responded after a little while.

"Why?" Brody asked.

Vanessa grunted. "I...you know..." She pointed to his wrists.

He looked down and saw the gauze and hung his head in shame. "I tried to kill myself."

"Again," Vanessa added in frustration. The room was silent again as Brody went to the dresser and pulled out something to wear. He sniffed the outfit first and noticed it reeked of alcohol; he grimaced but got dressed. Vanessa turned around to give him some privacy.

"I didn't feel right leaving you alone after you told me you have tried it before. So after you fell asleep, I cleaned up your room and stayed awake to make sure you didn't try it again," Vanessa explained, staring at the wall.

Brody snickered. "You thought third time's the charm, huh?"

Vanessa turned around, and much to her relief, he was dressed now. "This isn't funny, Brody, on top of your alcoholic tendencies, you are suicidal, and we need to talk about it."

Brody sneered, "I'm not suicidal."

"Oh yeah? Then why did I have to pick up your naked body off the ground and clean up your wounds? Don't make me get the police involved!" Vanessa growled, getting teary eyed.

Brody shook his head vehemently. "No, no police. The last thing I need is for my fans to find out because the authorities leaked it to the press. It will ruin my career."

"That is what you said last night too! Verbatim! Seriously, that is what you care about right now? Your career? You don't care about getting better?" Vanessa asked rudely.

"I don't expect you to understand. You aren't famous," Brody retorted. The room was silent once again. Brody sighed heavily. "What do we need to talk about? I feel fine right now."

"Yeah, but what about tomorrow? What about tonight? Or the next day or next month? This isn't a cold; it's not just going to go away with time. Suicide is a serious enough issue, but you are also a raging alcoholic and need help for that too," Vanessa told him seriously.

Brody looked around the room and grimaced. "You didn't happen to leave any alcohol here when you cleaned up, did you? I gotta gear up for tonight. I don't like being in big crowds without some liquid courage."

"It's all gone," Vanessa told.

"I can't be sober just like that," Brody protested.

"That's what I'm afraid of, so that's why we aren't going to the party tonight. You and I are going to stay here and detox," Vanessa said, locking the motel door with every lock on it and then closing the curtains before turning to look at Brody.

He looked panicked. "What do you mean we are detoxing?"

"I am starting the detox process on you today. I already called into work, and I am going to tell my parents we won't make it tonight. They'll understand," Vanessa said.

Brody sneered, "What makes you think you could help me with that, even if I wanted it?"

Vanessa's eyes lit up as she walked up to Brody. "It's my job."

"What do you mean, it's your job? How so?" he asked rudely.

"I am an addiction counselor," Vanessa told him matter-of-factly.

Brody looked at her gravely and then chuckled. "Then why do you work at Rocky's?"

"Rocky's is my summer job. I don't live locally anymore. I moved to India when I was nineteen. I serve with a ministry that helps addicts. We help them overcome their addictions and also find a relationship with Christ so they can experience true and lasting freedom," Vanessa explained. Brody didn't say a word. He didn't have to; the stunned look on his face said it all.

"I want to help you overcome your addiction to

alcohol—or at least start the process before I head back home to India—and in doing that, we can also help you with your suicidal tendencies," Vanessa said with passion.

Brody slowly backed up into the TV stand behind him. Now he felt trapped. "Is this an intervention?"

Vanessa furrowed her brow. "No, usually that involves family members telling you how your addiction has affected them, and a counselor would be present to take you to a rehab."

Brody snorted. "Isn't that what you are? Isn't that what you want to do to me? Send me to rehab?"

"No, I can't force you to go to a rehab facility. You have to want to be helped; otherwise, this won't work out," Vanessa reassured him.

Brody looked away, his jaw clenched. "Why do you want to help me? You don't even know me." He turned to look at her. "Why does it matter to you if I want to kill myself or if I want to have a drink?"

Vanessa looked into his scared eyes and smiled softly. "God doesn't want to see his children suffer needlessly. God created you to enjoy life to the full. How can you do that if you aren't healthy? It's my job to see the need and meet the need according to God's will. Jesus died on the cross for our sins so we don't have to continue to be slave to our sins, disappointments, hurts or deep, depressing pain. He died so we could live free forever." Vanessa spoke with such authority and passion that Brody's head was spinning.

"I don't know if I want to detox," Brody said.

"Do you want to keep doing life the way you have been? Do you really want to end your life?" Vanessa asked.

Brody was quiet for a few seconds. "Drinking is the only way I can drown out the pain," he confessed after some time, looking at Vanessa sadly.

"It doesn't have to be that way, Brody. I can help you escape this prison you keep putting yourself in," Vanessa said, putting her hand on his shoulder. Suddenly Brody dropped to his knees, crying heavy sobs. Vanessa knelt down next to him, praying silently over him and crying with him.

"I got up early Sunday morning, walked onto the ledge of my penthouse, and just stood there, looking down. I had every intention of jumping, but I couldn't. I was frozen in fear. I left that day to come here," Brody confessed, crying bitterly. "I don't feel like I have accomplished anything of worth in my life. When I die, will people remember me once my funeral is over? I want to know why I am on this earth. Am I here only to make music for people and then die? I want more than that!" Brody spoke with such brokenness.

"How do you know it was fear that kept you from jumping? You must have really wanted to end your life if you went a step further with the attempt last night. Do you want my opinion? I don't think you really want to end your life," Vanessa said.

Brody chuckled scornfully. "Then what was last night about?"

"I just think you are in a lot of pain and conflicted about whose voice you should listen to in your life. You won't get those things you are craving if you are gone, right? You need to listen to the voices that are speaking life into you," Vanessa added with all sincerity. Brody shrugged but didn't respond.

"Brody, you aren't here by accident," Vanessa started.

"Where? In Hampton Beach?" he asked.

"In Hampton Beach and on this earth. God made you special, and he has great plans for your life if you just surrender to him," Vanessa explained.

Brody chortled and shook his head in disbelief.

"I surrendered my life to Christ several years ago, and I do not regret it. My life has been very fulfilling, hard too, but I still love my life, even through the hard times—and there have been many," Vanessa added passionately.

"I don't know your God. Why would he want to spare me?" Brody protested, standing to his feet.

"None of us know him at first, but he is always there trying to make himself known to us. It's up to us to choose to hear him calling our names. You have a purpose in this life, and that is why he would want to spare you," Vanessa explained, standing to her feet.

Brody grimaced. "Don't get preachy on me, Vanessa. I was starting to like you."

Vanessa sighed. "I am just sharing the truth with you, Brody."

Brody groaned. "Well, I don't want to hear the truth right now. I want to drink."

"You won't find joy at the bottom of a bottle," Vanessa protested this time.

Brody shrugged. "Maybe not, but I will find freedom from my troubles."

"Yes, but it is only temporary freedom. I know a freedom that can last a lifetime," Vanessa told him boldly.

Brody chuckled at her expense. "Yeah, I know—your God offers me freedom. Look, Vanessa, thanks for keeping me alive and stuff, but I don't think this God of yours is for me nor do I like the idea of a detox," Brody said, sitting on the bed again.

Vanessa started tearing up, her fists clenched now. "Brody, I want to help you. I can't see another person I care about harming themselves again!" Brody looked at her, surprised by her statement. He could see she genuinely she was. She obviously had some hidden backstory attached to these feelings. Vanessa wiped away a few unexpected tears and then cleared her throat. "Don't you want to be free?" she asked, her voice wavering.

"Yes, but I'm scared," he confessed with eyes to match his nervous tone. "Detoxing sounds painful, and I've heard horror stories. You don't understand.... I've been drinking like a fish since I was nineteen years old. I'm going to have wicked side effects from this."

Vanessa sighed and touched his shoulder again. "I know what you are talking about. I have worked with many cases like yours. I won't lie and say it will be a walk in the park, but don't you think your life is worth the try? Remember, you want things in your life you don't have yet, so don't you dare tell me you would rather die. But if you don't fix this alcohol addiction, you will die. I can guarantee that."

Brody started to weep again. "Okay, let's do this."

"Okay, let me call my mom and tell her we won't be at the birthday party tonight," Vanessa said.

Brody looked at her apprehensively but nodded slowly, wiping the tears from his eyes.

Vanessa smiled. "I know it doesn't feel like it, but you made the right choice." She grabbed her phone and called her mom while Brody sat on his bed, wringing his hands anxiously.

Chapter Six

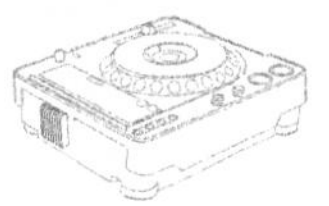

"AH! THIS HURTS! YOU'RE killing me!" Brody screamed out six hours into the detox process. He was shaking and occasionally throwing up in the trash can that Vanessa had given him earlier. He started to cry as Vanessa sat on the bed next to him, holding him and wiping his mouth with a cold washcloth, occasionally checking his pulse. It was definitely quickening.

"Brody, it's all right. You'll be okay. You can do this. God has you in his hands, and he is freeing you right now. Just relax and trust him," Vanessa said, running her hands through his hair.

Brody pulled away and sneered. "I don't care about God right now! I need a drink! Please, Vanessa, get me something—put me out of my misery!" He laid back on the bed and kept shaking. Vanessa sat him up as he started to dry heave. She prayed for him, even though he was groaning the whole time and couldn't really hear what she was saying.

Around the tenth hour of the detox process, Brody was exhausted. He had been throwing up non-stop and was starting to get a sore stomach as well as throwing up some blood.

His shaking became a little more intense, and now he was irritable and sweating so much he looked like he had just gone for a swim. Vanessa used a clean washcloth and occasionally rested it on his face to cool him down. He was still crying and begging for her to stop this. Again Vanessa spoke life into him and encouraged him to continue on.

Brody and Vanessa had been locked in the motel room so long that neither of them knew what day or time it was. Vanessa was mentally and physically exhausted, and Brody was beyond that by now as he lay on his bed, white as a ghost, sweaty, dry heaving, and crying. He had managed to sleep a few hours but suddenly woke up screaming, his eyes wide open and full of tears.

Vanessa ran to him and tried to calm him down as he screamed out, "A lion is trying to maul me!" Vanessa whispered in his ear many times that he was okay, that there was no lion; then she would pray for him.

After a few more hours of him randomly screaming out about various hallucinations, he finally fell asleep for a whole four hours straight before having audio hallucinations, so Vanessa just sat with him and sang praises to God over Brody. He would eventually stop, throw up, cry, and scream in frustration.

Vanessa stared at Brody, trying to keep her eyes open. She still didn't know what day or time it was; all she knew was that she was exhausted and wanted a shower. She saw Brody sleeping on the bed. She walked up to him and checked his pulse; the fast heart rate had finally slowed down to normal. She emptied his trash can and cleaned it out for the millionth time.

She yawned as she went back to the bed and grabbed the two washcloths. She rinsed those out too and brought them back to Brody. She touched his forehead; he was still a little warm but wasn't too bad. He was drenched in sweat, though, and so was his bed. She laid the washcloths on the bed and then took a deep breath, yawning again.

She suddenly started weeping silently; she didn't want to disturb him. She remembered everything they had endured. She had done this process many times, and it never got easier on her, only more painful emotionally. It was hard for her to see the person going through so much pain. She especially had a hard time watching Brody going through his seizures. She always felt helpless whenever someone had one. She heard Brody groaning, so she collected her emotions and stood to her feet and smiled. "Good afternoon."

Brody sat up slowly, wincing. "I have a headache."

"Yeah, that is probably going to be a thing for a while. How are you feeling otherwise?" Vanessa asked, sitting next to him on the bed.

He looked exhausted and beat up. "I'm tired and nauseous still."

"I'm sorry, but you made it. The worst of it is over," Vanessa tried to encourage him.

Brody tried to smile, but he was too weak. "How long have we been here?"

Vanessa shrugged. "We started Wednesday afternoon, and I just checked my phone. Today is Monday."

"Five days? Geez, won't your parents wonder where you are?" Brody commented.

"Nah, they knew I was here doing this," Vanessa told him.

"I am sorry you missed your dad's birthday because of me," Brody said next.

"He understands," Vanessa reassured him. "Do you think you are strong enough to get into the tub for a bath?"

Brody smirked. "Are you going to give me a bath?"

Vanessa snickered. "You wish. No, you will give yourself one. Do you feel strong enough walk?" He nodded slowly and tried to stand to his feet but immediately fell backward on the bed.

"Okay, I think you will have to just stay here. I will give you some soap and a washcloth and towel; you can wash off in here." Vanessa stood to her feet, grabbing a towel and warming up the washcloth. She handed him the towel, the soap, the washcloth, and a new outfit. "Here you go. I'll wait in the bathroom. Let me know when you are done." Vanessa went into the bathroom and splashed water on her face, taking some deep breaths and praising God for helping them through. She then looked at her phone and saw she had several missed calls from her parents, Daniel, and Kate.

She got on her phone and called her parents. "Hey, sweetie, how is it going?" her father asked.

Vanessa sighed and unexpectedly started crying. "It's good. The worst is out of the way. He might have a hard road staying sober, but I believe he has the fight in him to do it. I am exhausted, Dad."

"I know, sweetie, I know, but I am so proud of you for doing this, and I am sure he will thank you for it too. You did a great thing," her father encouraged her.

Vanessa heard Brody call her name. "Thanks, Dad. I gotta go now." She hung up, wiped her eyes, and left the bathroom. Vanessa took the washcloth, towel, and soap, and put them away in the bathroom, and then came back to sit next to Brody on the bed. "Do you feel like eating anything?" she asked. Brody grimaced. "Do you think you could drink some

Gatorade? Your lips look dehydrated; you need the electrolytes. I tried to give you as much water as I could, but you threw it up."

"Yeah, I'll see what happens. Let me have it," Brody said.

Vanessa stood to her feet and grabbed a Gatorade from the fridge. She handed it to him and prayed he could keep it down. "Don't chug it. Just sip for now," she reminded him. He did as she asked.

"Now what do I do?" Brody asked, sitting up slowly.

"Well, since you can't get up off the bed, I say you just sit here and rest. I will get the remote, and you can watch TV," Vanessa suggested walking, toward the TV.

Brody grimaced. "What if I have to go to the bathroom?"

"I can leave a container near you, or you can try to get up again if that happens," Vanessa suggested.

Brody snickered. "I'll take the second option. I don't want you to have to touch the you-know-what."

Vanessa giggled. "It wouldn't have been the first time, but okay, if you need to, I will help you stand up. For now, just rest; maybe that will help."

He laid his head on the pillow and closed his eyes. "I'm sure you're exhausted too, Vanessa, so if you need sleep, you can lay on the bed. Don't worry. I'm too exhausted to make a move." He let out a lackluster chuckle.

Vanessa yawned. "I may consider it." She walked over to the other side of the bed and laid down.

"Thank you for everything you did for me Vanessa. I am sure it wasn't easy on you either, but I appreciate your sacrifice," Brody said quietly.

"You are welcome, Brody. I was happy to do it," Vanessa said as she slowly fell asleep.

They managed to stay asleep the whole day. Now it was

Tuesday afternoon, a little over a week since Brody first arrived at Hampton Beach. Vanessa woke with a start, sitting up quickly. She saw Brody sitting up in bed, drinking a bottle of water he had found in the fridge. She smiled. "You were able to get up."

He nodded. "Yeah, and I went potty all by myself like a big boy." They laughed. "How are you feeling?" he asked as Vanessa stood up.

"I feel more refreshed. How are you feeling?" she asked next.

"I'm hungry," he said.

Vanessa smiled. "Glad to hear it. Why don't we go to my house and have some lunch? You've earned it." Brody nodded and grabbed his keys to his bike. "I don't think you should drive that just yet. Leave it here; I'll drive you over," Vanessa said. Brody nodded and winced as she opened the door. Vanessa shielded her eyes from the light too. Brody grabbed his sunglasses before shutting the door.

•

Vanessa pulled up to a two-story blue house with a large front yard that had an oak tree, many different flowers planted all around, and a tire swing hanging from the tree. They pulled into the gravel driveway behind another car.

"Who else lives here?" he asked.

"I live with my parents when I am in town. That car belongs to my brother. My mom must have told him I was coming home today," Vanessa remarked.

Brody groaned. "Do they know everything?"

Vanessa nodded. "My mom helped me stitch up your wounds, and my brother brought me the Gatorade and water the day after we started."

Brody groaned as they got out of the car. "Are they going to think less of me after this?"

She looked at him and saw him fidgeting. She touched his shoulder and smiled compassionately. "It's okay, Brody. My family will be thrilled for you that you overcame this. They won't think less of you—trust me." Brody smiled and nodded slowly As they made their way into the house.

"Vanessa and Brody are here!" Kate exclaimed, hugging Brody. "I am so proud of you!" Brody chuckled but didn't respond. Kate motioned for them to follow her into the kitchen, where both Brody and Vanessa were surprised to hear everyone cheer and shout, "Congratulations!" Vanessa beamed, and Brody was surprised by the kind gesture.

Daniel shook hands with Brody, and then Grace hugged him tightly. "I am so proud of you, kiddo. After you get some food in you, let's go check your wounds and make sure they are healing nicely, okay?" Brody nodded slowly but didn't speak.

Brody swallowed a lump in his throat as Vanessa's dad walked over to them slowly. He was a tall and slender man with many tattoos on his body and piercings in his ears. His long brown hair was pulled back into a ponytail. As he got closer, Brody couldn't help but feel like he knew who this was.

Vanessa's dad spoke in his gravelly voice, "Hey, Brody, I'm–"

Brody gasped as he figured out where he knew him from. "You're Heath Stewart, the guitarist for Jealous Creatures! Wow, my dad is a huge fan of your band! He has every album. I grew up listening to your stuff—your guitar solos are legendary."

Mr. Stewart smiled warmly and held out his hand to shake hands with Brody. "It's nice to meet you, Brody. Congratulations on your newfound sobriety. I'm sure you will find it is a much better way to live. You can call me Heath."

Brody chuckled nervously. "I don't think I can. I'm in the presence of a guitar god. Using your first name is not respectful enough, your majesty."

Everyone laughed. "You have made my day with all this praise, but before it all goes to my head, please just call me Heath. There is only one God in the world, and I'm not him."

Brody nodded and looked at Vanessa with wide eyes. "You didn't tell me you had a famous father. That's so awesome!" He looked at Heath. "I would love to talk to you about your life. You were such a legend. Why did you leave the business?" Heath put his arm around Brody, and they started toward the couch.

"I am going to make you two some sandwiches," Grace suggested, walking away. Daniel kissed Vanessa on the cheek. "I have to get to work now. I am proud of you, Sis. I remember my detox. You rocked that, and I am sure you rocked this one too."

Vanessa smiled. "Thanks, Daniel. God really showed up during this one." Daniel headed out the door.

Kate sat down at the kitchen table with Vanessa and they talked while Grace handed her a sandwich.

"Okay, how did it really go?" Kate asked, noticing Vanessa looked exhausted as she ate.

Vanessa hesitated before speaking. "It was intense. I can honestly say, out of all the detoxing sessions I have done, this was the toughest."

"Why?" Kate asked.

Vanessa looked at Brody and then looked at Kate again. "Because this one felt personal for me. It reminded me of the situation with Daniel."

"Aw, I'm so sorry this brought back bad memories for you," Kate said.

"Don't be sorry. Those memories helped me to stay in the game. And now look at him." Vanessa and Kate both turned to look. He was eating his sandwich and hanging on every word Heath said.

"He does look a lot better. He looks healthy, at least mentally; physically, he looks terrible. Make sure he eats enough to get back to health," Kate said. Vanessa nodded, and Kate grinned. "Now you can get to know him better."

"Oh goodness, Kate, you are always trying to set me up with someone every time I come home, and I keep telling you I am not interested. This time is no exception—especially Brody. He has too much on his plate right now," Vanessa explained.

"But he likes you. I saw the way he looked at you at the beach. A missionary can date, you know," Kate protested.

"Yeah, I know they can," Vanessa said.

"Has he tried asking you out yet? Is that why you look flustered that I am talking about this?" Kate asked next, grinning.

Vanessa looked at Kate, annoyed. "Yes, he has asked me out a couple times."

Kate giggled. "Wow, my best friend is on the radar of a mega star."

Vanessa snorted. "Mega star? How famous is he really?"

"You are so clueless when it comes to music. DJ Maddox—Brody—is probably in the top ten of the most successful DJs in the business right now. Last year he was a DJ in Vegas at a club in one of the top hotels, every weekend for five months straight. Plus he does lots of festivals. He even hosts a September show in Manhattan every year. He knows many famous people, not just DJs but other celebrities too. I can't believe he has tried to ask you out. That is an amazing accomplishment for you considering the last semi-famous person who asked you out was Tommy Tilly, the quarterback in high school."

Vanessa chortled. "I heard he's a doctor now. You know I have never been one to care about the romantic side of life." She glanced at Brody and then back at Kate. "I will admit he is handsome and slightly charming. I'm excited to see what he is like now that he is sober." Vanessa confessed, blushing. Kate giggled again.

"Relax, Kate. I'm focusing on my mission work right now. It takes a lot out of me, emotionally and physically. I can't afford to get unfocused. I only have enough energy to devote myself to one relationship right now, and I choose God," Vanessa explained with a grin.

Kate nodded. "Okay, but I think you could multitask two relationships easily. You were always good at multitasking when we were younger. A relationship with God is very important and worth maintaining, so I respect your decision."

Vanessa simply chuckled and hugged her.

Kate and Grace soon left to go to work too, so Vanessa and Brody sat at the table with Heath. "Sweetie, I told Brody he should live here with us until he decides to head home. He mentioned that you want to help him while you are home, which is a great idea. I told him about my struggle getting sober from drugs and alcohol and how I needed many people to help me. I told him I would help him as well. What do you think? Is it a good idea?"

"It's a great idea. I agree. He shouldn't be alone right now, and I'm glad I will be able to leave him in good hands too," Vanessa replied.

"What about Grace? Will she have a problem with a stranger in the house?" Brody asked.

"She won't mind. We always open our house to those who need help. She will be thrilled to help you in whatever way she can," Heath explained.

Brody looked at Vanessa, and she nodded in agreement. His eyes lit up. "Awesome. So I guess I should get my stuff from the motel now."

Vanessa grabbed her keys and drove him back to the motel.

"I am already feeling better, clearer," Brody said as they drove.

Vanessa smiled. "I'm happy to hear that. I wanted to let you know that your cravings won't be gone instantly, and you will be irritable from time to time. Also, the headaches may stick around for a while too, maybe six months. Just stay the course and don't fall back into what was easy. Remember everything you went through to get healthy."

Brody nodded. "I will. I don't want to go back. I feel better than I ever have, and it hasn't even been a whole week," he agreed as Vanessa pulled into the motel parking lot.

They got out of the car and walked to the room. "Do you think I could use your washer and dryer? I have to clean my clothes; they smell awful," Brody asked, putting his clothes into his bag.

Vanessa nodded. "Yeah, sure you can."

They finished packing, dropped the keys off at the office, and then walked over to Brody's bike.

"Do you think you'll be okay to drive?" Vanessa asked, concerned.

"Yeah, I'll be okay," he assured her.

Vanessa got in her car and waited for him to start moving before she left, following him closely.

Chapter Seven

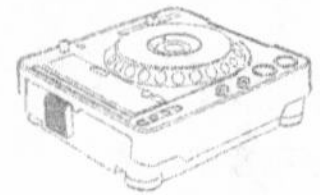

THE NEXT FOUR DAYS were tough for the family and Brody. Grace, Heath, and Vanessa took turns watching him like a hawk, at Vanessa's urging. She reminded her parents that Brody was heavily dependent on alcohol and that he would certainly be tempted to drink again, so they needed to be vigilant.

Brody felt very irritable during these days and found himself lashing out from time to time, even over the slightest comments. The family was happy to see that he was determined to keep his sobriety, but they were also concerned at how easily agitated he was. Vanessa assured them it was all part of the detox process and that they just needed to love him through it all.

Brody had a hard time seeing the silver lining to his newfound sobriety, so he stayed in his room most of the time, brooding or screaming out his frustrations. He had a headache almost every waking moment and occasionally still dealt with bouts of nausea. He also couldn't sleep well because whenever he closed his eyes, he saw alcohol. When talking to Vanessa about it, she reminded him that his desire for alcohol wasn't just going to go away; he would need to fight for his sobriety for a long time. This news didn't shock Brody—it made sense—but it was also very annoying to hear.

On the fourth day of his sobriety, Vanessa suggested they go for a jog on the beach, telling Brody that being near the ocean always helped her when she was in a bad mood. His irritability was at an all-time high that day, so at that point, he was willing to try anything. After this first jog, he found it was a great way to keep his mind off drinking and decided to make it a daily thing they did together.

Vanessa and her father walked through the church parking lot. "I really wish Mom had insisted on Brody coming with us to church today."

"You saw how grouchy he was at breakfast. That's why your mom decided to stay home and keep an eye on him. She was afraid he would go to the bottle if we all left him alone, and you know we can't make him go to church with us," Heath soothed her. Vanessa nodded and followed him inside. "I need to get inside now and start setting up for the service. I will see you later," Heath said as he walked into the sanctuary, and Vanessa slumped into a chair in the lobby.

After the service was finished, Vanessa started toward the lobby, and much to her surprise, she saw her mom and Brody standing there. She walked up to Brody and hugged him excitedly. "Wow! You came!"

Brody glanced at Grace and then back at Vanessa. "Yeah, I started making a few jokes about how a beer would taste good while watching TV, so Grace strongly suggested we go to church. She practically dragged me here. I'm glad I came though. I didn't know your father was a singer too. He's pretty good."

"What did you think of the sermon?" Vanessa asked next.

"Sermon? Oh, that. The guy who spoke looks like an MMA fighter. Hey, I wanted to talk to your dad. Would he be okay with that, or is he busy after this church stuff?" Brody asked, changing the subject quickly, much to Vanessa's chagrin. Vanessa motioned for him to follow her.

"Hey, Dad, guess who came," Vanessa said with a smile.

Heath's eyes lit up as he sat down on the stage and listened as Brody talked. Vanessa walked away reluctantly. She wanted to stay and see what Brody had to say, but Kate was calling her over.

Ten minutes later, Grace came over and told Heath they were ready to go to the diner. "Brody, come with us. You and I can ride in my truck and keep talking," Heath suggested.

After the diner, Heath and Brody started back to the house.

"Thanks again for letting me tag along with your family to the diner. I'm sorry I tried to order a beer with my meal. It's a bit of a habit," Brody apologized.

"I understand. When I was detoxing from my addictions, I had many times where I either relapsed or almost relapsed. It's a daily struggle, but it won't always be one. After a while, you won't even desire it anymore," Heath reassured him.

Brody chortled. "Yeah, when will that day come?"

"Everyone is different, but your time will come. Hey, I would love it if you came back to church next Sunday if you are still in town," Heath replied.

Brody smiled. "I'm staying in town until further notice. I am nowhere near ready to go back home. My life back there isn't exactly the best place for me to find sobriety, plus I like the feeling I have here in Hampton."

"Okay then, will you give some thought to the idea I mentioned on the way to the diner?" Heath asked.

Brody grimaced. "I suppose, but when would we start?"

"I have to talk to Grace first to get a start date. I'll let you know," Heath responded.

Brody nodded, getting out of the car. Heath started toward the front door as Vanessa walked out to greet them. She motioned for Brody to follow her to the backyard. They sat on the wooden swing near the big oak tree and listened to the peaceful sounds of nature all around them.

"How long do you plan to be in town?" Vanessa asked after some time.

"I'm not in a hurry to go home," Brody responded.

"Don't you think people will start to worry about you?" Vanessa suggested.

Brody shrugged and changed the subject. "When do you have to leave for India?"

Vanessa noticed he was deflecting. "I am only here from June 1 to September 1. Why?"

Brody shrugged. "I just wanted to know how much time I have to get to know you better; that's all. Only about two weeks...not much time, but it will do."

"You sure are smooth. I bet you have used that line on lots of women," Vanessa remarked.

Brody shook his head. "Nope, I haven't. In fact, I have never had an actual relationship. It's only ever been physical, and I didn't need to do much persuading to get with them. You are truly a challenge for me—in a good way of course. I like that you aren't easily excited by the way I look or my money and fame, and I like how my hitting on you does nothing for you."

"Thanks for the compliment...and I wouldn't say your hitting on me does *nothing* for me," Vanessa said with a coy smile. Brody looked at her, intrigued. "It irritates me," Vanessa said, giggling and nudging him playfully.

"Very funny. May I ask you about India? You said you are a counselor for addicts there, right?" Brody asked.

Vanessa nodded. "Yes, I am a counselor, and I assist in the detoxing process too. Once the initial detox process is done, the true healing can begin. That's when we tell them about the good news of Christ and how he will keep them free from their addiction."

"I can imagine it's very hard to deal with addicts all day. I know I have been a pain in the butt for you and your family since I got sober," Brody remarked.

Vanessa sighed. "Yes, it is hard, but it's rewarding too, and you aren't that bad, at least not to me. I have seen much worse."

Brody snickered in disbelief. "How can it get worse than how I've been feeling? You know I have had the shakes all morning, and my stomach has been gnawing at me for something to drink that isn't alcohol free. Every morning I wake up and hope that this sobriety becomes easier to handle. Actually, that is a lie because I don't really sleep. I still get night sweats and toss and turn all night. In all honesty, I am miserable."

"I am so sorry you are having a tough time, Brody. I know it can't be easy, but trust me when I say it won't be like this forever. After some time, you will find the withdrawal becomes less and less. You just have to be patient," Vanessa encouraged him. Brody simply grimaced at her as they swung silently for a few minutes.

"Vanessa, I want to get to know you better while you are in town," Brody blurted out.

Vanessa smiled shyly. "I would like to get to know you more too."

Brody was just about to respond when Kate walked into the backyard with intent. "Have you seen this?" Kate asked, concerned, as Brody and Vanessa stood up to greet her. She handed Brody her phone roughly. He started to scroll through different posts as Vanessa looked over his shoulder. Brody laughed.

"Why are you laughing? This isn't funny, Brody. Your fans think you are either dead or kidnapped!" Kate scolded.

"That's what makes this funny. It's only been two weeks. I'm just taking some time away from the limelight. Is that a crime?" Brody asked rudely.

Kate frowned. "Brody, why didn't you at least tell everyone you were taking time off? Post a pic, send a message—something, anything!"

Brody shook his head, getting agitated quickly. "I didn't want to, Kate."

"Why? You can't leave everyone hanging forever, Brody," Kate retorted.

Brody's nostrils started to flare, and his cheeks turned red. Vanessa touched his shoulder, trying to get him to calm down. She could feel the tension mounting.

"Hey, guys, Mom and Dad are trying to nap. Why don't we keep it down or just not discuss this right now?" Vanessa suggested.

"No! We will discuss this now! I'm frustrated with Brody, and he needs to make it right!" Kate protested, ripping her phone from his unsuspecting hands.

Brody grabbed at his hair and screamed unexpectedly, "I don't care about what you need right now, Kate! I am trying to stay sober, but you and your whining about my followers being worried about my whereabouts doesn't make me to want to stay sober!" Brody glared at Kate, and she stared at him with wide eyes. "I am a grown man, and I make my own decisions. You don't get to tell me what to do, so leave me alone!"

Kate started to tear up but didn't let the tears fall as she started to walk away. "Your fans are the reason you are successful! They have supported you—*I* have supported you—and you don't care about us? You aren't the only one in the world with problems, you know. You can't just shut down and ignore the world."

Brody groaned and looked at Vanessa, eyes flaring with hatred. "So do you hate me too?"

Vanessa helped him do some deep breathing to calm down before she finally spoke. "She doesn't hate you, Brody. She's hurt; that's all. You were rather ruthless. I know you didn't mean what you said. It was the withdrawal talking and frustration too; I get it. I'm sure she understands too, deep down. She just cares about you and your career and doesn't want to see it go down the tubes."

Brody started to get agitated again. "I want everyone to leave me alone so I can figure things out! It's not their life; it's mine. Doesn't anyone understand that?"

Vanessa sighed heavily, giving him a tight but brief hug. "You and my dad have a lot in common, Brody. My dad told me about his detox process; he also had a lot going on with that. If you want freedom in your life, then you need Jesus. He will help you with the difficulties of sobriety and everything else you are going through internally. If you don't want to burn too many bridges in your future, you should send a message to your fans. It doesn't have to be much, just a quick note to let them know you are okay."

Brody grimaced. “Okay, fine, but I’m shutting my phone down again after that. The silence has been great.… I should go try to talk to Kate. Do you have any idea where she is right now?”

“She might be with my brother working on one of his landscaping jobs. I’ll text Daniel and see if she’s with him. I’ll go with you,” Vanessa suggested.

Brody nodded. “You want to take my bike?”

Vanessa chuckled. “No thanks. We can take my car.”

“One of these days I will get you to ride on the bike with me,” Brody assured her.

Vanessa chuckled. “I doubt it. Last time I was on a bike, it didn’t end well for me.”

“Come on. Be adventurous. I’m a very safe driver—never had an accident in my whole life,” Brody reassured her.

Vanessa pondered the idea and then looked at Brody with a smirk. “Dad has his old helmet in the garage that I can use.” Brody got excited as Vanessa slowly made her way to the garage. He prepared his bike and put his helmet on.

Vanessa came back and chuckled in disbelief. “I can’t believe I’m doing this. Let’s get going before I change my mind.”

Brody chuckled again as he and Vanessa climbed onto the bike. “Make sure you hold onto my waist tight,” Brody said. Vanessa nodded quickly and did as she was told. Brody could tell she was nervous; she was shaking. He started the bike, and Vanessa clung to him tighter. Brody enjoyed the ride being so close to Vanessa.

Brody pulled up to a small shack. It was run down and had a “For Sale” sign in the yard. “So was it as bad as you thought it would be?” Brody asked.

Vanessa snorted. “It was terrifying. I don’t think I can do it again.”

Brody laughed. They spotted Daniel, three of his employees, and Kate working in the yard. Daniel stood up to greet them. "Hey, guys. Have you come to help?"

Vanessa smiled. "I'll help. He came to apologize."

Daniel laughed loudly and called for Kate to come over.

Brody watched as Kate glanced his way and then back at the ground where she was working and shook her head. After a little while, she got up off the ground and started toward him, arms crossed and a scowl on her face. She stood in front of him, not saying a word. Brody cleared his throat. Daniel and Vanessa walked away awkwardly.

"I'm sorry I hurt you, Kate. I'm dealing with a lot emotionally and physically. It has not been easy being sober. In fact, it's hell," Brody apologized.

Kate uncrossed her arms and sighed. "I forgive you. I remember seeing Daniel go through his detox from drugs. It wasn't pretty and neither were the months after."

Brody's eyes widened in disbelief. "Months! I can't live like this for months; I feel like crap!"

"Everyone is different, Brody," Kate reminded him.

He grunted. "I hate that phrase. I have heard it so much lately." There was a pause. "I've been really depressed lately, and I am also dealing with my alcohol withdrawal. That's why I'm staying away from social media right now; it's a major trigger for me and my anxiety, which is one of my main drinking triggers."

Kate smiled warmly. "I get it. Life can be tough, and sometimes it's easier to try to escape it somehow. I tried to commit suicide too."

Brody chuckled awkwardly. "I never said..."

Kate gave him a gentle smile. "You don't have to say it. If you have been in that dark place, you can tell when others are there too. Plus, who wears a sweatshirt in August?" She showed him the scars on her own forearm. He gasped, lifting up his sweatshirt sleeves to show her his wrists, which were no longer bandaged or stitched up but were now scarring.

"My parents divorced when I was twelve, and I haven't seen my father since then. My mom and I moved here from Boston. Vanessa and Daniel were the only ones who befriended me when I first got here. I spent so much time at their house that I became like part of the family. I started going to church with them, and after I became a Christian a year later, my mom would mock me. She was a heavy drinker, so whenever she was drunk, she would say awful things to me. It got to be unbearable after a few years, and I decided to end my life. My mom caught me in the bathroom with a knife to my arm, bleeding on the floor. She laughed loudly, cheering me on pretty much, saying, 'You are so weak. I am not going to call the cops for help. Maybe your God will!' She slammed the door shut and laughed loudly again as she walked away." Kate got choked up recalling this memory.

Brody frowned, realizing she understood more of what he was going through than he had thought.

Kate continued, "I dropped the knife then reached for my phone and called the police. Then I called Vanessa and told her what was going on. Her family met me at the hospital. My mom never showed up, and I haven't seen her since that day."

Brody hugged Kate. "That's awful. I am so sorry, Kate."

"It's fine. It's in the past, although that is one grudge I haven't been able to let go of yet. Anyway, I'm sorry I overreacted," Kate apologized.

"No harm done. I'm going to take your advice and make a quick post letting everyone know I'm fine," Brody promise her.

"Awesome! Well, I better go back to work," Kate said. Brody followed her, and Daniel showed them what to do.

Brody pulled into the driveway and helped Vanessa off the bike. They took off their helmets and looked at each other.

Vanessa chuckled. "Your hair needs help. It's all messed up."

Brody's eyes lit up. "Oh yeah? You should see your hair."

Vanessa gasped, "Does it really look that bad?" She reached up to smooth her hair.

Brody watched her and smiled admiringly. "Your hair isn't too bad. Anyway, I don't think anything could make you less attractive."

Vanessa looked at him and blushed. They locked eyes briefly before Vanessa started toward the house.

Grace and Heath were on the couch watching TV when they came into the house. "Hey, kids, if you're hungry, there are leftovers from dinner in the fridge," Grace offered.

"Thanks, but I'm going to shower and try to get some sleep," Brody answered as he started toward the stairs.

"So, Brody, we can start the Bible study this Tuesday, if you want, while the girls are at theirs. What do you think?" Heath asked as he turned to look at Brody. He stopped at the bottom of the stairs and nodded in agreement with the plan. "Great!" Heath said, turning back toward the TV.

Brody and Vanessa started up the stairs.

"You two are starting a Bible study together?" Vanessa asked, pleasantly surprised.

Brody nodded. "Yeah, your dad said he wants to read through something called John."

Vanessa smiled briefly, and then her smile turned to a frown as she looked at Brody, concerned. "Do *you* want to be sober, Brody? I heard you earlier when you were ranting, and you said you want people to leave you alone and that you are the one who calls the shots, not anyone else. Do you want to be free from your addiction? Did you only choose sobriety because you wanted to shut me up? Because after seeing you lying on the floor in the condition you were in and then seeing how alcohol was dragging you down, I just wanted to help you, but if you don't want the help, then..."

"Vanessa, you're rambling. Are you afraid I'm going to drink myself into oblivion again and try to kill myself?" he asked.

Vanessa was taken aback. "What? No...I just...I want to keep you..."

"Safe?" Brody finished. Vanessa nodded. Brody sighed and then looked at Vanessa longingly. "Vanessa, let me be real with you. You're leaving soon, remember? At some point, you are going to have to trust me." He reached out and took her hands in his.

"I want to stay sober, and I want to stay alive. Meeting you has given me a reason to stay alive. Being sober is hell right now, I will admit, but I want to be healed from this addiction and any other negative emotions that come from it, so I will stick to it no matter what," Brody said, staring at her intently.

Vanessa smiled. "I believe you Brody, but just for now, I am going to keep an eye on you. It will make me feel better. Is that okay with you?"

Brody smiled. "Sure. I don't mind getting to spend more time alone with you."

Vanessa blushed. "Good night, Brody."

Chapter Eight

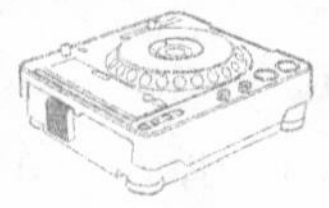

Tuesday morning rolled around. Vanessa had decided to quit her job earlier than she usually did after spending Monday in prayer about the decision. She was concerned about Brody being alone so early into his sobriety, and she knew her parents couldn't help out with the "babysitting" much longer, not with their busy schedules. She never told anyone, but keeping an eye on the newly sober residents at her clinic in India was one of the highlights of the job for her. She loved helping them find new life and purpose in their sobriety.

When Brody told Vanessa he was concerned he wouldn't be able to stay sober once he went back home, Vanessa felt even more at peace with her decision to quit her job. She suggested they take a walk on the beach and figure out his main triggers and social cues that made him drink. This would help him to find creative ways to keep his cravings at bay.

After they walked the beach, they walked the boardwalk.

"Thank you for taking the time to help me with my sobriety," Brody said as they walked.

Vanessa smiled. "Anytime. I really love to help. Do you feel a little more confident?"

He shrugged. "I don't know...maybe? I think I am going to need some time. I was a heavy drinker. Realistically, I can't just stop cold turkey and not feel the effects of it."

"Yeah, I understand. It will take some time for you. Just remember, some of the physical withdrawals you have could last a long time too. It's all part of the process. In recovery groups, they always teach you to have a higher power to look up to. There is no higher power than Jesus Christ, so try praying for his help too. Take things one day at a time. I believe in you," Vanessa encouraged him.

Brody nodded, and they walked silently for a little while.

"So are you excited about the Bible study tonight?" Vanessa asked after some time.

Brody chuckled. "I don't know if I would say I'm excited. I don't know what to expect, and I don't even have a Bible."

"There should be one in Daniel's room. My parents always keep a Bible in every room of the house. I'm sorry I didn't mention it before," Vanessa responded.

They passed by a rental shop, and Brody's eyes lit up. "Hey, you want to paddleboard? I saw people doing it yesterday, and it looked like fun. What do you say?"

Vanessa grimaced. "I don't know. I don't like the water much."

"Aw, come on. It will be fun!" Brody grabbed her hand and walked with her up to the rental booth. Vanessa couldn't understand how he was able to convince to her to do things she wasn't sure she wanted to do, but here she was, waiting in line for a paddleboard; it was the motorcycle thing all over again. She hoped she enjoyed this as much as she ended up enjoying the other.

Vanessa was hesitant to get on the board, but Brody did a good job of calming her down and encouraging her. She took a deep breath, prayed, and then stood to her feet shakily. They got the hang of it rather quickly. The water was calm, with only the occasional wave.

"This is really fun!" Vanessa commented after some time.

"Yeah, it's so peaceful out here," Brody replied.

"How old are you, Brody?" Vanessa asked suddenly.

"I'm thirty-two. Why? How old are you?"

Vanessa chuckled. "Don't you know you aren't supposed to ask a woman that question?"

"I remember you telling me you aren't like all the other girls," Brody joked.

"You got me. I'm twenty-eight. When is your birthday?" Vanessa asked next.

"I was born on March 22. What about you?" Brody asked.

"My birthday is January 10. Where do you live?" she asked.

Brody snickered. "Is this twenty questions?"

Vanessa smiled. "I want to get to know you better."

"I live in Manhattan when I'm not touring," Brody answered, smiling at her. They paddled farther.

"Where do you travel to?" Vanessa asked.

"I have done shows in small towns as well as big ones throughout the U.S., Europe, and Mexico. I'm really big in Europe," Brody said with a self-important grin on his face.

"I love traveling," Vanessa mused.

"Where have you traveled to?" he asked.

"My list is probably not as exciting as yours. I have only been to Texas, Hampton, and different parts of India. One day I would love to visit Europe," Vanessa responded.

"Where do you want to go?" Brody asked with a warm smile.

Vanessa's expression became bright with excitement, "I would love to visit Poland, the Czech Republic, the

Netherlands, and Italy too. Honestly, I wouldn't mind traveling all over the world if I were given the opportunity."

"I have been to all those places. They are truly exciting to visit, and each have their charms. You should try to transfer from India to one of those places with your ministry. I'm sure they need your help too," Brody suggested.

Vanessa just smiled as they paddled quietly for a few seconds.

"Did you always want to be an addiction counselor?" Brody asked, curious.

Vanessa shook her head. "No. Actually, when I was a child, I wanted to be a beekeeper. As I got into high school, I saw my brother's substance abuse issues, the suffering he was going through, and also the suffering all his loved ones were enduring, and it broke my heart wide open. I decided right then and there that I wanted to help as many people as possible that were going through what we were."

"I didn't know your brother had a substance abuse issue," Brody said honestly.

"His adoption story is very difficult, and that had a lot to do with it. If you ever want to hear about it, he'll be happy to tell you. He and my father never tire of talking about their transformation stories." Vanessa smiled. "Daniel and I are only a few months apart. We were in our junior year of high school when he finally quit his substance abuse and was going back to church regularly. God did something powerful in him to change his heart, but he won't tell anyone that part of his story; he says it was just between him and God."

"How did you end up in India of all places?"

"That was all God's doing. The day after I decided what career I wanted to have, I went to church with my family for a special event that the church was hosting. A missionary came to our church to speak about the mission work he did. He was currently living in Brazil and was helping people overcome their drug addictions and sharing the good news of Jesus Christ with the people. As soon as he said that, I knew this was for me." Vanessa smiled warmly at Brody as he turned to look at her.

"After the service, I went up to him and told him I wanted to join the program. He handed me a flyer and said that once I was out of high school, I could enroll in their program. I told God that I would go wherever he called me to go, no matter how tough a country it was. He sent me to India."

Brody smiled admiringly. "Wow, you are truly an amazing and selfless person. I don't think I could have taken a step out of my comfort zone like you did and go somewhere like that."

"Anyone can take a step like that if they have bold faith in Christ. Tell me about your family," Vanessa suggested.

Brody sighed heavily. "I have an older sister and my parents. My mom and dad live in Los Angeles; that's where I was born and raised. My sister, Regina, is three years older than me. She's a writer. I don't know where she lives now. We haven't talked in about five years. She's upset with me because I missed her wedding. I had a show I was supposed to do at the same time, and I chose the show over her. I don't blame her for being angry. She was always my biggest supporter, and I kind of spat in her face. My parents support my career, but that's probably because they like the money I send them monthly. I know my father uses a lot of it for booze. They call me, but usually it's to ask me for more money. It bothers me, so I don't talk to them too often."

Vanessa paddled and frowned. "Oh, Brody, I'm sorry to hear that. Maybe someday you will be able to mend fences with your family." Brody simply shrugged in between paddles.

"What kind of books does your sister write? Have you read any of them?" Vanessa asked.

"I think she writes teen fiction. I have her first few books. She sent them to me before our fallout. I haven't read them yet though. I'm not much of a reader," Brody confessed. They paddled some more in silence.

"When did you realize that you wanted to be a DJ?" Vanessa asked after a few minutes.

"I have always loved music with a kickin' beat. I would listen to lots of DJs when I was in middle school and high school. One day I thought, *I could do that*, so my parents got me a turntable—and the rest is history," Brody told her, grinning.

He paddled some more and spoke again. "I wasn't the best student in school; I barely made it out of high school. I only ever wanted to focus on my music. Once I graduated, I had a few odd jobs, but my focus was on making it big as a DJ. I finally got my first gig at nineteen years old, and a year later, I was asked to open for a festival filled with some of the greats in the business, guys that I grew up listening to. After that event, they all vouched for me with different venues, and I became a big deal in the making."

"That's awesome, Brody. "It's great to know what you want to do with your life at such a young age," Vanessa commented.

"Yeah, I just wish I still wanted to do it," Brody said, staring out at the horizon. "Don't get me wrong. I still love music and always love being in the studio, but lately it's like a burden—that scares me. How can someone know what they want for their whole life, get it, and then, out of nowhere, not want it anymore. Is that a real thing that happens?"

"Definitely. We mature, and then our ideas for our lives change. Like I said, I wanted to be a beekeeper as a child," Vanessa said with a chuckle.

"Yeah, I wanted to ask you about that.... Why a beekeeper?" he asked.

"I liked bees. I always dressed up as a bee every Halloween as a child. I don't know what the obsession was about," Vanessa said.

"Have you ever felt unfulfilled before?" Brody asked.

Vanessa looked at him with a nod. "When I first started serving in India, I was overwhelmed and homesick. I actually decided to head home five weeks after getting there. I was on my way to tell my leader about my decision when a young child from the street burst into the clinic, took hold of my hand, and laid a piece of paper in it before running off. There was writing on it in Hindi: 'You need to read James 4:17 before you make your decision, Vanessa.' I wasn't sure what to make of that situation. I didn't know this kid or where he had come from, and I hadn't told anyone except God about my choice. I went to my Bible immediately and read the verse: *Remember, it is a sin to know what you ought to do and then not do it.* I chuckled to myself, and I told God that his message was received and I would stay as long as he gave me the strength to."

"That is an inspiring story. I'm glad you didn't give up. Just think how many people you wouldn't have helped if you did, including me," Brody encouraged her.

Vanessa looked at him, pleasantly surprised by his answer. "Thanks. That really puts it all into perspective." They paddled quietly once more.

"You really take your God seriously, huh," Brody commented, glancing at her.

Vanessa nodded. "Of course. He is worth it. One day you will know this for yourself."

Brody chuckled in disbelief. "I don't know about that."

"God works all sorts of miracles, Brody," Vanessa told him, looking at him with a hopeful look.

Brody cleared his throat. "We should get ready to turn back."

Vanessa nodded in agreement and tried to turn around slowly. They started their journey back to the shore.

"Keep working on your sobriety. Maybe having a sober mind will help give you clarity in other areas of your life." Vanessa suggested.

Brody nodded slowly in agreement. "I have a serious question to ask you."

"Sure, what is it?" Vanessa asked.

Brody grinned. "Could this be our first date? I did rent the paddleboards after all."

Vanessa rolled her eyes playfully and chuckled, poking him with the paddle. "You never give up, do you?"

Brody poked her with his paddle too. "Some things are worth fighting for."

Vanessa stopped paddling momentarily, trying to stay steady on the paddleboard as she stared at Brody intently. He looked at her with a flirtatious grin, which made her blush and feel butterflies in her stomach. She decided to ease the tension she was feeling at that moment by lifting her paddle and pushing him into the water playfully.

He went in with a loud splash and a muffled gasp. Vanessa guffawed as he came up from under the water and shook her paddleboard with his waves. She knelt down, trying to steady herself so she didn't capsize as she continued to laugh. Brody stared at her, laughing too. Vanessa couldn't help but notice the radiance of Brody's genuine delight in the moment. He seemed carefree, something he had always wanted to be. She grinned uncontrollably.

"Oh, you think that was funny, huh?" he asked with a flirtatious smile.

Vanessa nodded, still giggling.. "Yes, it was very funny. You look cold. I bet the water is freezing," Brody smirked.

"I don't know. What do you think?" He grabbed her arm and tossed her into the water with a chuckle. She went in with a loud squeal and splash.

Vanessa came up from under the water, gasped, and looked at him with a surprised face. "I can't believe you did that."

Brody frowned. "I'm sorry, Vanessa. I got carried away."

Vanessa grinned and pushed him under the water briefly. "Not forgiven." She tried to get back on her paddleboard before he came back up, but she wasn't quick enough. He came up from the water and grabbed her leg. She squealed with laughter as he dragged her back into the water.

"Okay, okay, truce!" Vanessa yelled, looking at Brody with a flirtatious grin, practically in his arms because he was right there behind her.

Brody nodded, swallowing the lump in his throat. "Truce." They started at each other intently until Brody noticed Vanessa shivering. "Are you cold?" he asked.

She nodded. "Yeah, I'm freezing. I'm a wimp when it comes to cold water. That's why I don't usually go in the water."

"Then we should get out so you don't freeze," Brody suggested, helping Vanessa get back onto her paddleboard before getting onto his. They started paddling again, trying to shake the intense feelings they had just experienced but didn't express to each other.

"I really am sorry I dragged you into the water. You are going to be soaking wet and freezing for a while," Brody apologized.

"It's fine Brody, really. I had a lot of fun. Thanks for

encouraging me to do this. I think paddleboarding is now one of my favorite things to do," Vanessa said happily.

"Happy to hear it. This is a day I will always remember too," he said.

Vanessa smiled. "This isn't a date though."

Brody shrugged. "I had a hunch you would say that. It's still a great day regardless, and it helped to keep my mind off of you know what."

Vanessa blushed as they paddled to shore. "You haven't bought me a meal yet." Brody looked at her, intrigued. "This isn't a proper date until I get some grub," Vanessa said in a joking way to mask her nervousness about what she had just said to him.

Brody's eyes lit up with excitement. "I will buy you anything you want to eat."

"Let's get a doughboy. Have you had one yet?" Vanessa asked. Brody shook his head, holding his paddleboard and oar. Vanessa gasped. "Seriously? You haven't lived until you have tried one of these."

"Then we better get one now," Brody joked. They dropped off their paddleboards at the rental store and then went to eat. While standing in line, Brody's eyes strayed toward the open-air bar next to them where some people were sitting and having drinks. Vanessa noticed Brody staring at one table in particular; it was a group of young adults laughing and drinking while they ate lunch. Brody started to wring his hands, and his body tensed up.

Vanessa gently touched his hand and stirred him from his thoughts. He looked at her with sad eyes and frowned. "Thank you for being here with me. I know what would have happened if you weren't. I am too weak. I want to be sober, but it is a lot of work to fight off these nagging cravings."

They moved forward in the line, and Vanessa touched his shoulder gently. "Look at me, Brody. It will be okay. Take it a day at a time. Sobriety isn't a quick process for most people; it's going to take time. Don't beat yourself up for thinking about alcohol. Just recognize when it is happening, and make a positive change, like we practiced earlier on the beach." Brody nodded and smiled warmly.

They got back home before Vanessa's parents, so they changed out of their wet clothes and then sat on the couch and watched a movie together. By the time Vanessa's mom got home in the late afternoon, she saw them napping on the couch, Vanessa's legs draped on Brody's lap. Grace giggled to herself and started dinner. Vanessa woke up fifteen minutes later, startled that she was sitting that comfortably with Brody. She got off the couch quietly so she wouldn't wake him and went into the kitchen to help her mom.

"Hey, sweetie, sorry I woke you. Did you fall asleep right after work?" Grace asked, putting the bags of groceries on the counter.

Vanessa winced. "No, actually, I quit today."

Grace looked confused, so Vanessa explained. "You are truly devoted to your true calling. I am proud of you. So did you two stay on the couch all day?" Grace asked, pulling groceries from the bag.

"No, we went to the beach and paddle boarded; we just got home a few hours ago," Vanessa responded.

"Oh, is that the thing on the water with the board and oar? I have always wanted to do that. Is it fun?" Grace asked, boiling a pot of water for some noodles.

Vanessa nodded. "It was very fun, but the water was cold."

Grace handed her the sauce to put into the pot next to her. "Aren't you supposed to stay on the board?"

Vanessa explained to her mom what had happened, and Grace giggled. "I am so happy to see you two having fun together."

Vanessa tensed up. "What do you mean?"

Grace started to brown the ground beef. "I see how you to look at each other and interact with each other, and you just told me what happened today—that you considered it a date. Sweetie, I have never seen you show interest in someone before. It's nice to see, that's all. You know it's okay for missionaries to have relationships other than with Christ, right?"

Vanessa nodded apprehensively. "Yeah, but not with unbelievers."

"True. Don't give up on him, but guard your heart. Pray for him to stay sober and for him to come to faith. He seems open to Christ," Grace encouraged. Vanessa nodded, feeling an overwhelming sadness and confusion.

"He does, but I know that's not enough. Why do I have feelings for him when I have never felt strongly about anyone else? Why him?"

Grace put the noodles into the boiling water. "Sweetie, what do you see when you look at him?" Grace asked.

Vanessa looked over at him sleeping on the couch and smiled before turning to look at her mom again. "I see an overcomer, someone who will be a powerful influence in music and anything else he is called to do. I see a man of God who will change the world with his positive attitude and passion for life."

Grace teared up as she watched her daughter speak life over Brody. "This is why you like him—because you see who he can be. You don't see a person struggling with sobriety or someone who tried to end his life. You have always had the ability to see and treat people as you believe they will be one day. You see their flaws, yes, but you also like to lead them toward the truth that will set them free by loving them through their struggles and sin. You have a heart for people, and it's nice to see that you have a soft spot for *certain* people too, not just your family."

Vanessa laughed. "You just want your kids to get married so you can have grandchildren someday, Mom."

Grace laughed too. "That is the end goal of all parents, sweetie." Their laughter woke Brody, and he came over to see them.

Chapter Nine

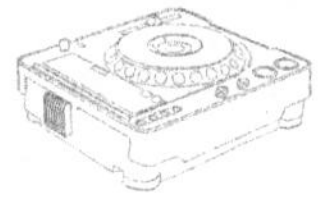

"HEATH WILL BE DOWN in a few seconds, Brody. Have fun with your Bible study, you two," Grace said as she grabbed her own Bible off the table and waved to Brody as she walked out the door. Vanessa bolted down the stairs shortly after. "Bye, Brody. Have fun, and keep an open mind and heart. I look forward to hearing how it went when I get home!" she said, waving quickly as she left.

Brody killed time by looking at the pictures on the mantle over the fireplace. He saw a few of Heath and Grace at their wedding; Vanessa and young Grace looked a lot alike. Next he saw some pictures of Heath when he was in his rock band days. The last few were of Daniel and Vanessa: some baby and young kid pictures, Daniel's graduation photo, and Vanessa's graduation photo. He blushed and touched her picture gently. Just then, Heath came downstairs.

"Okay, are you ready?" Heath asked, making his way to the couch. Brody nodded and sat down, holding a Bible awkwardly in his hands. "I see you found the Bible and notebook we have in Daniel's room," Heath commented.

"Yeah, I did. I will leave it here when I go back home," Brody assured him.

"No, the Bible and notebook are for you. We can always get a new Bible and notebook for the next person who stays in that room. Okay, let's open up to John chapter one," Heath said, flipping through his Bible and then showing Brody how to find books of the Bible with the table of contents. Heath started reading.

"I have a question, Heath," Brody interrupted. "What is sin? This John persons says that Jesus came to take away the sins of the world. What does that mean?" Brody interjected.

"That is a great question. Let's go to Genesis chapter on through three," Heath said with a smile. Brody used his table of contents, found the book, and turned there quickly.

Heath asked Brody to read it out loud. Brody was nervous at first, but Heath assured him he would do great.

"This is some heavy stuff," he said, sighing. "I have some more questions now. First off, why did God let us live in our sins if he loves us so much? Why didn't he just fix us right there?" Brody asked.

"Well, he gave us free will, and in order to 'fix us,' he would have to override our free will. Since he loves us so much, he didn't want to do that. He lets us hang out in our sins until we no longer want to. That is when we start searching for what is missing from our lives, and it will ultimately lead us to God. *That* is when he can truly heal us from the inside out," Heath explained at length.

"Kind of like my situation, although I wasn't looking for God when I got here. I'm still not sure that I am, but I am willing to try anything to fix it, even this God of yours. Okay, my next question: Why would God send his only son to die for us sinners if his son didn't deserve to die? According to this second chapter of Genesis, it sounds like we deserved to die. He would have been justified in letting us burn, so why did he send Jesus?" Brody asked.

"He sent him so we could all have a chance to live in eternity with him. He missed that fellowship he once had with Adam and Eve in the garden. They would be in each other's presence all the time. He wanted that connection with us again. Without a sinless sacrifice, Jesus, the Lamb of God as John the Baptist called him, we wouldn't be able to have that connection with God again, because God can't be in the presence of sin," Heath replied.

"What do you mean he can't be in the presence of sin? So what happens if a Christian makes a mistake? God leaves them until they apologize or something?" Brody asked.

"No, as Christian, we should try not to sin, but we are humans and will make mistakes. As believers, we have the sacrifice that Jesus Christ made for us to make us right with God. Once we place our trust in Christ, we can come to him and ask for forgiveness and repent of those sins. People who have not accepted Christ's free gift of eternal life do not have that covering. Their sins aren't forgiven and cleansed. They don't have the desire to do what is right, and they don't want to repent for it; therefore God can't be around their willful sins. Does that make sense?" Heath reiterated.

Brody nodded sadly. "Yeah, I get it now. You mean people like me, who keep doing bad things without remorse, are the ones he keeps a distance from, right?"

Heath patted him on the shoulder. "That is correct, but it doesn't have to stay that way. As we just read in John 1:12, 'But to all who believed him and accepted him, he gave the right to become children of God.' What this tells us is that God loved you enough that he sent Jesus to rescue you from your sins, when he died on the cross and then rose from the grave three days later. If you accept that gift, realize you did nothing to deserve it, and truly repent from your sins, then Christ comes into your heart and changes you day by day." Brody was deep in thought for a while, and Heath prayed for him during the silence.

"So I have a new question: If God can't be in the presence of sin, how does anyone get saved. Aren't we all unworthy of being in his presence before we come to repent?" Brody asked after some time. Heath grinned. He loved Brody's provocative questions.

"You're right. He can't get close to us while we are sinners. But here is the beauty of how much God loves us: He calls to us," Heath started. Brody looked at him quizzically. "He whispers in his loving voice until we can finally hear him, and as we hear him and make strides to start listening to his call, we start to leave our old ways behind and start to follow his voice. Before we know it, we are in the presence of God because we are now his. All his calling for us and our searching is what draws us to each other. It's like a relationship with a significant other; you don't become close unless you communicate with each other and listen to each other," Heath explained, a glimmer in his eye.

Brody smiled. Even though he didn't fully understand everything Heath said, he could feel the passion in his words.

"Jesus was willing to be the perfect sacrifice needed to fulfill God's plan, and because of that, we are all able to be called children of God when we accept the sacrifice that Jesus made on the cross. We get the chance at a new and healthy life and an eternity in heaven," Heath finished.

Brody nodded slowly. "I'm still confused, mostly by all the words. It seems like a college course to me; I feel I should have taken notes."

Heath smirked. "I felt the same way when I was searching for God. I'm sorry I didn't try to speak in the same way my mentor spoke to me. I will reiterate in an easier-to-understand sort of way."

Just then Heath heard Grace and Vanessa walking up to the door. "I will try to get the girls to go upstairs, and then we can continue to chat," Heath said, standing up to greet them at the door.

Brody waited on the couch, looking at his Bible and writing a few things down in his notebook. Heath told the girls he was still working with Brody and wondered if they would head upstairs so they could talk privately. Vanessa was reluctant at first because she wanted to see how things were going, but it was more important to her that he get the most out of this Bible study.

Heath went back to the couch and cleared his throat. "The man who ministered to me long ago said it to me like this: 'Heath, you are a sinner. You have broken God's commands, and you need God's forgiveness so you can be saved from eternal death. You need to ask Jesus Christ to come into your heart so he can help you.'"

Brody chuckled. "Yeah, I think that is straightforward enough for me to understand. Thanks for dumbing it down for me."

"I'm glad I could help, and I really enjoyed tonight's study. If you have any more questions before we do our next study, don't hesitate to ask me. You can call or text me anytime too, even when you go back home to New York," Heath assured him. Brody nodded. "Okay, let's pray and head to sleep," Heath suggested.

Vanessa heard the footsteps of someone coming upstairs and was about to open her door, but then she heard her father talking to Brody and decided to stay in her room, realizing she wouldn't get the chance to talk to him tonight. She turned off her light and went to sleep reluctantly.

That night Brody had a hard time sleeping. After lying in bed for hours, he sat up, turned on the light next to his bed, and sighed heavily, rubbing his weary eyes. His stomach started grumbling, and he thought about sneaking downstairs to make himself something to eat. He looked at the clock next to him: one in the morning.

He climbed out of bed and snuck downstairs to the kitchen. He had started to rummage through the fridge when he heard footsteps on the stairs. He stood up quickly and shut the fridge door, a piece of watermelon hanging from his mouth, his eyes wide with alarm.

Vanessa giggled at the sight. "I thought I heard someone down here."

Brody chuckled in embarrassment and bit off the piece of watermelon in his mouth. "I was hungry. Did I wake you?"

"Nope, I was up," Vanessa answered, opening the fridge back up. She pulled out a bag of grapes and some cheese and motioned for Brody to sit at the kitchen table with her. They sat there and snacked.

"Why were you up?" Brody asked.

Vanessa looked at him with a shrug of her shoulders. "Just couldn't sleep. So why aren't you asleep?"

Brody popped a grape in his mouth. "Why don't you go first and tell me why you weren't sleeping."

Vanessa chuckled nervously. "Why do you want to know? It has nothing to do with you."

Brody's eyes lit up. "Liar, I can see it all over your face. You were thinking about me, huh?"

Vanessa blushed. "No, I was not."

"Okay, okay, I won't pry. I have been having bouts of insomnia since I gave up alcohol. It sucks, but with my line of work, I'm kind of used to not sleeping much. I'm still trying to force myself to sleep though," Brody confessed.

"Have you had any other symptoms?" Vanessa asked.

Brody shrugged. "I don't think I have noticed any symptoms other than insomnia and irritability. That is why sometimes I will skip breakfast and stay in my room for a few extra hours. I need to relax first. I have noticed that in the mornings is when my irritability is highest."

"I'm sure those are tough symptoms to have. Try drinking some warm tea before bed; it might help with the insomnia. It's in the cupboard over there," Vanessa said, pointing behind Brody. He nodded. "For the irritability, I suggest taking deep breaths before you react," she added with a smile.

Brody nodded slowly, smiling at Vanessa admiringly. Vanessa smiled back, blushing. It was hard not to; his smile was electric. The room was silent for a few minutes as they ate and exchanged glances.

"So how is it being sober?" Vanessa asked finally, breaking the tension of the moment.

"I'm enjoying the clarity and focus. It has given me a new perspective on how to approach things I want out of life," Brody confessed.

Vanessa smiled warmly. "That's great. I am very happy for you. I can tell you are different. I see it in your eyes."

Brody leaned in toward her and smiled flirtatiously. "You see it in my eyes? What do you see?"

Vanessa swallowed a lump in her throat and gazed into his eyes. It gave her the chills as she saw his pupils dilating, indicating he found her attractive. She swallowed another lump in her throat and blushed. "I see hope for your future in your eyes."

Brody leaned back in his chair and smiled. "Did you see anything else in them?"

Vanessa chuckled nervously. "Nope."

He chuckled in response. "You seem a little tense for someone who only saw hope." Vanessa tried not to let on how anxious she was during this conversation. "I saw something in your eyes too," Brody told her, grinning.

"Oh yeah? What did you see?" Vanessa asked waveringly.

Brody paused for what seemed like forever before he finally spoke. "I'm going to keep it to myself. Besides, I think you already know what I saw."

Vanessa chortled. "Oh yeah? Why do you think that?"

Brody smirked. "I saw the same thing in your eyes that you refuse to tell me you saw in mine." Vanessa swallowed another lump in her throat as Brody stood to his feet. "We should try to go back to sleep now that we have some food in our bellies," he suggested, picking up the grapes and cheese.

In the morning, Brody woke up and saw a note on his bedroom floor near the door. He grabbed it and read it with a grin on his face:

> *Morning, Brody. I wanted to see if you would like to go to dinner with me this evening. Yes, to answer your question, it would be another date. Meet me at Rocky's around 6 if you want to go. Vanessa*

Chapter Ten

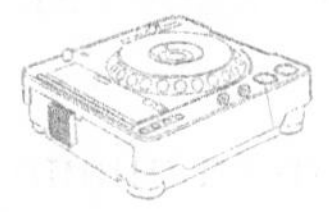

Brody arrived at Rocky's a little before six and waited outside. He wore a dark green dress shirt tucked into black jeans. His hair was slicked back into a classic undercut hairstyle, and he wore a nice pair of shoes and glasses he had bought in town earlier in the day. He thought he was looking pretty good, and then he saw Vanessa walking out of Rocky's wearing a beautiful knee-length yellow dress with lace sleeves and a pair of heels. Her hair was swept to the side and curled slightly at the ends, and she wore a little make-up and some earrings. He swallowed the lump in his throat and smiled nervously as she walked over to him, waving.

"Did you show up to work dressed like that? I'm sure you had a lot of sales if you did. You look amazing, Vanessa," Brody said shyly.

"Thanks for the compliment, but no, I was off work at five. I used that extra hour to get ready. You look nice too. Green is a good color on you, and you shaved your stubble," Vanessa complimented him.

"Yeah, I figured it made me look too scruffy."

Vanessa shrugged. "I don't know. I kind of liked it, but you look good either way. I didn't know you wore glasses either."

"I don't. I didn't want anyone to recognize me, other than you of course," Brody commented.

"So where are we going anyway?" she asked.

Brody looked at her, fumbling over his words. "You asked me out, didn't you? I thought you had a place in mind."

Vanessa chuckled. "I'm just messing with you. I know where to go. You can drive my car, and I will give you the directions."

The restaurant was fifteen minutes away. He parked on a grassy knoll and then helped Vanessa get out of the car carefully, catching a whiff of her perfume. He couldn't nail down the fragrance exactly, but he was intoxicated by it.

"This place has the best ribs," Vanessa commented as they walked toward the entrance.

"Are you going to eat ribs looking like that?" Brody asked, holding the restaurant door open for her.

"I know how to eat without making a mess," Vanessa said with a sly smile as she walked in. They sat down at a high-top table and looked over the menu before the waitress came by and took their drink order.

"Wow, can I eat one of everything? This menu is stellar," Brody commented, rubbing his belly.

"You can afford it if you really want to," Vanessa commented with a giggle.

Brody chuckled. "I was a total jerk flaunting my money like that when I first met you. I'm sorry I refused your kind offer that day I arrived, if it means anything to you; I felt bad that I upset you."

Vanessa blushed. "It's okay. It's in the past." The waitress came and took their orders.

"This place is small and secluded. I like it," Brody commented after the waitress left.

"I know you don't want anyone to recognize you right now, so I figured this would be a great place. Not many people are here on a Wednesday night. I haven't been here in years, so I had to ask my parents if it was still open."

Brody looked at her admiringly. "Thanks for the consideration to make this night special for us."

Vanessa sipped her tea with a shy smile.

"So do your parents know we are on a date tonight?" Brody asked suddenly.

Vanessa looked at him and nodded. "Yes, of course. After I asked my mom about the restaurant, she asked why I wanted to know, so I told her."

Brody looked surprised. "And they didn't try to stop it?"

Vanessa snickered. "Of course not. Why would they? They trust me, and they seem to like you."

Brody smiled. "And what about you? Do you like me?"

"It must be difficult being famous to the point you are afraid to go anywhere for fear of being seen," Vanessa said, deflecting.

Brody nodded. "Yeah, it's not easy, but it comes with the territory. You get used to it after a while, but then one day it makes you crazy."

"I am sure fame can weigh heavily on a person," Vanessa remarked as the waitress brought them their iced teas. They sipped their drinks silently.

"So what made you want to have a second date with me so soon? Am I that irresistible?" Brody asked flirtatiously.

Vanessa chuckled, "No, I mean yes, I mean...I wanted to get to know you more. That's why I asked you out tonight." Vanessa didn't like how his advances were making her trip over her words; it was showing him her cards.

Brody chuckled. "You already grilled me about my life on the first date. What else do you want to know about me?"

"I'm going to ask you about those women you have mentioned before," Vanessa said, looking a little hesitant. Brody gulped and felt her sentiments in his soul. He felt the same hesitation to tell her anything. Their food came at that time, and Brody was happy for the distraction. Vanessa prayed over the meal, and they started eating.

"Why do you want to know about that stuff anyway?" Brody asked, looking disgusted.

"I don't want details. I just want to ask some questions that I would ask any guy I went on a couple dates with. If you want to date someone, you have to be open with them about everything, right?" Vanessa asked.

Brody nodded. "Okay then, if you ever want to have a healthy relationship with someone, you have to learn how to talk about uncomfortable things, like past relationships. It's healthy for a couple to be open and honest with each other," Vanessa continued.

Brody grinned. "Are you saying we're a couple?" Vanessa laughed nervously but didn't respond. "I don't think I have ever been totally honest and vulnerable with a woman, not like I have been with you. Go ahead and ask your questions, Vanessa," Brody said, moving on.

"You said you have been with many women…more than ten?" Vanessa asked.

Brody winced as he nodded, ashamed.

Vanessa smiled, "Thank you for your honesty. Did you have romantic feelings for any of them?"

Brody snorted. "Honestly, I don't even remember most of their names, and if I saw them on the street, I don't even think

I would recognize them. I was drunk out of my mind most of the time."

Vanessa saw the disappointment written all over his face as he answered. "So you have never had a *real* relationship with a woman?" Vanessa asked next.

Brody shook his head and sipped his tea.

"Thank you for being honest with me, Brody. I am sure it was hard, but I appreciate it so much. You can ask me some questions now if you want," Vanessa suggested.

"What's your history?" he asked.

"I dated someone in middle school for two days. Then in high school, I went to prom with a different guy each year. Aside from that, I haven't really been interested in dating. I was always too focused on other things. In school, I was focused on my studies, and then when I went to the mission field, my focus shifted to my mission work."

Brody sighed. "Well, at least your story is cleaner than mine."

"Don't belittle your story, Brody. God wouldn't want that. He can do amazing things with your past if you let him," Vanessa encouraged him.

Their dessert came, and they started eating.

"How can he use my past? It's so…gross," Brody wondered after the waitress left.

Vanessa smiled. "Many people in India who have gone through our program have asked me that same question, so I will tell you what I tell them. God doesn't make junk, he doesn't make mistakes, and he turns ashes into beauty. He will take what you think is broken, and he will turn it into something that has infinite value because you mean so much to him. He is willing and able to put the time and effort into creating you anew."

Brody looked at her and felt himself choking up, but he tried not to show it as he responded. "Well, that was a very loaded answer. Thank you…very encouraging." Brody finished his dessert.

"Thank you for dinner. you didn't have to pay for it though; I don't mind paying. I asked you out after all," Vanessa said as they walked out the door.

"I have never had the pleasure of treating a lady to dinner before. I was happy to do it," Brody said with a grin.

Vanessa smiled back and then looked over at some benches near the grassy knoll, "Do you wanna sit?" Brody nodded, and they made their way to a bench.

"If you could do anything else for a job, what would you do?" Vanessa asked, looking very interested in his answer.

Brody sat quietly for a few seconds. "I don't know. Being a DJ is all I have ever wanted to be. It would take an act of God to change my mind. What about you? If you were no longer a missionary, what would you do? Would you continue doing addiction counseling in America?" Brody asked.

Vanessa sighed. "Now there is a question." Brody could tell there was more she wanted to say, so he stayed silent until she spoke again. "Most days I love what I do and don't want to do anything else, and then there are days when something big happens to us out there—the area I work in can be hostile sometimes—and it makes me wonder."

"Makes you wonder what?" Brody asked.

Vanessa looked at him hesitantly. "It makes me wonder if God is telling me my time there is over. I have stayed there a lot longer than many others have. Usually the people in my field of work will only stay for a period of five to ten years, and then they go home—unless they feel God telling them to stay longer; then they will stay their whole lives. I am not sure

I am being called to a lifelong ministry out there. My job is very taxing emotionally and physically, as you witnessed first-hand, and some days it is more than I can take. I really have to rely on God's strength to make it through most days." Vanessa paused before speaking again. "Lately I have felt God telling me something in my life is going to change soon. I don't know what that means yet though." Vanessa looked at Brody for a reaction.

"Are you in danger there?" he asked, concerned.

"Oh, I don't know why I even mentioned any of this to you. Please don't worry about it. Just forget I said anything please," Vanessa all but begged.

Brody snorted. "Should I ask your family about it instead? I'm sure they would tell me something."

Vanessa chuckled. "Not if they don't know anything either."

He furrowed his brow but didn't speak.

Vanessa sighed. "I haven't told my parents about any of the backlash we get in India. I don't want to worry them, and I don't need them trying to keep me here. I am already battling the idea of staying here on my own; I don't need help."

"Don't they already know what missionaries go through?" Brody asked, confused.

Vanessa shrugged. "I don't know. They probably have their suspicions. I just don't want to worry them. I'm their little girl, you know?"

Brody nodded slowly. They stayed silent for a while, listening to the distant waves.

"Whatever has happened to you must be severe enough to make you think God is calling you to stay home permanently, right?" Brody commented, breaking the silence.

Vanessa looked at him sidelong. "The local gangs have tried to set our clinic on fire a few times. They have kidnapped some people coming to our clinic for help and have been making death threats for several years to the clinic workers." Brody frowned. "Yikes. Have they done anything to you personally?"

"I have been threatened with bodily harm, and at one point, an angry pimp tried to rape me as I helped one of the women he owned leave him. But I took self-defense classes in Texas, so I know how to take care of myself," Vanessa said, looking at Brody with sadness in her eyes.

"I can see why you are wondering if you should take a break or move on," Brody said.

Vanessa felt immediate guilt for having those thoughts. "Maybe it is all my own nerves. Maybe I am just scared of persecution. I'm telling myself that it's God who wants me back home, but it's really me wanting it so I can stay safe." She looked at Brody and saw he couldn't understand her babbling. She smiled and cleared her throat. "Please don't mention this to anyone. I haven't even told Kate about this. You are the only one I have confided in. Not even anyone back home in India knows how I have been feeling."

Brody smiled reassuringly. "I won't say anything." He paused. "How long have you been a Christian?"

"I grew up in the church, but I didn't accept Jesus into my heart until I was in high school. I always had an interest in him and the Bible, but I didn't make it personal until my junior year of high school, around the time of Daniel's healing," Vanessa explained.

"My family was never religious. I grew up completely disconnected from any sort of spirituality, except for my grandma. She would read the Bible to me and my sister whenever we saw her, but she didn't live like you and your family do. She didn't look any different than anyone else in my family did when you looked at her life." Brody paused and looked at

Vanessa with a smile. "At this point in my life, I will try just about anything, even God."

"God is always worth a try; he won't let you down. He is all you will ever need in life," Vanessa said sincerely. Brody looked at her with a warm smile. "May I ask you a tough question now?" Vanessa asked, her face indicating it was probably not easy for her to ask it any more than it would be for him to answer it. He nodded. "Why do you act like a womanizer? Why didn't you stop chasing after women when you started feeling it wasn't making you happy?"

Brody grimaced. "Going for the jugular, huh?"

"Sorry, this has been on my mind for a while now," Vanessa responded.

"I wasn't a cute kid growing up. I know, looking at me now, it's hard to believe," he started with a smirk. "I got picked on a lot, believe it or not. When I was a little kid, I had a crush on a girl. She said I had cooties and would get all the girls to run away from me. When I got to junior high, I had crooked teeth that needed braces and acne all over my face, so the girls did about the same thing to me—but worse. I would get flat out ghosted to my face when I tried to talk to a girl. Once I hit high school, I just gave up talking to girls and was a loner." Brody glanced at Vanessa. She was frowning, empathizing.

"In my senior year of high school, I left my ugly duckling phase behind, and I was more of what you see now. When I started making my own music in my senior year, I saw that girls at school were showing interest. From that point on, girls would flock to me. As a young adult, once they heard what I did for a living, they liked me even more, so I just ran with that, remembering all the girls in my past who dissed me. That gave me a greater desire to play with more heart. I didn't quit, because it had become a big part of my identity that I couldn't let go of. I was known for having a girl with me every night, and I didn't want to upset that balance. If I did, then people would have noticed there was a shift in my mindset and started asking questions I wasn't prepared to answer," Brody told her honestly.

Vanessa could feel the pain in his voice, and she hugged him, surprising him. "It must have been hard doing the same thing you always did even when you didn't want to do it anymore." Brody shrugged as Vanessa let him go. She continued, "I used to be a big people pleaser. It wasn't until the day I found Christ that I realized I only needed to please one person: God. That really took a load off my mind."

"I wish I could please only one person too," Brody said in a half-joking way.

"You can, you know. If you accept Jesus into your heart, you only have to please him," Vanessa reminded him, nudging him playfully with her shoulder. Brody smiled but didn't respond.

"So who is Brody Maddox if he is not what is portrayed to the world?" Vanessa asked.

Brody looked at her and sighed heavily, shrugging. "Heck if I know. I haven't been him in so long."

Vanessa nudged him again and grinned. "If I may say so, I think I am seeing him tonight...and have seen him since you came to stay at my house." Brody looked at her, intrigued. "Kate showed me your photos and past videos on your social media pages," Vanessa started.

"Oh gosh, I was such a douche in all those. Please don't judge me off of that. That's not me at all," Brody protested.

Vanessa nodded in agreement. "I know. That is where I was going. Since you have been here, you have been nothing but nice, a little shy but also flirtatious, curious, and funny—and you seem very relaxed and down to earth. I see a powerful spirit in you, Brody, one that wants to change the world but isn't sure how to do it yet. You seem to have a passion to thrive, which is good, and you're deeper than you let on. I see you are more than what you put on social media, and I hope you are starting to see it too."

Brody's eyes welled up with tears unexpectedly. "I think you forgot to add I'm a sad-sack."

Vanessa laughed and wiped away his tears for him. Brody smiled and touched her hand gently. Vanessa felt her heart skip a beat, and there was an awkward silence as they looked at each other longingly. Vanessa pulled her hand away slowly. "Maybe we should head back to Rocky's so you can get your bike. It's getting late."

Brody nodded reluctantly, and they headed to the car.

Brody parked the car in the parking lot by Rocky's, turned the engine off, and then turned to Vanessa. "I had a great time," he said as he handed her the keys.

"Yeah, I did too," Vanessa said, taking the keys, her hand brushing against his momentarily. She got goosebumps. "Well, we should go back to the house now," Vanessa said, opening the door and starting to the driver's side with intent.

Brody stepped out of the car and waited until Vanessa was right in front of him. He reached out and touched her hand gently, looking at her longingly again. Vanessa's heart fluttered, and she didn't move her hand away this time, even though her mind was screaming at her to move.

"I wish you didn't have to leave, Vanessa. I have never met anyone who makes me feel like you do," he said passionately. Vanessa's stomach flip-flopped, and she turned away from him, moving her hand. "I know, and this thing between us isn't helping the feelings I have about staying."

Brody's eyes lit up. "Then stay. We can see where this thing goes between us, and you can evaluate your life's course."

Vanessa pondered the idea momentarily and then shook her head. "I made a promise to God that I would serve him wherever he calls me, no matter what. I can't quit simply because I am feeling exhausted or burned out."

"Maybe God is calling you to stay here with me," Brody suggested, hopeful.

Vanessa furrowed her brow. "I don't think so, Brody."

"Couldn't you just extend your stay until after the new year. After all, you wouldn't want to miss the holidays with your family, would you?" Brody begged, giving her a flirtatious grin.

Vanessa snickered. "I'm never here for the holidays. Also, you aren't planning on staying away from your life until next year are you?"

Brody took hold of Vanessa's hands again and smiled. "I don't care about all that. I just want to be with you longer."

Vanessa was flattered. She felt the exact same way, but she didn't want to show him her true feelings so she pulled her hands away gently.

Brody sighed. "I just find it really ironic that the one girl I finally feel any sort of emotional attachment to is leaving soon. It's a cruel joke your God is playing on us."

Vanessa chuckled inadvertently. "Yes, it does seem cruel."

Brody brushed his fingers against Vanessa's arm and then looked at her with an intense gaze. "Do you like me, Vanessa?"

Vanessa's heart was pounding now. "Of course I do."

"More than just a friend?" he added.

Vanessa swallowed a lump in her throat and then opened her mouth to speak, but Brody shook his head slowly.

"You don't need to answer. It's not fair to put you on the

spot like this. It's probably best for me that you don't answer anyway since you're leaving. We should head back to the house," Brody said, walking to his bike. He started it up and put on his helmet. Vanessa got into her car and drove away, conflicted.

Vanessa pulled in right after he did, and they stared at each other awkwardly as they walked up to the front door. Vanessa grabbed her house keys and started to open the door. "I hope this situation doesn't put a dent in our ability to be friends, Vanessa," Brody said seriously.

Vanessa turned to look at him, surprised. "Of course it doesn't. Why would it?"

Brody shrugged. She opened the door quietly, and they walked inside toward the stairs. Brody started up, and Vanessa followed him. She touched his shoulder softly to get him to look at her before he opened his bedroom door, and he turned around with distraught eyes. Vanessa felt butterflies in her stomach as she echoed his sentiments. Suddenly she leaned forward and kissed him softly on the lips. Brody didn't have time to react before she pulled away and went into her room quickly. Brody was dumbfounded and elated as he went into his bedroom. Vanessa leaned against her door and collapsed to the floor, crying silently.

Chapter Eleven

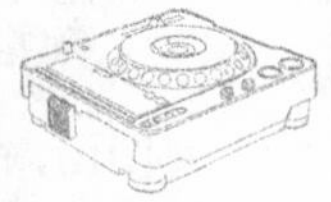

BRODY WOKE EARLY THE next morning at about seven o'clock and sat in bed, grinning uncontrollably as he relived what had happened with Vanessa last night and hoped it wasn't just a dream. After some time, he got up and started to Vanessa's room. He noticed her door was open, so he went downstairs. Only Grace and Heath were at the kitchen table.

"Good morning, Brody. How did you sleep?" Heath asked.

"I slept great," Brody replied.

"Have some breakfast, kiddo," Grace said, handing him a banana nut muffin.

"Thanks, Grace. Where's Vanessa?" he asked.

"She said she wanted to take a walk on the beach before she went to work," Heath told him, stuffing his face with a muffin.

"Oh, I see...do you mind if I take this to go?" Brody asked. Her parents shook their heads and watched as Brody left.

Brody walked the beach until he finally found her in the spot where they'd had their heart to heart. He took a deep breath and approached her, feeling butterflies in his stomach now.

Vanessa turned away from the ocean and saw him coming. "Hey, Brody."

"Hey, are you avoiding me?" he asked, jokingly. Vanessa chuckled but didn't respond. "I will take that as a yes. Why?" he asked, confused.

Vanessa turned back to the ocean. "I needed to think. Why are you here?"

"I wanted to talk about last night. You left it on an interesting note," Brody said with a smile.

Vanessa winced. Unlike Brody, she had kind of hoped what had happened was only a dream.

"I like you, Vanessa, a lot, and after your kiss last night, I am willing to bet you feel the same about me. Am I right?" Brody asked, standing closer to her.

Vanessa turned to look at him, slightly annoyed. "You already know that, but you also already know I am not looking for a romantic relationship. I live very far away, and long-distance relationships don't usually work out."

"Why don't you stay here then? You already said you feel like maybe your time there is over. If that's the case, it won't be so long distance with me being in New York and you being here in New Hampshire," Brody wheedled. Vanessa sighed heavily, and Brody could tell she didn't quite like that idea either. "Okay, so if that doesn't work for you, we can just see how it goes between us while you are in town and go from there," Brody suggested next.

Vanessa furrowed her brow in disapproval and turned back to the ocean.

"Oh, come on. It's not that awful of an idea, is it? You are only here for thirteen more days, so it wouldn't be a long commitment, and if it didn't work out, we could go our separate ways and wouldn't have to see each other again," Brody explained.

"And what if it *does* work out between us? What then? I don't want to take my mind off of what I am doing in India, not even for a second. A romantic relationship is a distraction that I don't need right now," Vanessa said, glancing at him before turning back to the ocean.

"You think I'm a distraction? I'm sorry, but if your mission work is something that matters to you, I shouldn't be able to deter you from it," Brody snapped.

Vanessa frowned and turned to face him. "I'm sorry. I didn't mean to insult you, Brody. This is all very overwhelming for me." She started weeping, much to his surprise. "I wasn't expecting to fall for you." Brody smiled at her statement. She continued, "All I am saying is that a relationship takes focus and drive, and right now I don't want to try to divide my loyalties between you and God." They stayed quiet for a minute.

"Kiss me," Brody blurted out, staring at Vanessa.

Vanessa chuckled awkwardly. "What?"

"I said, kiss me. If there isn't a spark, then we can forget the whole idea," Brody suggested coolly.

"That's not how things work, Brody. This isn't a rom-com. Love and relationships aren't meant to be built on feelings and in-the-moment type stuff."

Brody took a deep breath. "Yeah, I don't want to cheapen anything when it comes to you, Vanessa. You make me want to be a better man. That's why I like you so much."

She groaned loudly from the depth of her internal struggle and started to cry again.

Brody could tell she was really weighed down by this situation, so he paused before he did or said anything else. After a few minutes, he reached out to grab her hand; Vanessa didn't fight him. He caressed her hand while Vanessa closed her eyes and cried more tears.

"I don't want this thing between us to go away," Brody whispered.

Vanessa could feel her heart pounding as she pulled her hand away slowly. "I feel like you want me to be the missing piece for you in your life. I can't be the driving force for you, Brody. What if we didn't work out? Are you going to go back to who you said you didn't want to be anymore? You need someone more stable to be your everything, someone like–"

Brody grimaced. "You're going to tell me I need this Jesus guy, aren't you?"

"Brody, we both need to make God our everything before we come together. It's the only way we would work out. Instead of pursuing me, why don't you pursue God? I guarantee he is more worth your time and effort than I am," Vanessa said. Brody turned away, arms crossed over his chest, obviously upset.

He turned back to her after a little while with a sly smile and then leaned in and kissed Vanessa on the lips until she backed up, surprised. His eyes were wide with possibility as he watched Vanessa, unsure what she would do or say. Vanessa's heart was beating so loudly she could barely think.

"Why did you do that?" Vanessa asked, eyes narrowed.

"I'm sorry. I had to," Brody protested with a chuckle.

Vanessa shook her head. "No, you didn't! You could have respected what I said and left it at that. We could have left what happened last night in the past and tried to move on from there!"

Brody couldn't believe how angry she was. "I'm sorry. I–"

Vanessa was shaking now. "No, don't say another word!"

It got deathly quiet. Brody felt his stomach tighten as he

frowned and looked away. Vanessa didn't move. She didn't do anything except take a few breaths and try to collect herself.

"Look at me please," Vanessa said finally in a softer tone.

Brody looked at her expectantly. Vanessa's face was expressionless, but her eyes betrayed her and gave Brody some encouragement. After a moment, she touched his face gently. He closed his eyes, enjoying the feel of her delicate skin on his face.

"You put me in a tougher spot now, Brody," Vanessa confessed.

Brody's eyes widened. "What do you mean?"

Vanessa turned to stare at the ocean. "I'll stay." She glanced at Brody as he started to chuckle in excitement. Vanessa giggled to see how thrilled he was. "Just for the rest of the year, though, so we can see what happens between us. It will also give me time to process what I think God might be calling me to do about India."

Brody cheered loudly and spun Vanessa around. She giggled and grinned. He put her down slowly and looked into her eyes, running his hands through her hair and holding her close. "I am excited to see where this goes, Vanessa."

Vanessa smiled nervously. "Me too." They kissed briefly. Brody took Vanessa by the hand and walked her down the pier to Rocky's so she could go to work.

Brody didn't see Vanessa again until her shift was over that evening. He waited for her outside Rocky's so he could take her out for a surprise dinner. They walked to the other end of the boardwalk to get pizza.

Once they finished dinner, they took a walk on the beach and talked more about Jesus and the Bible, specifically the first chapter of John. Brody confessed to her that it was more confusing to him than he let on to Heath. Vanessa was happy to see he was genuinely interested in learning about God and tried her best to help him understand what he was confused about.

Vanessa told Brody that on her break, she had emailed her leader and asked for permission to stay longer. Brody was thrilled and wanted to know what they said, but she told him she was still waiting for a response. They were both anxious to get a follow-up email. They left the beach and walked back toward Rocky's so Brody could pick up his bike.

Before he got on, Vanessa stopped him. "Please don't say anything to anyone about us dating, okay?"

Brody looked confused. "Why? I think your family would approve of me."

Vanessa blushed. "That isn't it. We are still new, and I don't even know if we can be an official couple yet. Isn't there a specific timeline for that or something?"

Brody chuckled. "I don't think so."

Vanessa shrugged. "Well, neither of us knows how to have a real relationship, so let's just keep it secret for now, okay?"

Brody took her hand in his, kissed it, and looked at her with intent. "I get it. You want to see where this goes before we tell people. Don't worry. I will keep it quiet. I am just glad I get to be with you."

Vanessa had butterflies in her stomach as she walked to her car.

Brody was on cloud nine as he arrived at home. He sat on the couch with the family and watched TV. As he sat there, he quietly did something he had never done in his whole life before: He prayed. *God, thank you for bringing Vanessa into my life. Please help me to treat her in a way that would make you happy.*

Chapter Twelve

Brody arrived at Rocky's Friday evening to pick up Vanessa for dinner but didn't see her car in the parking lot. He went inside and talked to Rocky and found out that Vanessa had left not long ago. Apparently she seemed very upset about something and said she had to go home quickly. Brody was concerned, so he drove back home.

"Grace, is Vanessa here?" Brody asked, walking into the house, frantic.

Grace looked at him with a slight smile. "No, Brody, she isn't here."

"Rocky said she left a half an hour early from her shift and said she had to go home; we must have just missed each other. He said she seemed upset." Brody told her, genuinely concerned. He noticed Grace's face looked apprehensive. "What's wrong, Grace?" Brody asked gravely.

She sighed heavily and answered his question. "Vanessa said she had to go back to India now."

Brody looked at her in disbelief. "She did?"

She nodded. "I had just finished making dinner when she came bursting into the house weeping. I asked her what was going on, and all she said was that she needed to pack right that minute and leave. I was worried about her, so I followed her upstairs and tried to get her to talk to me, but she ignored me and focused on booking a flight to India. She left for the airport a few hours ago."

Brody drummed his fingers along his crossed arms, trying not to show his seething anger. "I see.... It must have been something *really* pressing to make her leave like that."

"I suppose so. I'm sorry you didn't get to say goodbye to her. Her father, Kate, and Daniel will be sad too," Grace said, turning around to start plating dinner.

Brody tried not to let his burning anger turn into intense sadness as he spoke. "Well, I guess our plans for tonight are shot."

Grace frowned. She could see he was distraught about it. "I'm sorry, kiddo. You are welcome to have dinner with us."

Brody smiled sadly at the offer, "That's okay. I'm gonna head out and do my plans anyway. I will see you later, Grace." Brody left quickly, leaving Grace troubled.

Brody had been gone for several hours, and Grace and Heath were concerned. Brody's bike was in the driveway, so they knew he was on foot, which worried them more. Heath decided to go looking for him and was just about to leave when Kate and Daniel barged in, holding up a slumped over Brody. He was drunk and apparently sleeping. Heath and Grace frowned at each other before going to help.

"Kate and I had just left the boardwalk, and we saw him in Rocky's parking lot, lying on the ground and mumbling about how he wanted answers," Daniel said, dropping Brody onto the couch gently.

"I'm just glad that we found him and not the cops or someone with a camera," Kate said sadly.

"I thought he was doing good with getting sober? What happened?" Daniel asked.

Grace frowned. "Vanessa left."

"What? Why? She doesn't usually leave until September," Daniel asked sadly.

Grace explained what had happened earlier with Vanessa and then how Brody had left.

"Aw, poor guy took her leaving really hard. You know he liked her, right?" Kate asked.

Grace nodded sadly.

"Thanks for bringing him back. Daniel, help me carry him into the bedroom," Heath said, lifting Brody's head and shoulders while Daniel followed his dad with Brody's legs.

"I can't believe he gave up sobriety for Vanessa. He is going to have to detox again, but at least it won't be so long and difficult—or at least I hope not," Daniel commented as they moved slowly up the stairs.

Heath replied, "Vanessa is an incredible young lady."

Daniel smiled. "Yeah, I know, Dad, but you know what I mean. He fell for her hard, and they barely knew each other for two weeks."

They laid Brody down on the bed, and Heath smiled. "The first time I saw your mom, I knew I wanted to date her, although we didn't date until a year after. Don't you remember how it happened with you and Kate? You two clicked right away."

Daniel grinned. "That was different, Dad. We were teens filled with pubescent emotions."

Heath chuckled. "Everyone has emotions, and everyone feels different things in different ways and at different times. Your grandparents on your mom's side got married at sixteen and were together sixty-five years. You know, Vanessa liked him too."

Daniel nodded slowly. "Yeah, I could tell."

"Sometimes you just know," Heath concluded. They walked out of the room and started down the stairs.

The next morning, Heath came into Brody's room with a cup of coffee and was surprised to see him packing. "Going somewhere?" he asked.

"I've decided to head home. I already called my agent and told him to get a free concert together to make up for the last few weeks. The concert is Sunday night, so I need to get back home now to prepare," Brody said, trying to sound convincing that this was what he really wanted to do.

"So back to business, huh? How are you feeling after your bender?" Heath asked.

Brody glanced at him in between packing. "I have a wicked headache, but I can deal."

"I thought you wanted to stay sober and wanted meaning in your life," Heath reminded him, putting the cup of coffee on the desk next to him.

Brody shrugged. "Maybe it was my depression talking, or maybe I was just caught up in the moment of being around Vanessa. It doesn't matter. She's gone, so it's time to go back to reality."

Heath cleared his throat. "What about our Bible study? We just started. We still have much to learn. Are you giving up on that too? Were you just humoring me to get to my daughter?"

"No, of course not. I like hanging out with you, and I did want to hear all that God stuff and be sober...but what is the point now?" Brody asked in a gruff tone.

"What do you mean?" Heath asked.

Brody sighed heavily. "What's the point in trying to get to know God now? He took Vanessa from me—he obviously doesn't think I'm good enough for her."

"I am sure that her departure had nothing to do with you, Brody. In her ministry work, these things happen sometimes. In the first few years of her work out there, she didn't even come home, and last year she left a few weeks early because someone at the center needed her," Heath reassured him.

Brody snickered in disbelief. "Yeah, I still don't see the point in staying here and taking up space in your home to learn about a God who dangles a great woman in my face and then takes her away as we start to develop feelings for each other. Did you know Vanessa was going to stay longer so we could date? Apparently her God didn't approve of us liking each other. He doesn't seem like someone I would like to get to know better if he is going to be cruel like that."

Heath smiled. "It was pretty obvious you two liked each other, and I don't think God took her away because he didn't think you were the one for her. I am sure something big happened, and she had to go back. Whatever the reason, don't you still want something more in your life than what you were escaping from?" Heath asked.

Brody swallowed a lump in his throat before answering. "No, I don't feel that need anymore."

Heath looked at him with a sharp eye. "So you are fine going back to your old life? The wild parties and late nights?"

Brody swallowed another lump and simply nodded. Heath could clearly tell Brody didn't mean it, but he didn't push him. There was an awkward pause.

"Well, I gotta finish packing. I have a long drive ahead of me," Brody said softly.

"Before you go, I want to give you something," Heath said, grabbing Brody's Bible. He started to skim through it and then jotted down some notes in the notebook next to him. Brody watched with a quizzical look. When Heath was done, he closed the Bible and notebook and handed them to Brody with a serious look on his face.

"Don't leave this here. When your hurt and anger toward God go away, you are going to find that God is the only one you ever really needed, and you will need the Bible to lead you in the right direction," Heath assured him, standing up and pushing in the chair. "Remember, Vanessa isn't your savior; *God* is. Vanessa was just the vessel he chose to use in your life to help you overcome your situation. Don't close your heart up to God because of this."

Heath picked up the coffee cup and handed it to Brody. "Try to stay sober too, Brody. Life will be better for you that way. Don't forget the pain and struggle you and Vanessa went through during your detox process. I wrote out some verses and chapters of the Bible for you to look up whenever you have free time. Good luck. We will be praying for you." Heath patted Brody on the back and then lingered by the door before finally leaving. Brody looked down at the Bible and notebook and then the coffee in his hands and sighed.

Chapter Thirteen

BRODY GOT BACK TO his penthouse, put the key in the door, and hesitated before opening it. The penthouse was silent and unwelcoming. He sighed heavily and walked in, shutting the door behind him. He went to his room and started unpacking, thinking about his rash decision to leave Hampton. There was a sense of loss—until he thought about the situation with Vanessa again. Suddenly he scowled and started to feel his seething anger resurface. "Why did you take her from me? Why couldn't you just let me have her until the end of the year?" Brody growled, clenching his fist and raising it toward heaven.

His agent, Chuck, knocked on the front door and, once in, started talking business, so Brody tucked his anger away and tried to stay focused on the task at hand. Chuck had scheduled Brody to do an interview over the phone with a popular magazine to clear up his sudden disappearance. Brody reluctantly agreed to do the interview after Chuck made it very clear it wasn't really a suggestion.

His agent went into the living room to set up for the interview while Brody took a quick shower. Brody came out of his bedroom ten minutes later, dressed in sweats and a ratty T-shirt, his wet hair disheveled.

"You couldn't get dressed up?" Chuck asked, disgusted.

"Chill, dude. It's only a phone interview. The only one who will see me is you, and I could care less what you think of my outfit. I'm comfortable, and that's what matters to me," Brody said disrespectfully, slumping down onto a barstool.

Brody looked at a piece of paper lying on the counter with a furrowed brow. "What's this?"

"Your notes for the interview," Chuck said, scrolling through his phone.

Brody tossed the paper at him. "I don't need talking points. I will just answer the questions on my own, thank you."

Chuck caught the paper in midair. "Listen, turd, you were gone for almost three weeks, nowhere to be found. I didn't even know where you were. Your fans all thought you were dead. This magazine is paying you big bucks for the first scoop as to what happened to you. I know you told me the truth, but that is because I made you tell me; however, it is not what we are going to tell all your fans. It's not good for business."

"Why not? It's the truth," Brody protested.

"We can't tell everyone you were so depressed you tried to jump off your building, and then, when you chose not to go through with it, you decided to run away and slice your wrists open instead. How will that look? It will paint you as an unstable person who needs mental help, and you will lose your fan base. No, stick to the script, or you can kiss your two-day concert goodbye, because it's sponsored by the people doing this interview," Chuck warned.

"Two days? It was just supposed to be Sunday," Brody reminded him.

Chuck was staring at his phone again when he answered.

"Yeah, I added a show tonight. I also signed you up for a Labor Day weekend festival going on in New Mexico, and before you complain about the schedule, don't worry about it; you can do it. You really have no choice; you owe it to your fans. Learn to love it. You are going to be very busy until at least mid-September with shows." He looked up from his phone briefly. "Get ready. They're calling in five." Chuck walked away, his nose buried in his phone once more.

Brody felt the anxiety bubbling up to the surface, mixed once more with seething anger. He felt the growling pangs of needing alcohol start to creep up into his mind, so he reluctantly took Vanessa's advice and took a few deep breaths to try to stay calm then looked down at the papers and grimaced.

The interview was over after fifteen minutes. The magazine got their fake scoop, and Brody's career was saved. It was a win–win…sort of.

Brody crumpled up the paper he was forced to read off of and tossed it at Chuck's head. "If I'm supposed to do a show tonight, I need some rest now. Get out."

Chuck chortled. "You have awful manners, you ungrateful turd. I have bent over backward trying to salvage your career after this episode of yours."

Brody opened the front door and smirked. "Why should I thank you? This is your job, isn't it? I'm tired. I need rest if you want me to perform at my best tonight."

Chuck shook his head in disgust as he started for the door. "Brody, you better stay put, you hear me?"

"Yeah, yeah, I hear you. I'm not leaving," Brody responded, slamming the door in Chuck's face. Brody took a deep, labored breath and went to his room. He flopped onto his bed and started to cry.

True to what Chuck had said, Brody had been busy every day since he got back home three weeks earlier, doing shows or interviews for radio stations throughout the U.S., Mexico, and even one in Europe. Many of his friends and colleagues asked him what had happened to him. He would lie and tell them he just needed a mental break. They would buy the lie, hook, line, and sinker.

Reluctantly at first, Brody started to drink again to mask the pain of missing Vanessa and almost to spite her for leaving him, but he didn't sleep around anymore, no matter how much the girls tried to come at him. If he looked at any woman, all he saw was Vanessa's face staring back at him, and it made his heart ache all the more, which drove him to drink even more.

The saddest part was that he didn't want to do these things anymore. His heart ached, his mind screamed for him to stop, but his emotions were so strong against God and Vanessa that he fought his better judgement and continued doing life as he always did. Whenever he was at an afterparty or a show, he would drink, but he would hear his heart screaming at him to stop.

He hadn't been home much during the last three weeks, but whenever he was at home or alone in his hotel room, he found himself crying over Vanessa leaving or reluctantly reading the Bible passages that Heath had left for him in that notebook and then scoffing at them. He also started listening to some Christian techno bands that Heath had written down in that notebook for him to check out. At first he was only doing it to humor Heath should he ever call to ask him about it, but in the end, he didn't mind the music.

Now it was time for his final show of this long stretch, the one he put on every year on the last Friday of September.

Usually this show brought him the most money and increased his fan base a lot too. It was one of his favorite times of the year, but this year was unlike every other year. This year's concert was going to be free of charge for his fans, just like every other concert he had been doing since he got home. As Chuck put it, "he owed his fans." That phrase echoed in Brody's ears every time he did something for his fans now. It was no longer because he *wanted* to do it; it was because he *had* to do it. Now it was all a burden expected of him.

Brody stepped off the stage as the crowd chanted for one more song. Brody didn't have it in him to do another. He hadn't slept much in the last several weeks, and he hadn't been consuming anything except alcohol and finger foods. He was nauseous now as the chanting got louder and resonated in his ears, making him wince. He put on his fake smile and stepped back out on the stage. This was his final performance until further notice, after all, and he wanted to make it epic and keep suspicion away.

After the final song, some of the groupies and a few of his friends took Brody out to celebrate, like they did every year. Brody just wanted to head home, but his friends begged him not to break tradition. They finally wore him down, but it wasn't really that hard to do at this point though.

Brody got home at noon on Saturday and laid on his bed, exhausted and seething. He had a hangover again. He closed his eyes and took a three-hour nap before waking suddenly to hunger pangs. He went to the kitchen and cooked himself a hot pocket, the only thing he had in his freezer. While it was cooking, he rounded up all his alcohol and tossed it into a garbage bag, putting it outside on the patio. He grabbed his food from the microwave and ate it while sitting on his couch, staring into nothingness like a zombie and musing about Vanessa and the lost possibilities.

After eating, he tried to go back to sleep. He tossed and turned for an hour before falling asleep briefly. He gave up and went back to the kitchen to grab a glass of water, hoping to get rid of the hangover. He walked back to his room and grabbed his phone out of his pocket to make a call.

"Hi, Brody. How's life?" Heath said nicely.

Brody settled back onto his bed, leaning against his headboard, and answered, "Sorry I haven't reached out since I left. I've been on a mini tour. Last night I finished my last show until mid-October." Brody sounded frustrated as he realized he only had a few weeks to relax before he had more concerts to do.

"That's okay. How are you feeling? How's the sobriety?" Heath asked next.

Brody winced. He didn't want to disappoint him. "I'm fine.... Actually, that's a lie. I'm not doing so well. Life sucks worse now than it did when I ran away to Hampton." Brody sighed heavily before continuing. "I told myself I wouldn't drink when I got back here, and I haven't been able to keep that promise. I am so miserable, and when I feel like that, all I know to do is drink the feelings away. No one here is rooting me on to stay sober either, so that doesn't help. On a positive note, I haven't been drinking nearly as much as I did before I got sober."

"That's a positive step. Do you want to talk about what's bothering you?" Heath asked.

Brody explained everything that had happened since he came back and how he regretted coming back in the first place.

"I am sorry to hear you are hurting so much, Brody. What can I do to help?" Heath asked.

Brody groaned. "I don't know…."

Heath took a second to pray for wisdom before answering. "Brody, only Jesus will give you peace and fulfillment in life. Vanessa wasn't supposed to be the reason you wanted to be sober or find meaning in life. You wanted those things before you met her, didn't you?"

"Yeah, well, maybe the meaning of life stuff. I didn't want sobriety until she mentioned it, but honestly, after having it, I do miss it now," Brody confessed.

"Okay then, you have to remember Vanessa won't save you from your addictions and pain. She is a human, and just like the rest of us, she is flawed and will make mistakes or hurt you. Look what happened when she left you; you crumbled under the weight of your pain and went back to some of your old ways. You weren't sober for the right reasons; you were doing it for her. Now that she isn't here, you have to figure out if you really want lasting change because only God can be the long-lasting help that you need in life. You have to repent from your sins and allow God to change you from the inside out if you want to be truly free. Do you still have your Bible?" Heath asked.

"Yeah, hold on. I'll get it," Brody said as he grabbed it off the TV stand in his bedroom and then sat back down on the bed. "I've been reading everything you wrote down for me to read. I'm in Luke now," Brody explained.

"I'm glad you have had time to read, even with your busy schedule. Okay, what we are reading isn't part of what I wrote down for you. I was saving this for the day you reached out to me with a heart that seemed really ready to change. Turn to Romans 10:9–10," Heath instructed him. Brody flipped pages until he got to that section and listened as Heath read, "If you confess with your mouth that Jesus is Lord and believe in your heart that God raised him from the dead, you will be saved. For it is by believing in your heart that you are made right with God, and it is by confessing with your mouth that you are saved."

Brody chuckled. "It's that easy to become a Christian? Is this repentance thing easy too?"

"The word repentance means sincere regret or remorse. It means, as a Christian, if you truly want your life to change, you need to do a one-eighty away from what you once did and follow what the Bible says to do. More importantly, you need to follow Jesus's commands. It is hard to repent. It's a daily surrender of all your bad habits, addictions, attitudes, and thoughts," Heath explained.

"So becoming a Christian means I can't be a DJ anymore?" Brody asked, concerned.

"Not necessarily. Have you listened to the Christian DJs listed in your notebook?" Heath asked.

"Yeah, I started listening to them last week. Some of them are amazing! They could perform on any of the stages I perform on," Brody admitted.

"See? It is possible to keep your job. It just means you need to do what you do differently. The wild partying, striving for fame and fortune as if they're your idols…those are the things you need to give up," Heath replied.

Brody sighed heavily but didn't respond.

Heath continued, "Coming to Christ isn't about what you *can't* do as much as it is about doing what pleases God and the overwhelming joy you will feel walking in his will. There is freedom in obeying Christ, and I think that is what seems hard for people to grasp: How can someone have freedom by obeying someone?"

Brody snickered. "Yeah, it does seem like an oxymoron to me."

Heath chuckled. "I get it. I thought so too at one point, and then I realized that once you start to read the Bible more and let it penetrate your heart, you find that your passions will align with God's passions. I will be honest with you and tell you that if you choose to follow Christ, Satan will do everything he can to get you back into your old lifestyle. Also, you will lose friends and maybe even family members over this decision. It's not an easy thing to stay in the will of Christ. The Bible says, 'Remember that if the world hates you, it hated me first' in John 15:18. Also, in Matthew 10:39, it says, 'If you cling to your life, you will lose it; but if you give up your life for me, you will find it.'"

Brody stayed quiet, pondering everything Heath was telling him.

Heath continued, "Life will not be easy as a believer. I never want to make you think it will be all fluffy puppies and rainbows. There will be backlash from the enemy, tough times, but also great times. Your relationship with Christ will be rewarding if you keep trusting God through everything that happens." Heath paused for a moment. "Do you have any questions? I know I talked your ear off, and it was all heavy stuff."

Brody sighed. "I don't think so. You spelled it out pretty well for me. If I want to see lasting change in my life and freedom from addiction to alcohol, I need Christ."

"That is a great way to sum it up. Do you think you are ready to come to Christ?" Heath asked in a hopeful tone.

Brody laid his Bible down on the bed before speaking. "I don't know.... Yes, I would like to be sober again—in fact, I already threw out all the alcohol in my house—but being a DJ is all I have ever known; it's all I ever wanted to be. But at the same time, I don't feel content doing it anymore. I also have millions of fans and friends that I have made throughout the years. I don't know if I am ready to let any of that go. My fans and followers will hate me. What if I can't be a DJ anymore? Who am I if I'm not DJ Maddox?"

"You can't please everyone, and the beauty of being a Christ follower is that the only one you need to please is Christ himself. He gave you a Bible full of ways to do that," Heath replied.

Brody scoffed, "Vanessa told me that too, about only having to please Jesus."

Heath sighed. "You will have to let go of your bitter feelings toward Vanessa and God when you do finally come to Christ."

"I'm upset that she led me on and played with my heart like she did," Brody confessed, shocked that Heath could sense his bitterness over the phone.

"I don't think she played with your heart on purpose; I could tell that her feelings for you were real. I believe that she had every intention of sticking around to date you, Brody. I know my daughter, and she keeps her word unless circumstances get out of her control," Heath assured.

Brody smiled warmly, but then he scowled. "In my opinion, her relationship with Christ got in the way of our happiness."

"On the contrary, she has it right. God is always supposed to come first for us believers. She is a missionary first and foremost. Serving God in that capacity is supposed to come at a price, and maybe you were the price she had to pay to show God she served him first." Heath spoke compassionately but honestly as well.

Brody sighed. "I really miss her, Heath. We just clicked. I can't wait until her next visit to see her again. It's too hard on me. And you know what's annoying? I admire her for staying true to her commitment to God, even if it means I don't have her with me. That kind of commitment level just makes her even more attractive."

Heath chuckled loudly. "Love stinks sometimes, huh?" Brody snickered in reply.

Heath continued, "Remember, you were created on purpose and for a purpose, Brody. Maybe your skills as a DJ play into God's plans for you, and maybe you and Vanessa will be together in the future. But even if those things don't happen, God can give you a new direction that will be better than anything else you ever thought possible. You will never know if you don't take a step of faith and trust what his word says in Jeremiah 29:11: 'For I know the plans I have for you, declares the Lord, plans to prosper you and not to harm you, plans to give you hope and a future.' Coming to Christ costs us something big—our pride, selfishness, and devotion. I had a very hard time giving up my life before coming to Christ, so I understand your hesitation."

"Thanks for talking through everything with me," Brody replied.

"When you are ready, it will happen for you. Coming to Christ can't be forced," Heath added.

"Well, I'm going to head to bed. I haven't slept much since I got back here. Goodbye, Heath. Thanks for chatting with me," Brody said with a yawn.

"Anytime Brody. Maybe try to find a church to go to tomorrow morning. Goodbye."

Chapter Fourteen

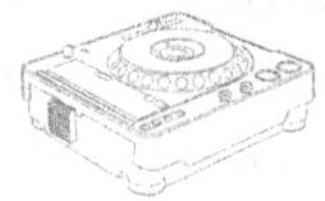

BRODY MANAGED TO SLEEP all Sunday and into Monday afternoon with only about five hours awake during that time. He wasn't sure how he was able to pull that off, but he was happy about it, knowing he needed the sleep to refresh him. He spent the rest of Monday reading his Bible and watching TV, until around eight at night, when some friends invited him out to their house party. He reluctantly went and told himself he would have fun without drinking. He was going to take back his sobriety.

Brody finally arrived home around one o'clock in the afternoon on Tuesday, his head pounding from all the alcohol he had drank. He beat himself up for that the whole ride home. He went to take a hot shower, hoping to get rid of his pounding headache and guilt. While in the shower, he threw up and then collapsed on the tub floor, crying pathetically.

He got out of the shower after cleaning up the mess, slipped into some shorts, and then crawled into bed and tried to sleep off his feelings of shame. He tossed and turned until he fell asleep an hour later.

He didn't sleep well at all; in fact, all he did was toss and turn, wince, and whimper the whole night, as if he were in pain. He woke suddenly close to six in the evening with a heaviness on his chest, a loud gasp, sweat dripping from his body, and tears filling his eyes. He jumped out of bed and raced out of his penthouse and to his motorcycle like a madman. He drove away frantically, trying to see through the relentless tears.

He rapped at the Stewarts' door multiple times before Grace looked through the peephole and said in disbelief, "It's Brody." She quickly opened the door. "Brody, why are you here so late? Is everything okay? Where are your shoes and your shirt? You shouldn't ride like that on a motorcycle. What if you got into an accident?" Grace ushered him inside and noticed he was trembling.

"Why are you trembling, kiddo? What happened?" Grace asked, concerned. Heath touched her shoulder, and she nodded. "I know. I'm mothering him too much right now. I'm going to head to bed now," Grace said, touching Brody's cheek gently before kissing the top of his head and walking away.

Brody walked over to the living room and paced the floor for a few minutes before finally sitting on the couch next to Heath.

"I had a dream…no, actually it was a freaking nightmare! I was standing on stage in front of millions of screaming fans. I was on the last song of my set, music blasting and a drink in my hand. A woman stood next to me in a tiny dress. She motioned for me to follow her, so I did. Before long, we were standing on a high mountain, kissing and drinking. All of a sudden, she smiled at me eerily and then wrapped her arms tightly around me so I couldn't breathe and jumped off the cliff. As we were falling in slow motion, I looked at her and she laughed maniacally, but it didn't sound like a woman's voice; it sounded like a scary creature, which is what she turned into—a thing with soulless eyes and claws digging into my skin, making me bleed." Brody started to touch his arms, as if he were looking for scars.

"I was still falling at this point, and then I heard voices, not just the evil laughter. It sounded like a news update about me committing suicide, and then I heard people chatting about my life and how sad it was that I was gone too soon. They said how much they loved my music and all the other superficial things that people say when a celebrity dies. Next the creature laughed again, but this laugh was more scornful. The creature whispered in my ear, 'Looks like you were just another blip on the radar, nothing special after all.' I screamed as we hit the ground, and then I woke up," Brody added, tears forming again and his trembling getting more noticeable. Heath touched Brody's shoulder softly.

"It was so real! I could hear myself screaming out. I felt the claws in my skin. I was scared...really scared. Shoot, I still am! I drove over here as soon as I woke up. I don't know what I expected you to do about it. I just couldn't understand what happened, and I didn't have anyone else to turn to," Brody confessed, wiping his eyes as more tears fell. He jumped to his feet and started pacing again, running his hands through his hair.

"It sounds like it was a spiritual attack, Brody," Heath finally said.

"A what?" Brody asked with a quizzical brow. Heath explained what he meant by that, and Brody shuddered. "Yeah, it was totally that! What do I do now? How do I get it to go away?"

"There is no way to stop it Brody. You have been trying to

find meaning in your life, and Satan doesn't like that because he knows it means you will find God. He is trying to keep that from happening. The good news is that God is fighting for you too, and he never loses. These spiritual attacks happen in different ways all throughout a devoted follower's walk with Christ. The only thing you can do now is make your choice: Do you want to fight this battle on God's team or alone?" Heath asked.

"I don't want to live two lives anymore; I feel like a fake. I hate my life. I'm not happy, and even listening to dance beats doesn't get me hyped anymore. I put on a facade on stage, but it's exhausting to pretend you're happy when you aren't. I want joy and purpose, and for the love of everything, I want to be sober! Just keeping it real, I'm scared what might become of my career if I ask Jesus into my heart, but I think I'm more scared of what will happen to me if I leave here tonight without Jesus. I feel like this nightmare was sort of like a warning for me from God," Brody confessed, wringing his hands nervously as he processed his thoughts out loud while still pacing.

"It could very well be that. He does love you that much that he would do something like that for you," Heath encouraged him.

Brody sat back down finally and looked at Heath with defeated eyes. "I don't know what to do." He collapsed onto Heath's shoulder, and they cried together.

This situation brought Heath back to where he had been before he came to Christ. He, too, had felt desolate, like he was at a crossroads or past the point of no return.

After a few minutes, Brody sat up and smiled nervously. "I want Jesus. My life sucks without him. I don't know what will happen in the future, but I would rather fight with him than against him."

Heath laid his hand on Brody's shoulder and looked at him

seriously. "Asking him into your heart won't be a quick fix. It will take hard work on your part and a whole lot of faith and trust in God." Brody nodded slowly, and Heath continued. "This decision will most definitely cause division in your life and relationships, and these spiritual attacks will keep coming, maybe even intensely depending on how hard you pursue Christ's will for your life. But with God's Holy Spirit in your heart and godly counsel, you will overcome. I just want to reiterate these points so you understand what you are choosing and don't feel misled or anything."

Brody sighed heavily as he swallowed the lump in his throat and started to get choked up. "Whatever God has to offer me has to be better than feeling empty and meaningless like I feel right now. I choose God."

Heath grinned, choking up. "Let's pray then."

They closed their eyes, and Heath prayed silently for him while Brody spoke from his broken heart: "God, please accept me. I want you to fix me. I hate my life the way it is, and I don't want to leave Hampton Beach without you in my heart. I want to make something of myself that will make you smile. I want you to give me purpose and fulfillment. Please come into my life, forgive me, and clean my heart of all the drinking, idols, and womanizing. I'm sorry I hated you for taking Vanessa away, and I'm sorry for the bitter feelings I have toward her too. Please forgive me for that and anything else I may not be able to recall right now. I believe you sent your son, Jesus, to die on the cross for my many sins, and I believe he rose from the dead three days later, breaking my chains of sin and addiction. Thank you for changing me. I know it won't be easy, but I am ready to be used in a purposeful way. Amen." Brody's eyes lit up as he finished speaking. He hugged Heath and laughed loudly, standing to his feet.

"I feel…I don't know how to explain it. I feel high. Is that appropriate to say?"

Heath stood up and patted him on the back. "I said the same thing to my mentor when he helped me come to Christ. I know exactly what you mean. It's an amazing feeling, right?"

Brody nodded, exhilarated.

"Realize it won't last forever. Just like a drug high, you will want to keep chasing this one, but I encourage you not to do that. Chase after Jesus instead of your emotions. Our emotions won' always steer us in the right direction, but Jesus will." Heath got choked up and hugged Brody tightly., "Welcome to the family, Brody!"

Grace tiptoed downstairs holding folded clothes in her hands and smiled. "Hey, guys, is it okay for me to come down here now? I brought you some clothes, Brody."

Brody raced over to her and hugged her tightly, taking her breath away. "I'm a Christian now!" he said ecstatically.

Grace laughed joyfully. "Praise the Lord! What great news!" Brody hugged Grace again and ran upstairs excitedly. Grace looked at Heath with a glimmer in her eye. "I guess he is staying the night with us."

Heath laughed, tears welling up in his eyes. He nodded in agreement and hugged Grace as they headed off to bed.

The next morning, Grace and Brody talked while Heath washed the dishes after breakfast. Grace wanted to get to know Brody better. She felt bad that while Brody was staying with them, she had never gotten the chance to really chat with him alone. She asked him everything from what he was like as a child to how he got into the business he was in and how his relationship was with his family. After he mentioned he and his sister had a strained relationship, she suggested he take care of that right away and told him about Matthew 5:23–24, which talked about making amends immediately with someone who had something against you.

Brody grimaced. "Yeah, I remember reading that, and it did remind me of my situation with my sister. I should call her soon."

Grace grinned. "No time like the present."

Brody smiled and nodded. She kissed his cheek and walked off to help Heath put away the leftovers from breakfast. Brody grabbed his phone and started dialing his sister's number as he went out the back door and walked to the backyard swing.

After a half an hour, he came back inside. "I was able to start the process of mending fences with her. She is happy to hear I am now on the track to doing well. She and her husband, Bill, had a baby not too long ago too, a girl. Her name is Candace; she's three months old. Regina is going to send me some pictures of her."

"That's wonderful! Maybe you will be able to see them soon too. Where does she live?" Grace asked.

"She lives in Denver now. I guess her husband was just transferred there. Well, I better head back home," Brody said, looking around the room. "Where's Heath?"

"He had to go to work. Do you really have to leave now? You just got here, and I know Heath will be sad he missed saying goodbye," Grace said dejectedly.

"I'm sure my agent is going to be looking for me soon, and if he doesn't find me, he will have my head," Brody told her.

"Let your agent know where you are going to be staying. You could use a break, am I right? Heath said you have been working nonstop since you got home," she suggested.

"Okay, I will talk to him and see what he thinks," he said, heading out the back door again while dialing his agent's number. After ten minutes, he came back inside.

"Good news. I convinced my agent that I need some downtime after all the concerts. He wasn't too thrilled about the idea at first, but I assured him I would be home by Sunday night and would call him as soon as I got back or he could call the cops on me," Brody told her as he approached the couch where Grace was watching TV.

"That's wonderful! Now you can have dinner with the family tonight. Pastor Brian and his wife are coming over too. Everyone will be thrilled to see you and hear your great news about your faith," Grace said with a grin.

"Awesome! I'm excited to see everyone too, but do you mind if I go crash now? I won't make it until tonight if I don't. I guess my body still needs to catch up on sleep," Brody said, stifling a yawn.

"Yeah, of course," Grace answered.

Thursday morning, Brody woke to the heavenly scent of bacon. He got dressed and went downstairs. "Good morning, Grace. Is that bacon I'm smelling?" Brody asked, helping her set the table.

"Sure is. Come and eat. It's just us this morning. Heath went to work already. Brody sat down, and Grace prayed for the meal before they dug in.

"So what are your plans for the day?" she asked.

"I was thinking of going shopping in town. I need to wear something other than these borrowed clothes for the rest of my time here," Brody answered, shoving a piece of bacon in his mouth.

Grace smiled. "That sounds like fun."

"Do you want to join me?" Brody asked.

Grace chuckled and swallowed the bite in her mouth. "I'm sorry. I can't. I work at the YMCA today."

"That's cool. What do you do there? It's a rec center, right?" Brody asked next.

"Yeah, that's right. I run a Zumba class."

Brody's eyes lit up. "That's awesome! I bet you have loads of fun doing that for a job."

"Yeah, it's pretty fun. You should come with me today and join a class. It's a fun way to work out," Grace suggested, sipping her coffee.

"I don't think so. I have to work on getting sober again, and I don't know if that will help. Plus someone will recognize me and try to put the video on social media—then the world will see I suck at dancing," Brody joked.

"I don't think anyone would recognize you in today's class. Thursdays are senior classes," Grace said with a chuckle. "Also, I think exercise is good for anyone, even someone who needs to detox from something. Come on. Just try it. If you feel sick or something, you can always stop."

Brody ate another pancake and mulled over the idea. He finally nodded. "Okay, maybe I will join you. What time is your class?"

"I start one in an hour, but I have another class at two. That gives you plenty of time to go shopping first," Grace suggested.

"Great, I will be there. Just text me the address," Brody said, scribbling his phone number on a napkin for Grace. As he helped her carry things to the sink, he asked, "Would you like me to do the dishes?"

"Oh, aren't you sweet. No thank you, dear. You go ahead and shop so you will be ready to sweat later," Grace responded with a smile.

"Okay, I will make sure I stretch too so I don't pull anything," Brody joked.

Brody collapsed into a chair and breathed heavily, sweat dripping from his body. He chugged water from his bottle and gasped for air afterward. A few seniors from the class came up to him, patted him on the shoulder, and congratulated him, which didn't make him feel any better considering they were all standing and walking normally.

After everyone left, Grace came up to him, wiping her face with a towel. She sat next to him and patted him on the knee, handing him a towel. "You did better than I thought you would."

"I think I only lasted as long as I did because I didn't want to be shown up by a bunch of healthy seniors. I will be very sore tomorrow in places I didn't even know about, but at least I still have my pride," Brody confessed.

"Would you like to get a victory snack?" Grace asked. Brody nodded and followed Grace to a small ice cream shack that was walking distance from the YMCA. They ordered their ice creams and sat at a picnic table.

"What will you do once you go back home?" Grace asked.

"I don't know. I haven't really thought about that. I have just been trying to figure out the Bible. It's not easy to understand," Brody responded.

"Sweetie, you don't need to know it all. If you did, you would be God. We are supposed to pray that the Holy Spirit would give us wisdom and insight about what we are reading. If you do that, I guarantee it will be easier to read the Bible because you won't feel you have to know everything, only what God wants you to know at that moment." She encouraged him, taking a bite of her ice cream.

"Psalm 119:105 says, 'Your word is a lamp unto my feet

and a light for my path.' This is one of my favorite verses. When I don't know what to do, he reminds me of this, and then I pray and ask for his guidance. If you have never read Psalms, you should. There are many wonderful nuggets of wisdom, praise, and love in them, as well as the book of Proverbs. In fact, the book Proverbs has one chapter for each day of the month; there are thirty-one. Isn't that amazing? I just think God is so wonderful." Grace spoke so softly and sweetly.

"You remind me of my grandmother. She was such a sweet woman. She died when I was twelve, but she would read the Bible to me once in a while when I would visit as a kid. I didn't remember anything specific until you mentioned Proverbs. She used to read that to me," Brody mused. Grace smiled warmly.

They headed back to the YMCA so Brody could get his bike, and then they arrived home just as Heath was getting home from work. They made their way into the house from the driveway, sharing stories about the day. Heath was impressed at how well Brody had done at the Zumba class.

Once in the house, Brody went upstairs to drop off the things he had bought earlier, took a shower, and then helped Grace get all the ingredients ready to make her famous crab bisque. He was excited to try his hand at cooking; he had never done it before, so it was going to be a brand-new experience for him.

Around five o'clock, Daniel and Kate came over. They were excited to see Brody was still in town and made plans to hang out with him the next day for lunch. They also asked how he was doing with getting back on track with his sobriety. Brody mentioned how he hadn't had a drink since late Monday night and was already feeling some detox symptoms—lack of sleep, shakes and sweats, and nausea whenever he even thought about drinking. They were happy to see he was not suffering too much and offered to help keep him accountable in any way they could. Daniel even asked if Brody would help him finish a landscaping job after lunch the next day. Then Grace called everyone to the table for dinner.

"Brody, are you going to be in town on Sunday? Could you help my team set up for the play we are doing during the service? We need to be there around eight in the morning," Daniel asked him, biting into his corn on the cob.

"What is this play about?" Brody asked, sipping his water.

"Pastor Brian is talking about the transformation of Saul to Paul. The youth group is putting on the play as part of the sermon," Daniel explained.

"The youth group has been practicing for weeks now. They are so excited," Kate chimed in.

A transformation, huh? Maybe I will get something out of this that will inspire me about what I should do next in life, Brody thought, stroking the stubble on his chin. "It sounds very cool. I'll be there to help," Brody answered.

Chapter Fifteen

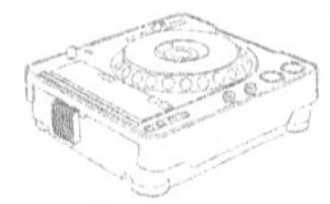

Brody left the church service and headed back to New York, pensive and teary eyed. The play had been very moving; that was the part that captured his attention the most during the whole service. He especially liked the part where Saul, a very wicked man, was knocked off his horse by God and called into service, where he received a new name too. It made him think about how he used to go by DJ Maddox, but since he had met the Stewarts, they called him Brody. He also felt a little like Saul, being kicked off his high horse and called to something different, but in his case, he wasn't as sure as Paul was on what to do with his life. God hadn't come to Brody in a booming voice and told him what his plan for his life was.

When he arrived home, he went straight to his bedroom and sat on his bed with a highlighter, his Bible, and a notebook. He started reading his sermon notes and then read Acts 9:1–31. After reading the passage, he grabbed the highlighter and highlighted everything he just read. Then he read it all once more, out loud this time. After that, he grabbed his notebook, and a pen and wrote a simple question down: What have you chosen me to do?

He closed the notebook and turned in his Bible to the book of Proverbs. *One chapter for every day of the month.* He heard Grace's words echoing in his mind while he searched for the day's date. After reading the chapter, he grabbed his phone and dialed Heath's number.

"Hey, Brody, did you make it home safe?" Heath asked.

"Yeah, I did, thanks, and yes, I did contact my agent too. He seemed very surprised I actually kept my word," Brody told, clearing his throat before speaking again. "I don't want to be a fool."

"Okay, what do you mean by that?" Heath asked, chuckling.

"I was reading Proverbs, and it said a wise person listens to others and asks advice. I haven't been able to stop thinking about the sermon today. What do you think God wants me to do with my life now? I doubt he wants me to continue doing things as usual, and if I don't have direction soon, my agent will have me doing life the way I always have until I can't hear anything from God," Brody explained, worried.

"Well, then you should start praying hard and honest about what you want and then ask God to help line up your heart with whatever he wants you to do. No one can tell you what to do; you have free will. You can do what you want, what someone else wants, or what God wants. Just remember, only God has a perfect plan for you," Heath told him.

"But will he talk to me like he did to Paul on that road to Damascus? Will it be a loud voice so I know it's him talking?" Brody asked, hopeful.

"No, I don't think so, but you will have a peace about whatever he is calling you to do. That is how you know it is God calling you to something. Even if you don't want to do it or you are scared, you will still have a peace that can't be explained. God never asks us to do anything that goes against what he says in the Bible, so that is another way to be wise and determine what is from God and what is from Satan," Heath replied. There was a pause.

"I have felt pushed to do something since I asked Jesus into my heart, but I have been pushing it aside because I am nervous about it. If I do it, I don't know what my next step is from there. How can I go forward if I don't have another step to take?" Brody asked.

"It sounds like you might have to exercise your faith. The Bible says we walk by faith, not by sight. If God wants you to do something but there isn't a sure thing on the other side, take a step of faith, do it even though you're afraid, and he will give you direction when it's time to move again," Heath suggested.

Brody sighed heavily. "Okay, I guess I need to shut my phone off and start praying now. Thanks, Heath. I will chat with you later. Good night." Brody shut his phone down and then knelt on the ground next to his bed and prayed. He prayed so long that he fell asleep with his face buried in his bed.

He woke up abruptly, looking around bewildered. He winced as he got up off the floor. His legs had fallen asleep but started to tingle as he headed to the kitchen. He looked at the clock on the microwave and saw it was nine-thirty at night. He yawned and searched all his cupboards for something to eat—nothing. He looked in his fridge—nothing. He looked in his freezer next and saw one more hot pocket, so he grabbed it and put it in the microwave with a grimace. *I need to go shopping soon and get better food,* he thought, waiting for the hot pocket to finish cooking.

After finishing his food in three bites, he went back to his room and grabbed his Bible. Deciding to read the book of Psalms, he started with chapter one. He read until he couldn't read anymore and went to bed close to midnight. As tired as he was, he tossed and turned until three in the morning and then sat up in his bed with intent.

He turned on the light and grabbed his phone, turning it on. His phone started to ping with notifications from his agent and friends. Right before the notifications stopped, he received one from a new source.

He had forgotten that he had downloaded a Bible app and set it up to give him "verse of the day" notifications. He opened the app and saw today's verse, Psalm 34:4: "I prayed to the Lord, and he answered me. He freed me from all my fears."

Brody swallowed the lump in his throat, closed out the app, and scrolled through his newsfeed on his social media accounts. He saw post after post from his friends and others he followed and smiled warmly before slowly frowning. He opened the Bible app again and started to browse through the past daily Bible verses. Several of them impacted him, and he jotted them down in his notebook to ask Heath about them later. A few verses really stuck with him and resonated with how he was feeling at the very moment of reading:

> Romans 12:2: Don't copy the behavior and customs of this world, but let God transform you into a new person by changing the way you think. Then you will learn to know God's will for you, which is good and pleasing and perfect.
> Proverbs 3:5–6: Trust in the Lord with all your heart; do not depend on your own understanding. Seek his will in all you do, and he will show you which path to take.
> 1 Corinthians 10:31: So whether you eat or drink, or whatever you do, do it all for the glory of God.

After reading many verses, he knelt down on the ground next to his bed, took a deep breath, and started to pray, tears falling down his cheeks. "God, I'm scared. I think I know what you want me to do and I know I need to take a step of faith, but I am so scared of what will happen. I read in one of these daily verses that we live by faith, not by sight. Heath said that to me earlier too. You have brought me here to the start of a healthier life, and I don't see why you would steer me wrong now. So I will believe that you have great plans for me, just like you did for Paul. I give you my will that I thought I wanted for my life, and I surrender to your will. Amen." He opened his eyes and grabbed his phone apprehensively.

Chapter Sixteen

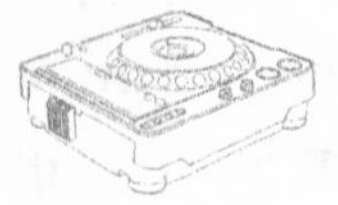

"After my twelve-thirty Zumba class, do you want to meet me for lunch? I wanted to talk to you about some decorating ideas I have for the house," Grace asked as she and Heath drank their morning coffee.

"Yeah, I think I can do that. What decorating ideas do you have? Not for the backyard, right?" Heath asked.

Grace kissed his cheek. "Don't worry. The backyard is your and Daniel's project."

Their quiet morning was interrupted when Kate burst into the house and ran straight over to them. "Oh my gosh, have you guys seen this? Oh wait, of course you haven't; I'm sure you don't follow him on social media. Look! Brody uploaded an epic video last night!" Kate exclaimed, pulling it up on her phone. She held it out to show them the video.

In the video, Brody was sitting on his bed. He took a deep breath and then started to speak: "Hey, guys, so I am currently filming this at three in the morning because I can't sleep, not until I get this off my chest." He ran his hand through his hair, and they could see nervousness on his face as he spoke. "I lied to you all about my disappearance last month. I wasn't taking a break at a spa. You, my fans, have been my life for almost thirteen years and you deserve the truth, so here it is." He took another deep breath, but this one was longer and labored as he wrung his hands.

"I have been dealing with depression for a long time.... No, that's not the right phrase. 'Dealing with' implies that I knew I was depressed and was seeking help. I didn't know I was depressed until the day I was going to try to jump off my penthouse building...the same day I went missing."

"Pause the video," Grace said with a furrowed brow. Kate paused the video, and Grace pointed to the screen. "What are all those little hearts and smiley faces doing there?"

Kate chuckled. "They are people's way of showing support and love."

"Oh, but a few don't look like they are showing him love," Grace remarked.

Heath grunted. "Grace, dear, let's watch the rest of the video please. I have to go to work soon." Kate turned the video back on.

"I got panic attacks before my shows, cried myself to sleep, and felt empty inside, plus I drank a whole lot. I have an alcohol addiction too. During my disappearance, I decided to get sober. The detox was brutal but I am glad I did it. I did have a minor relapse earlier this month, so now I am back on track to getting sober again. I can proudly say I haven't had a drop of alcohol since Monday night. Anyway, back to my original thought... While standing on the edge of my building, I realized that wasn't what I wanted to be remembered for—having a stellar career and then just ending my life in such an awful way. I wanted more in life, and I wanted to know that my life truly mattered." Brody leaned forward, and they could see the hope coming into his eyes as he smiled.

"I got off that ledge and drove straight to Hampton Beach in New Hampshire. I didn't tell anyone I was leaving or where I was going, and I am so sorry that I kept you all in the dark about it as long as I did and that it caused you so much grief; that was not my intention. I wasn't thinking of anyone but myself at that point, and I think that was a good thing, because I found true healing in Hampton Beach."

Brody grinned big now. "I met someone in Hampton Beach, and before you start getting all mushy and thinking this is going to be a post about a girl, hold on. I met Jesus, and he changed my heart through a girl named Vanessa and her family. Because of their kindness to me, I was able to find the love of Christ when I asked Jesus into my heart. I can't describe the feeling I have right now—it's something you have to experience for yourself—but it is amazing and overwhelming." He grinned from ear to ear, his eyes welling up with tears.

"I love you all, and I always will. Being a DJ has been my lifelong dream come true, and it was made possible by all of you. Thank you so much. That being said, I have decided I am leaving the DJ business so I can learn where God wants me to go from here. I want my life to glorify God now. I thank you all for your support for my career all these years, and if you continue to support me, that is awesome. And if you don't, I understand and still have love for you. This is just what I feel God calling me to do, and I am going to be obedient. Thank you all for taking the time to listen to my video. God bless you. Bye." He leaned forward to shut off the video.

Grace had started crying. "Wow, that is a big step," Grace said, choked up, and Kate nodded.

Heath stood up with a look of concern. "Grace, I'm going to have to reschedule our lunch. I'm going to go see Brody. I think he is going to need support soon," he said, kissing Grace before leaving.

"Does he think something is going to happen to Brody?" Kate asked.

Grace hugged her. "I think he is concerned that Brody's agent might try to dissuade him from this decision."

"Yeah, I can imagine his agent won't be too happy with this news. I have to go to work now, but I will talk to you later," Kate said, hugging Grace.

Grace started praying for Brody to stay strong in his decision while she finished getting ready for her day.

"Get up, maggot!" Chuck growled as he leaned over Brody's bed and tossed cold water onto him.

Brody shot up and gasped, "What the heck?"

Chuck started rifling through Brody's closet. "You need to get up and get dressed now!"

Brody stood to his feet, yawning. "Why? What time is it?"

"It's ten in the morning, and we have a lot of damage control to do now," Chuck said, shoving clothes into Brody's chest with a look of contempt. "Get dressed and dry your hair; it's soaking wet." Brody took hold of the clothes and walked into the bathroom.

"Why do I need to do damage control?" Brody asked, drying his hair with a towel.

Chuck laughed scornfully. "Are you drunk? How can you not know what I'm talking about?"

Brody came out of the bathroom combing his hair. "The video I posted? There's nothing to do damage control about. I've made up my mind, Chuck," Brody told him, putting his comb down on his TV stand.

"No, you couldn't have made up your mind, not without talking to me first. Remember, I'm here to help you stay away from mistakes that will kill your career. This stupid video—that was a horrible move that will kill and bury your career before noon if we don't get on top of this situation like it's a beautiful woman."

Brody grimaced at the metaphor. "Come on, Chuck. Listen, I don't want to do any damage control, okay? I made my decision, and I'm proud of it."

Chuck got on his phone and started clicking away, ignoring him. "Okay, we need to leave now. I booked you with three different radio stations and a TV station. You're going to tell them you were very drunk when you made that video," Chuck commanded, reaching for Brody's arm to drag him away.

Brody shook his arm. "No, Chuck. I'm not lying to my fans anymore. They deserve better than that." Brody left the room and went into the kitchen to drink some water. Chuck watched him with contempt, but Brody had a pep in his step and a smile on his face.

"What were you thinking? I can't believe you did that video without consulting me first. Don't you know how this will affect your career?" Chuck asked, annoyed.

"Didn't you watch the video? I quit, so it's okay," Brody said, sipping his glass of water.

Chuck stood rigid and pointed a finger in Brody's face. "No, it's not okay! I have spent the last thirteen years making you into the megastar you are now, and this is how you repay me? You are such an inconsiderate brat! You don't even give me the courtesy of telling me first that you plan to crap all over all the hard work we did for your career!"

Brody laid his empty cup on the counter and patted Chuck's shoulder, "Hey, Chuck, I am sorry that you are so upset, but it is *my* career and I am okay with this. I have other plans in mind."

Chuck rolled his eyes, laughing hysterically. "Yes, I heard. I had a great laugh at your expense."

He leaned in closer to Brody and glared at him with scorn. "So you want to glorify God with your life now, huh? Do you really think a person with your history can do such a thing? You drink like a fish and sleep with any woman who comes near you. If I were God, I wouldn't want you."

Brody started to feel overcome with negative emotions and looked away, hurt and full of doubt.

Chuck continued, realizing he had Brody vulnerable enough to get him to bend to his will. "If you couldn't change yourself all these years, why do you think you can change now—or change the world, for that matter? You can't change who you are just because you found religion."

Brody hung his head, feeling worthless now.

Chuck snickered. "See, you are already doubting that you can do anything good, so why not just quit while you still can? Let's fix this mess you made. The true fans will stick with you even after this, and if you still have a career, we can build it up better than it was before—more fame, more girls, more alcohol, more money, more whatever you want. In fact, you just got asked to be a part of that epic Halloween festival in San Bernadino, the one that you have been trying to get into for years. They have finally asked you to be a part of it. Isn't that exciting?"

Brody's eyes lit up. "Really? They asked for me? You didn't have to beg them or bribe them to take me?"

Chuck chuckled. "No, of course not, kid. You are very good at your job, and you have paid your dues. It has all led up to this one show. You know that this show is for the big leagues only. Once you get asked to be a part of this, the world is your oyster." Brody's heart pounded with excitement and confusion, and it was written all over his face. Chuck saw the vulnerability and pounced. "See? It's all coming together for you, Brody. Don't leave the business, not now that you are so close to the top."

Brody was silent for a long time, conflicted. This was a career advancement for sure and an achievement he had only dreamed of. He had tears in his eyes as thoughts of his future career success ran through his mind, clouding out the Bible verses that had encouraged him earlier. Finally he lifted his head, ran to his patio, and started to rummage through the trash bag. Brody pulled out a half-drunk bottle of rum and started to gulp it down.

Chuck laughed. "So much for staying sober, huh?" Brody finished the bottle and dropped it onto the patio before running to the sink and throwing it all right back up. Brody started to cry uncontrollably.

Chuck looked at him with annoyance. "Why did you do that? I don't think that would have messed up your sobriety that bad."

Brody cleaned off his face and looked at Chuck. "I said I wasn't going to drink anymore, and I meant it." Brody walked out of the kitchen and stood next to Chuck. "I can't do this Chuck...."

"Can't do what?" Chuck asked, livid.

"I can't live this life anymore. I don't want to. The fame, the fortune, the women, the alcohol, the late nights...it's all meaningless to me, and I don't want it anymore!" Brody explained with a glimmer of hope in his eyes and passion in his voice.

Chuck slammed his fist onto the kitchen island loudly and

then poked Brody hard in the chest, making him stumble backward into the island. "Look here, bane of my existence. I never liked you. In fact, you always act like a pain-in-the-butt teenager who never grew up! You signed a contract with me, so I can sue you for all you got if you don't comply. Now let's go!" he shouted with disgust in his eyes as he grabbed Brody's arm again.

Brody shook him away and squared his shoulders. "No! I am not going, and no threats, name calling, or bullying from you or anyone else will *ever* change my mind! James 4:17 says, 'Remember, it is a sin to know what you ought to do and then not do it.' I have chosen Christ, and I am not backing down on that, even if I have to suffer for the decision. I may not be a perfect person now, but in Christ, I have the chance to change for the better. That means more to me than all the money or fame in the world."

Chuck glared at Brody for a while before grabbing a glass on the counter and tossing it at the wall. The sound of shattering glass echoed in Brody's ears.

Chuck's eyes flared with hatred. "Oh, you will suffer for sure, Brody! One day you will look back and see this was a huge mistake. You will beg me to come back to you, but I won't be there! I will just kick you to the curb and tell you to let your *God* save your career. I will talk to my lawyer as soon as I leave here. Don't you dare leave this state before I have you served, you ungrateful and entitled piece of crap!"

In this moment, Brody noticed something in Chuck's eyes that he'd never seen before; it was sadness. Brody's face dropped as Chuck emptied his pockets of anything that belonged to Brody and tossed it onto the kitchen counter, angrily muttering to himself.

"Chuck," Brody said after a few seconds.

Chuck was already at the door, his hand on the knob. "What? Did you change your mind? I knew threatening you with a lawsuit would get your attention."

Brody shook his head. "No, I didn't change my mind, but I just realized something...." Chuck looked at him, intrigued. Brody continued with a sad smile. "I know I wasn't one of your easiest clients. As you said, I acted like a piece of crap toward you."

Chuck raised a quizzical brow and started back toward Brody, motioning for him to continue.

"I have never forgotten how much you believed in me, even when I didn't believe in myself. I also realized you have sacrificed your whole life for mine. It reminds me of the sacrifice that Jesus made for us sinners. It's not quite on the same level, but I kind of get it now, Jesus's sacrifice, that is," Brody rambled, looking at Chuck with compassionate eyes. "I have never thanked you for all your years of service to me and I know this came out of left field, so allow me to leave you with a parting gift to show you my gratitude for all your amazing years of devotion. I want you to have this penthouse. You can live in it or sell it, whatever you want."

Chuck was genuinely surprised by the gesture. Brody could see his scowl start to melt and a hint of a sincere smile start to form. "Are you serious?"

"Yeah, I don't need it anymore. I'm planning to move to New Hampshire. Honestly, I wouldn't even have what I do if it weren't for you and your hard work. Giving you this place would be the least I could do for you. If you still want to sue me too, I don't blame you," Brody explained. Chuck stared at Brody for the longest time.

Finally Chuck sighed heavily and hung his head. "I won't sue you. I was just angry. I also didn't mean it when I said I didn't like you. You are like the son I never had." Chuck tried not to show any emotion. "Your penthouse is too generous. I...I can't accept it, especially not after how I talked to you. I don't deserve it."

Brody grinned. "That's the beauty of God's grace. No one deserves it, but he is always willing to give it to us if we ask for forgiveness and turn to him."

Chuck started to get choked up. "Grace or not, I can't take such an elaborate gift from you. I think you'll need the money from selling this place to get settled into your new life anyway."

Brody shook his head. "I'll be okay financially. I've been putting away a nest egg since my very first show."

Chuck paused before speaking again. "Can I have your motorcycle instead?"

Brody laughed loudly. "Ha! You have always wanted that thing. Sure, you can have it. I was thinking of getting a car anyway."

Chuck wiped away a few tears that had managed to fall and walked up to Brody, hesitant before he smiled and hugged him tightly. "Have a good life, kid. I wish you the best, really."

"Thanks. I wish you the best too, Chuck. You were a great agent," Brody said as they let go and Chuck left.

Brody fell asleep on his couch after Chuck left and slept there for a few hours before someone knocked at his door. He was startled awake and stumbled to the door to find Heath standing there. He grinned. "Hey, Heath, I wasn't expecting to see you. Why are you here?"

Heath walked in. "I saw your video. Bold move. I thought you might need some emotional support when Satan tries to mess with you about this."

Brody chuckled. "I think I already had that moment." He told Heath everything that had happened earlier.

Heath smiled. "I'm very proud of you for standing up on your own two feet, and even though you tried to drink, you immediately regretted it and expelled it. That was a good step toward self-control."

"Thanks for the encouragement. I just think the Holy Spirit gave me the strength. I was of no help in this situation. I also think he used Vanessa to help me too," Brody started. Heath looked at him intrigued, so Brody explained, "I was about to cave into Chuck's demands until I felt the Holy Spirit kick me in the butt. He reminded me of something Vanessa and I talked about while paddleboarding, a Bible verse, James 4:17."

Heath chuckled. "Yeah, I am familiar with that one. Very convicting, isn't it?"

Brody nodded in agreement. "Well, since you're here, you want to help me pack? I plan to sell this place, so I need to pack up all my personal belongings. The furniture stays. It came with the place," Brody told him.

"Yeah, I can help. What do you need me to do?" Heath asked.

"Well, the first thing I want you to do is grab that awful trash bag of alcohol off my patio and toss it in the trash as far away from me as possible," Brody said, pointing Heath in the direction he needed him to go.

Heath chuckled. "I'll take it to the dumpster outside." Brody nodded and went to work packing his bedroom.

When Heath returned, Brody had finished packing his clothes. "I have a question to ask you, Heath. Do you mind if I were to live with you and Grace for a while, so I can finish the detox process? I also don't feel comfortable being on my own right now. I could stay in Daniel's old bedroom, and of course I would pay you rent," Brody added.

Heath smiled warmly. "I have to discuss it with Grace, but I am sure she will not have a problem with it. We wouldn't make you pay rent either, but we would give you rules we would expect you to follow, just like we would do for one of our own children living under our roof—no drinking of any kind being the number one, in your case especially."

"I am okay with any rules you give me. I just want to be free from my chains of addiction and feel comfortable enough to live on my own again," Brody replied as they continued working.

Chapter Seventeen

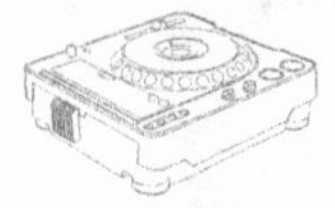

BRODY PUT HIS FINAL box on the ground and then sat down on the bed, frowning. He heard footsteps coming up the stairs and perked up. Heath knocked on the open door and then walked in and sat next to Brody.

"Settled in?" he asked. Brody nodded, but Heath could tell something was going on with him and waited for Brody to speak.

"I'm nervous that I made a hasty decision about leaving the music business. I have already been getting texts and phone calls from friends asking me what that video was all about and if I meant what I said about leaving. A few of my friends have already started trying to talk me out of it or make me feel stupid for my choice," Brody confessed.

"You're scared for the next chapter of your life. I was there too when I was coming out of the business. I wondered if I would be successful and financially stable, and I worried if anyone would remember me in a year. It took me years of being in God's Word and surrounded by his people before I finally realized I needed to give my hopes for my life to God and let him do what he needed to do. Once I did that, my heart changed. I started to notice that the fame and fortune I cared so much about didn't matter to me anymore. All I wanted was what God wanted for me," Heath encouraged him, patting Brody on the shoulder. "It won't be easy to surrender your life to Christ. It's a daily struggle and takes intentionality, but it will be worth it all in the end. God is with you, and so are we."

Brody smiled. "Thanks. That helps a lot. I'm going to organize my room and do some reading before bed." Heath got up and walked out the door, shutting it behind him. Brody frowned momentarily and then walked over to his boxes.

Brody had been living with the Stewarts for two weeks now, and they were hard weeks for him, not because of the rules or that the Stewarts were difficult to live with but rather because he was having trouble staying sober with all the backlash he was getting from critics, friends, fans, groupies, and past lovers who didn't approve of his choice to leave the business. Their comments, phone calls, and voicemails weighed heavily on him and hurt his heart. He cried himself to sleep most nights during the first week.

He was going to tell Heath about the overwhelming pain he was going through and how it stirred up an intense desire to drink but decided to keep it to himself and learn to reject the desires on his own. He didn't want to burden anyone with his situation.

During the second week, Brody's best friend, Michael found him in Hampton Beach and tried to persuade him to come back with him to do the San Bernardino concert with him. He even left Brody a copy of the poster. DJ Maddox was one of the top performers listed.

Brody's heart ripped in two as he thanked Michael but told him his mind was made up. Michael had some rather choice words for him and his God. Brody greatly knew that life wouldn't be the same as before, but he also didn't like losing his best friend or saying no to the biggest event of his life. He still knew it was the right thing to do. After that encounter, the desire to drink intensified, yet he still chose to keep quiet about it.

Now, three days before the huge concert, all he wanted to do was not think about it. But between texts from friends and people on social media tagging him in posts about the upcoming event, it was impossible to forget.

He groaned loudly as he tossed his phone onto the bed. "I need a drink," he muttered to himself, walking quietly downstairs. He wanted to get out of the house without any questions from Heath and Grace. He smiled when he saw they were watching TV. He snuck out of the house through the back door and went for a walk around the block.

He tormented himself while he scrolled through his social media and saw more comments and messages begging him to reconsider. He pulled up the map app on his phone and looked for the nearest liquor store. It wasn't far by car, but by foot, it would take him at least ten minutes. He decided it was worth the trip, so he continued walking in that direction.

As Brody rounded a corner, he received another text message from Michael telling him he had one last chance to change his mind before his life blew up in a huge pile of ashes. Brody groaned and searched through his contact list for Chuck's number. He was about to dial but hesitated and put his phone back into his pocket just as it started to ring. He looked at the caller ID. It was Michael. He didn't want to hear anything he had to say. Michael had been relentless lately and not very kind either. Brody denied the call and kept walking with intent. Only eight more minutes to go until his liquid salvation would be in hand.

He walked into the liquor store and picked up a bottle of vodka, paid for it, and then went to the other side of the building to drink it. He pulled the bottle out of the paper bag and twisted off the top, his mouth all but salivating at the thought of the liquid freedom from his pain. He put the bottle to his lips but didn't let the contents enter his mouth. He heard God talking to him at that moment: *I've got you, Brody. You don't need to do this.* He started weeping bitterly and dropped to the ground. "God, if this is what you called me to do, shouldn't I be at peace right now?"

He wiped his eyes and put the bottle on the ground next to him. "I don't regret asking you into my life, and I really feel you want me to leave everything behind. I felt very free when I initially made the announcement, but now? Now I don't know what I'm feeling. Maybe I'm just scared because you haven't given me my next step. What am I going to do with my life now?" Brody put his face into his knees, sighed heavily, and then stayed silent for a while.

Finally he stood to his feet with intention, clenching the bottle in his hands. He poured the contents of the bottle onto the ground. "I refuse to believe you have anything less than your best for my life. I am tired of the past trying to draw me back in and making me feel like I made a mistake. I know I didn't. Help me, Lord, please. I am weak, but I am ready to follow your leading fully. I don't want to be a slave to the bottle or to my career. My whole life, all that I am, is yours. I hope you are ready for that." Brody took the bottle and paper bag and tossed them into the trashcan as he started walking back home, his head held high and a boldness in his heart now.

Brody was five minutes into his walk back to the house when he saw a semi-rundown building. He looked at it, perplexed, and started to walk over to it. The store windows were boarded up but a few planks were coming off, so he peeked inside. He saw a nice space; it was long and wide, full of potential. He heard a still, small voice speak to him: *I never said you would be finished with music, Brody.*

He walked into the house through the front door and saw Grace staring at him nervously. "Hey, Brody, where have you been, kiddo? I got worried when I went upstairs to see if you wanted something to eat and you were gone. Heath went out looking for you not long ago," she said, hugging him.

He smiled back. "Sorry. I went for a walk. I needed clarity. The last few weeks have been tough on me," Brody confessed. Grace motioned for him to sit on the couch with her. He was about to tell her everything when Heath came into the house. He looked relieved when he saw Brody.

"Hey, where were you?" Heath asked. Brody realized the torment he had put on them with his disappearance and frowned. "I am so sorry I worried you two." He explained everything to them about the last few weeks and the tipping point earlier that day. He also told them about his transformation at the liquor store.

Grace sighed. "That is a lot to have on your plate. I'm sorry, Brody. I am proud of you for not giving into the temptation to drink." Brody smiled. "So do you feel better now?" Grace asked.

Brody nodded. "Yeah, actually I do. I really feel like I have been freed from my desire to drink now."

Grace hugged him. "Good. I'm glad to hear it."

Grace and Brody looked at Heath. He was rather quiet, which concerned Brody. He was sure he would have to march upstairs and pack his things.

Finally Heath hugged Brody so tightly it knocked the wind out of him. "I'm glad you and God were able to figure things out together." He looked at Brody solemnly. "You have to take your relationship with God seriously now that you told him you're all in. Start serving at church somewhere, pray and read your Bible often, and don't forget to take your sobriety seriously too. After what you just told us, I think you are finally on the right track to doing that. Please don't ever feel like what you are going through will burden us. We are here for you always. Remember that."

Brody's eyes welled up with tears as he looked at Grace. She nodded in agreement with Heath's statement. Brody grinned and looked back at Heath. "Okay, I am sorry again. Thank you for your support and for not giving up on me. Last week I signed up for the audio production team, and I'm just waiting for someone to get back to me about it." Heath patted his back with a smile.

Brody spent the rest of the day thinking about that building he had seen. He talked with Heath after dinner that night and asked what he thought of the idea of turning it into a studio. Heath thought it was a good idea, and if it needed as much work as Brody said it did, then it would keep him busy while he worked on his sobriety.

Brody couldn't wait until morning so he could put an offer in for the place. His offer was accepted the same day, and he spent the next few weeks working on the place. Some guys from the audio production team offered to help him set up the audio equipment, and Kate, Daniel, Grace, and Heath helped whenever they had the time. Brody's goal was to be finished before he visited his sister for Christmas.

While he renovated the studio, he also renovated his life. In November, he started to attend the new addiction ministry that was started by a couple guys at the church, Chad and Matty, who had overcome their own addictions and wanted to help others do the same. Brody thought it could be a good tool for him to stay sober even though he hadn't felt the desire to drink at all since that day behind the liquor store.

Chapter Eighteen

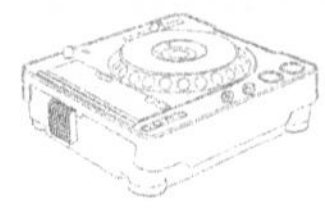

"WHO WANTS TO SEE the new studio?" Brody asked, walking into the house with a grin.

"It's ready? I want to see it!" Grace exclaimed, grabbing Heath's hand and rushing out the front door. They followed Brody to his car and drove to the building.

Grace gasped as she stepped out of the car. "Oh, Brody, the outside is wonderful. I can't imagine how beautiful it is on the inside." They walked in and looked around. Brody showed them everything and let them go in the sound booth too, which brought back fond memories for Heath.

"You did a great job. This place is awesome, Brody," Heath said with a pat on Brody's back. "Now you are ready to make your first single as a re-birthed artist."

Brody looked confused. "You want me to make a song?"

"Isn't that what you created this space for?" Heath asked with a chuckle.

Brody nodded nervously. "Yeah, but I don't...I wouldn't know what lyrics to use."

"Write about how you have been feeling the last almost three months or about your conversion. There are many things you could sing about. You have written your own lyrics before, right?" Heath asked.

Brody nodded. "Yeah, totally. I just haven't written lyrics with substance before; all my lyrics were superficial," Brody confessed.

"Well, I'm sure you will do well. There is no pressure or timeline. Just write what God wants you to write and when he wants you to write," Grace chimed in.

Brody nodded. "Okay, I think I can do that. I used to write lyrics really quickly. Maybe I will get lucky with that skill again. I'm up for the challenge."

"Let's head back to the house. We need to set up for my birthday party before all the guests arrive," Grace said with a chuckle, heading out of the building.

Heath followed her, nudging Brody. "She gets so excited for her birthday, even though it is so close to Christmastime. She told me all her friends and family would bunch her Christmas and birthday gifts together when she was a child, but she didn't care. She still got excited every year because it was close to the celebration of the birth of Jesus."

Brody chuckled. "Grace is a remarkable woman. You are a lucky man, Heath." Heath nodded in agreement as Brody closed the door.

Brody woke up around seven the next morning, grabbed his luggage, and started downstairs. He saw Grace sitting at her laptop. She was reading through something on her computer screen very intently. Brody walked over to her and put his arm around her. "Good morning, Grace."

She patted his hand. "Good morning, kiddo. How did you sleep?"

"Really well. I was worn out after your party last night.

Who knew charades and Pictionary could be so tiring?" he said, chuckling. She giggled and went back to what she was reading.

Brody leaned in. "What's this?"

"This is a monthly email I get from the mission leader for Vanessa's region in Southeast Asia. This is how I get updates about Vanessa," Grace explained.

"I see," Brody said. She nodded. Brody's eyes scanned down to a magazine near her computer desk, and he picked it up. "What's this?"

"That is the ministry's magazine I subscribe to. They mention those being persecuted for their faith either through imprisonment, harassment, or uprooting of their families or those who have been killed and their families who were left behind. Her ministry gives to the families of those who have been martyred too," Grace told him, looking at Brody with a smile.

"It sounds very encouraging and sad at the same time," Brody commented.

Grace nodded. "It is definitely both those things, but it is a good way for me to say informed on what is going on around the world and how to pray for missionaries who are suffering."

"Does Vanessa ever try to call you guys around Christmas? She mentioned to me a while ago that she doesn't get to video chat or call because where she works and lives is so remote. It must be hard to not be able to contact her often."

Grace looked at him. "Yes, it's hard to not hear from her, but we were well aware that was how it would be before she left. She tries to make a trip to a place with good Internet reception at least twice a year so we can see her. Usually she tries to video chat around Easter and Christmas."

Brody frowned. "I won't be here. I'm gone until January 3."

"Well, she doesn't call on those days specifically, just around those times of year. I haven't gotten the email with the scheduled time yet. I will let you know with enough time to come home early if you want to be here for the conversation," Grace assured him.

Brody smiled. "Okay, thanks, Grace."

"I made you some muffins for your trip. They're on the counter," Grace said, shutting down her computer.

"Thanks," Brody said, stuffing his face with a muffin.

Just then Heath came downstairs and smiled. "Good morning, Brody. I'm glad I caught you before you left. I wanted to give you your Christmas gift," Heath said as he handed Brody his gift. Brody started to rip the wrapping paper off the box while Grace ran to the pantry and grabbed her gift for him.

Brody's eyes lit up as he opened the box and revealed a leather-bound notebook with his name engraved on the bottom of the cover.

Brody looked at Heath in awe. "Wow, this is cool."

"It's for you to jot down lyrics. You'll start having ideas everywhere, and it's a good idea to have a notebook handy," Heath said.

"This is a very thoughtful gift. Thanks, Heath," Brody responded.

"Okay, my turn," Grace said with a twinkle in her eye as she handed Brody her present.

He opened it and saw that it was a homemade cookbook. His eyes widened as he skimmed through it.

Grace smiled. "They're recipes for all the meals and snacks you have told me you liked. When you end up having your own place, you will be able to make them whenever you want."

Brody hugged her and gave her a kiss on the cheek. "Thank you, Grace. This means a lot to me. Maybe we can make some of these together the first time so I don't mess them up."

"Sure, kiddo, that would be lovely. Have a good trip. Tell your folks we say hello, and give that sweet baby a hug from me. She looks so cute in all her photos you showed me. I wish I could squeeze those adorable, chubby cheeks," Grace said with a laugh.

"We will miss having you with us for Christmas, but I am sure you are excited to see your family for the holidays," Heath chimed in.

Brody shrugged. "Yeah, I guess so. I am excited to see my sister, but my parents…not so much. I don't think they will take my transformation or my quitting the business as well as you all did…or even as well as my sister did. I haven't talked to them in a long time, and I'm sure they will not be happy to know the checks are no longer coming in for them, because their son is no longer making the big bucks."

"Just pray for them. I'm sure it won't be so bad," Grace encouraged.

Brody smiled. "Okay, I will. Thanks. I better leave now. Pray for me." Brody waved as he left.

Chapter Nineteen

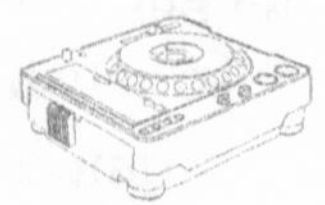

JUST AS BRODY HAD thought, his family wasn't too thrilled to hear he had left his lucrative career behind to pursue religion, and surprisingly, they weren't as proud of him for giving up alcohol as he thought they would be. In Brody's mind, this didn't bode well for his vacation, so when Grace called and said Vanessa was calling a few days before he was scheduled to leave, he was all too willing to cut his trip short.

Brody walked into the house and saw Kate and Daniel sitting at the dining room table. They waved. "He's here, Mom," Daniel said, shaking hands with Brody as he came over.

Grace came downstairs and hugged Brody. "Hey, kiddo. Happy New Year's! How was the flight?"

"It was a nice one. I took a nap." Brody said.

"I am so excited!" Grace said with a giggle as she sat down next to Heath.

Kate nodded. "Me too. What about you, Brody?"

Brody swallowed a lump in his throat and sat down in his chair. "I'm nervous but also excited."

Vanessa called not long after everyone was seated. Grace barely let it ring before answering.

Vanessa was sitting at a table in a small, dimly lit room with beige walls. She grinned and waved. "Hey, everyone, Happy New Year!"

"Happy New Year, sweetie. How are you? You look tired. Are you getting enough rest? Have you been working too hard out there?" Grace asked.

"Yes, Mom, I'm sleeping just fine. We had a hard day today, so I'm more tired than usual," Vanessa said, clearing her throat.

"Hey, Vanessa, Happy New Year! How's the weather there? Really hot?" Heath asked.

"Yes, it's very hot. I like it some days, but other days it's unbearable. How is the weather there? Is it snowing yet?" Vanessa asked.

"No, not yet. I know you love the snow, so if it were, I would have moved the computer so you could see it. I miss you so much, sweetie, and I love you too," Heath said with a grin, blowing her a kiss.

Vanessa blushed and giggled as she blew him a kiss. "I love you and miss you too, Dad."

Vanessa chatted with her brother about his business, and then she and Kate chatted about how Kate left the arcade and got a job as a receptionist for a real estate office that had just opened up in town not too long ago. Vanessa was very excited to hear she was at a place she enjoyed working at. She always knew Kate hated working at the arcade.

"Sweetie, someone else is here to chat with you," Grace said, turning the camera toward Brody. He waved awkwardly, and Vanessa gasped and grinned as she waved back. Grace turned the camera back toward herself. "Sweetie, are you sure you are okay? I was reading the most recent email from your ministry, and it seems like there is unrest in certain places."

"I'm fine, Mom. Don't worry about me. I am so glad you all are doing well. I love you guys. Do you guys mind if I have some alone time with Brody? I would like to catch up with him alone." Vanessa asked, glancing at Brody shyly.

"Of course, sweetie. Come on, guys. Let's give them some privacy," Grace said, ushering everyone away with a giggle. Kate nudged Brody playfully.

Daniel looked at Brody. "Hey, do you mind if I talk to her alone real quick? I have something I need to tell her before I lose my nerve." "Sounds mysterious. Sure, go ahead," Brody said as he stood up from his chair and walked away.

Daniel sat down and started chatting. Everyone watched from the kitchen. They couldn't hear the conversation, but they saw Vanessa get excited by whatever was said. Shortly after, Daniel got up from the chair and motioned for Brody to come over.

Brody's hands started shaking and his heart skipped a beat as he sat down in front of the screen, smiling at Vanessa. Daniel and Kate waved to the screen as they left. Heath kissed his wife, waved to Vanessa, blew her a kiss, and told her he loved her and then left as well to go to church for the worship team rehearsal. Grace said her goodbyes too and then went upstairs. Vanessa and Brody were finally alone.

Brody stared at her longingly. "It's so good to see you, Vanessa. You are a sight for sore eyes."

Vanessa blushed. "Thanks. It's great to see you too. Your stubble grew back, I see."

Brody chuckled and stroked his chin. "Yeah, I keep it this way because I remembered you said you liked it."

Vanessa blushed again. "I'm glad you aren't upset with me."

"Why would I be upset with you?" he asked.

Vanessa looked away. "You know, because I left after I said I would stay. I'm sure you thought it was because of the feelings we have for each other that I left, but I can assure you it wasn't that at all."

Brody chuckled, embarrassed. "Yeah, I did think that...for a while actually, but everything happened the way it did to bring me to the place I am at right now."

Vanessa listened intently as Brody explained everything that had happened since the day she left. Vanessa started to tear up. "Wow, Brody, that is a great testimony! I am so glad God used my disappearance in a good way for you. My faith has been increased since I got back here, so we both won I guess. I am proud of you for going to the addiction group at church. It's amazing someone finally made a group for that. I always thought we needed one."

"Thanks, Vanessa. That means a lot to me. Maybe when you come to visit again, you can come to the group with me, you know, to check it out. I'm sure everyone would be encouraged by your story and mission work," Brody suggested.

Vanessa paused. "So I have some news, and since you are the only one here, I will tell you and you can relay it to everyone else. I may be coming home sooner than summer...and more permanently. I can't go into details, but it's a very strong possibility," Vanessa said with excitement.

Brody's eyes lit up. "Seriously? That would be totally awesome! Your family will be thrilled—and so will I. Now we can date officially, and we won't have to worry about leaving each other since we both will be local."

Vanessa glanced away, nodded, and then looked back at Brody with a grin. "I look forward to that very much. Listen, I need to leave soon, but I wanted to say I'm glad my family is there to help you on your spiritual journey. I'm also excited for your future in music. I can't wait to hear one of your songs."

"I haven't written any yet," Brody admitted, feeling dejected.

Vanessa smiled warmly. "You will. I believe in you, Brody."

His face lit up. He paused before speaking, looking at Vanessa lovingly. "You are so special to me, Vanessa; I want you to know that. Now that I am focusing my life on God, I see that I didn't have a correct affection for you. But I do now, and I look forward to your coming home so I can show you how much you really matter to me, in a healthy way. I wouldn't be who I am today if it weren't for your influence in my life. Thank you so much for helping me when I was at my lowest point in life."

Vanessa cried happy tears and blushed as Brody blew her a kiss. She giggled and blew him a kiss back. "I'm glad I didn't give up on you either. You are going to do many things to change the world this coming year, Brody. I feel it in my soul."

There was a momentary pause. Vanessa looked away once more and nodded before looking back at Brody. "I have to go now. Please remember to keep everyone in India in your prayers. As my mom mentioned, there is something going on out here. I am fine—don't worry about me—but there are places around here that are very hostile right now. God bless you and my family, Brody." They lingered before finally shutting the call down.

"You are lucky the warden wasn't here today. That phone call was way over the allowed time for foreign prisoners," the guard said in Hindi.

Vanessa stood up, bowed in respect, and spoke in Hindi as well. "Thank you again for allowing me more time. I will make up for it with extra time in the yard tomorrow."

The guard ran his hands over her hair. "That is not necessary. You are a pretty girl. I am happy to help you—this time only." The guard stared at her with a serious look on his face.

Vanessa bowed in respect again with a slight smile and spoke in English this time. "I thank you again, Ronit."

The guard smiled back and also spoke in English. "You are welcome, but do not use my first name when we are near other guards or prisoners. They will think I am showing favoritism toward you, and I could lose my job." He escorted Vanessa back to her cell.

"You lied to your boyfriend and family," Ronit said, speaking in Hindi again. Vanessa looked confused, so he explained. "You told them you were fine and weren't in danger, but here you are in prison for this faith you wear so proudly."

Vanessa smiled and replied in Hindi, "God is by my side. He is looking out for me, even in here, so I am not afraid. I did not want to worry them needlessly. I will be fine. God is my protector." Ronit was silent as they passed a few oncoming guards.

"Is that the reason you asked the visitors two months ago not to put your name on their list of prisoners? So your boyfriend and family wouldn't be informed?" he asked, seeming to be genuinely curious. Vanessa nodded as they approached her cell.

"I suppose it is a kind gesture," he said, opening the door to her cell and nudging her in gently. She bumped into a couple other missionaries inside the crowded cell. He was about to leave, but she reached through the bars and touched his hand softly. Their eyes met. He looked at her, surprised and with a clenched jaw. He knew that they could both get in trouble if it looked like he was fraternizing with a prisoner.

"Thank you again for your kindness and letting me speak

with my family. My soul is rejuvenated knowing my family is doing well and that Brody, my boyfriend, is now a believer," Vanessa said with the biggest grin, having called Brody her boyfriend.

Ronit moved his hand away and chuckled. "It seems you touch lives wherever you go then." Ronit walked away slowly.

Chapter Twenty

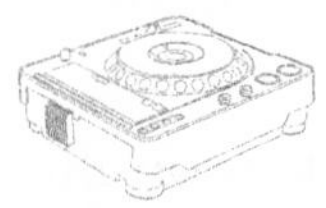

TWO DAYS AFTER VANESSA'S video chat, the family received a group email from Duncan Miller, the leader of the Southeast Asia ministry team.

> *Dear Families,*
> *Thank you for all your dedication and prayer for our teams in Southeast Asia. No doubt you are aware of the massive unrest that has been happening in that area for the past few years now. It has reached a head in the last several months, and because of that, we have been told it is no longer safe. The governments out there have called for the removal of all missionaries, so effective immediately, all of our teams will be called back to the United States indefinitely. I am sure you are all excited to see your missionary, and we are excited to send them home to you, but before we do, we will keep them with us at our Texas headquarters for a few weeks to a month. We are doing this so we can tend to any illnesses or wounds that may have been inflicted.*

Also, we want to make sure we can account for all our missionaries before we start sending them home. By the end of February, we hope to be able to send your missionaries home. Again, thank you for always praying and supporting the mission work, and may God bless you all.
Duncan Miller

This was the best New Year's news the family could have received; however, Grace was also apprehensive about it too. After all, the email did mention illnesses and injuries. Heath tried to assure her that it was probably just standard procedure when the missionaries come home. Grace agreed but still was worried, so she tried to occupy her time while she waited for a follow-up email by tidying up Vanessa's room and organizing things. Heath spent his time tuning up Vanessa's car.

Brody was on cloud nine after hearing the news. He was so glad she would finally be out of danger. Ever since she had told him about what had been going on with her and the locals, he had been concerned for her safety; he was grateful he wouldn't have to be concerned any longer. He also realized that soon he would have Vanessa in his arms again and they could begin dating. This gave him more drive to stay close to God, keep sober, and work on a song to impress Vanessa with. He still hadn't come up with any new music. He had been in his studio feverishly trying to come up with one song but still nothing. He hoped her coming home was a good enough incentive to get his writing mojo started. Unfortunately for him, not even Vanessa's return was enough to spark his creativity. After the second week of January, there was still no music.

Brody sat in his studio chair, rocking and twirling it around, tapping a pencil on his forehead and grunting periodically. He was drawing blanks trying to come up with lyrics, and it was starting to grate on his nerves. His lyrics from his old music may have been superficial, but at least he was able to come up with them. Why was it so hard to come up with lyrics that meant something to him?

He had already tried several times to create lyrics out of his transformation, but nothing was meshing. He decided to wait on the Lord for the perfect time. He looked at the clock on the wall. It was almost time for his group, so he reluctantly shut everything down and left the building.

"Hey, Brody, I couldn't help but notice you were rather distracted today. Is everything okay?" Chad asked, walking outside the church with Brody after the meeting and putting his jacket on.

"Yeah, sorry. I'm frustrated about something," Brody said, putting his jacket on too.

"Does it have to do with your sobriety?" Chad asked.

Brody smiled. "No, that's going well, praise God. I can't seem to write a song, and it's bothering me. Maybe I'm really finished with music. I have been trying so hard, but nothing is happening for me." Brody put his beanie on his head and looked up at the sky; it was starting to snow.

"Maybe the problem is that you are trying too hard. How long have you been trying to write a song?" Chad asked.

"Since Christmas," Brody answered, frustrated.

"Have you been trying nonstop, or are you taking breaks to focus on other things?" Chad asked next.

"What other things should I be focused on?" Brody asked.

"You should be focusing on your relationship with God

above all else. I am sure if you did that, the lyrics would flow easier and in his timing," Chad suggested.

Brody unlocked his car and opened his door. "I do focus on God a lot. I pray all the time, I do Bible studies on Tuesday nights with Heath, and I come to church weekly. I also do this group and serve What else am I not doing?"

Chad sighed. "I hear a lot of *do*, but I'm not hearing you say you are listening to God or resting in him. In order for a healthy relationship to work, what do you need?"

"Love, devotion, trust, communication...oh, I see where you're going with this. You think I am too focused on doing things for God that I am missing the chance to let him talk to me and share his heart with me so I can understand what he wants from me. Is that what you are getting at?" Brody asked.

Chad smiled. "Bingo. It's hard to sit back and just rest in the presence of God, especially when we are busy doing things *for* God, but sometimes we get in the way of progress when we get too far ahead of him. I understand your hunger to use your gift for God. It's very commendable, and I am sure God wants to use it...but when the timing is right. Trust him, love him, communicate with him, and let him communicate with you. This is the best advice I can give you. I don't know if it will fix your mental block, but it can't hurt it either, can it?" Chad asked with a chuckle.

Brody sighed and nodded. "I know I need to work on my listening skills. Thanks for the reminder, Chad."

"Anytime, Brody. Have a good weekend. See you Sunday," Chad said, waving as he walked away.

Brody drove slowly through the pelting snow and was almost home when he felt God tell him to take a turn down a different road. *What am I doing this for, God? I should get home. It's getting hard to see.* He was halfway down the street

God wanted him to go down when he saw a car farther ahead that had their hazard lights on. He pulled up behind it and saw a short, heavyset young woman standing outside trying to flag him down. She raced to Brody's car and waved as he rolled down the window.

"I'm sorry to disturb you, but I need your help switching my tire out, if you are able. I was on my way home, and the tire popped. It's horrible timing. My newborn is in the car sleeping, and my husband is worried about us. I called him to let him know what happened. He was going to come help, but he has a hard time seeing in the dark; he's blind in one eye. I'm sorry. I don't know why I'm telling you all this, as if you care." The young woman babbled on as Brody stepped out of his car, smiling.

"I don't mind helping. Do you have everything you need to change a tire?" Brody said, following her to the trunk of her car. They pulled out everything they needed and started toward the passenger tire. Brody took a moment and prayed, *God, please help me. I don't know how to change a tire. I have never had to learn that.* He took a deep breath and tried to do what he needed to, even though it was dark, the snow was falling, and his gloveless hands were really cold. The woman knelt by him and watched him carefully, which made him even more nervous.

"Thank you for helping. I hope I didn't inconvenience you at all," the young woman said softly after a few minutes.

"Nah, it's fine. I was on my way home from a church group," Brody said, finally getting the old tire off.

"Oh, you go to church? Which church?" the young woman asked next.

"I go to Christ Church of Hampton Beach. Have you heard of it?" Brody asked, grabbing the new tire.

She nodded slowly, "Yeah, I went there once a while ago, but I didn't feel I belonged there."

"Why did you feel that way?" Brody asked, intrigued.

She sighed. "Honestly, I felt judged."

"I see. Well, you shouldn't let haters get the best of you," Brody encouraged through strained breath as he tried to stay warm and tighten the tire bolts.

The young woman smiled. "What group were you at today?"

"I go to a recovery group for addicts," Brody said.

Her eyes widened. "What kind of addicts?"

"Any kind is welcome. It's a place where we help each other find true freedom in Christ from our addictions," Brody told her as he stood to his feet and blew into his hands to get them warm.

"I think I could benefit from a group like that. Thank you for your help," she said with a soft smile.

"You're welcome. What's your name? If you want to come to group, it's every Friday at seven," Brody offered, shaking her hand.

"My name is Anne, and maybe I will take you up on that offer sometime. I did like the church when I went, but a voice in my head made me feel I was being stared at and judged; it made me afraid to be there," Anne confessed, walking Brody back to his car.

"My name is Brody. It's nice to meet you, Anne. I know that feeling. I felt the same way when I first showed up at the church. I have a very sordid past. I realized later that the devil was trying to keep me from finding God. He likes to keep us in our shame so we won't be effective and in God's will." Brody opened his car door. "If you feel like pursuing God, come back to the church and ignore that voice. Call out to

God more than you listen to the fear, and come to the group. I am usually there every week, so at least you will have a friend."

Anne smiled again, tears in her eyes, and she unexpectedly hugged him so tightly he gasped. She waved goodbye and went back to her car.

Brody sat in his car until she drove away. He put his hands in front of his heater to get them warm and grinned. *I'm glad I listened to your prompting, Lord. I enjoyed helping her. If this is what it means to be open to listening to you speaking, then my ears are open. I want to do whatever you want me to do. I love the feeling I have right now of obedience and pure joy.*

The rest of January went by fairly quick for Brody, mostly because instead of trying to come up with a song, he focused on going deeper in his relationship with Christ. He spent every night reading his Bible, praying, and then staying silent so God could talk. He also started to journal in one of the many notebooks he had in his room. He found this was a good way for him to get his thoughts out to God and also look back to see where God had answered prayers or had responded to something he had written down.

During this process, Brody also found himself being led by God to help strangers around the town from time to time. Some of them recognized him from his former life and would ask what happened to him, which would give him the chance to share his testimony with the person. He realized quickly he loved doing this. Every time he shared his story, he saw the depth of God's love for him, which encouraged him to focus on God's will all the more and spurred him on to keep sharing his testimony.

By the beginning of February, Anne had started coming to the church with her husband, Dean, and their newborn daughter, Millie. She told Brody that the day he helped her change her tire had changed everything for her. She and her husband gave their lives to Christ the first day they went back to church, and Anne joined the addiction group, much to her husband's surprise. He never thought she would go to a support group for her food addiction, but she said ever since she had her daughter, she wanted to be healthy and full of energy. She knew being extremely overweight wasn't healthy for her small frame, so she wanted to get some help and joined a gym and the recovery group.

For Valentine's Day, Heath surprised Grace with tickets to go to Hawaii the next day. They deserved a vacation, but Brody was also a little apprehensive about them leaving since this would be the first time he was all alone in the house. He knew he wouldn't drink, but he was still anxious about the idea of being alone.

"Have fun on your trip, guys," Kate said, hugging Grace.

"I bet you two are excited to get away from this snow for a week," Daniel said, hugging his parents.

"Yeah, it will be wonderful. I can't stand the snow," Heath said with a chuckle.

Grace giggled and turned to hug Brody.

"The house will be very empty without you two here," Brody admitted sadly.

"Aw, kiddo, you will have fun being alone. I'm sure of it," Grace said, patting his face.

He nodded and turned to Heath. "Don't worry. I will stay sober and make good choices."

Heath chuckled and hugged him. "I trust you. Have a good time while we're gone."

They had started out the door when Grace's phone went off with an email alert from Duncan. She read it quickly and cheered loudly as she told the family Vanessa would be coming home around the first week in March.

"Yeah! I can't wait to see her! We are going to the spa together. She has wanted to do that for years, and I have been putting her off. Not anymore," Kate said as she waved to the Stewarts as they got in their car and drove away.

Brody was grinning ear to ear. He was finally going to get to see Vanessa again. The thought kept him sober and encouraged the whole week they were gone.

At the start of March, the family still hadn't heard anything from Duncan. This worried Grace, so she emailed Duncan to see if she would get a response back. By March 15, Grace was not only worried but frustrated because she hadn't received a response to her email questioning when Vanessa would be home. After much deliberation with Heath, she finally decided to call Duncan and left a message at his office: "Hi, Duncan. It's Grace Stewart. I know I have been bugging you a lot in the last few weeks, but I just wanted to know if you had received my email because you haven't responded to it yet. Please call me as soon as you can or email me and let me know what day we can expect Vanessa. Thanks." She hung up and went back to mixing her cake batter.

Kate walked into the house as Grace was pouring the batter into a cake mold, a stoic look on her face. "Hi, Grace. Daniel said he will be here soon. He went home to shower after work," Kate said.

"Okay, sweetie. Will you open this oven door for me please?" Grace asked quietly.

Kate nodded and rushed to help. She couldn't help but see Grace was upset. "What's wrong?"

Grace groaned. "Oh, I haven't heard from Duncan yet. I

don't want to cause concern during the little birthday celebration we are doing for Brody today, so I am trying not to dwell on it, but it's been eating me alive for days."

Kate hugged her. "I have been concerned too. I feel like we should have heard something by now. I am sure he is just busy. He is helping hundreds of missionaries get home, right? I'm sure it's a daunting task."

Grace nodded. "I agree, but you know me—I like to worry." They went to work finishing up dinner for Brody's birthday celebration.

Daniel had just finished putting the cake on the table when Brody pulled into the driveway. Grace lit the candles and held the cake in her hands with a grin. They bombarded him by the door and sang "Happy Birthday" while Grace held the cake with thirty-three flickering candles on it. Brody grinned as they finished the song and blew out his candles. They cheered loudly and sat down at the table to eat dinner while giving him their gifts.

"Thanks, everyone, for the wonderful gifts. I'm so happy to be here with you all," Brody said while eating.

"So are you excited to see your family soon?" Kate asked.

Body grimaced. "I'm happy to see my sister and her family."

Daniel snickered. "But not your parents?"

Brody sighed. "I know, I know, it's bad. My sister has warmed up to my new lifestyle, but my parents haven't. I don't want to see them. We butted heads a lot during Christmas and haven't talked since then. I don't know what to expect this time around. Plus, how do I tell them that I went from having a very successful career as a DJ to working at the local diner?" The family looked at him with furrowed brows.

"I got a job. I went to the diner for lunch yesterday and saw they needed part-time help. So I am working there

Wednesdays, Thursdays, and Saturdays. I was starting to go stir-crazy not having things to do, and right now I'm not even able to make music. I needed something to do with my time rather than stay in my studio day after day with nothing to show for it," Brody explained.

"That's great, Brody. I'm glad you found something to keep busy," Heath said with a smile.

"I'm sure your parents will be happy if you are happy, but if they aren't happy to hear about your new job, just be yourself. They can't argue with you if you are respectful and kind like you usually are," Kate suggested. Brody smiled and nodded.

Kate and Daniel had just left, and Brody had gone up to bed since he had an early flight. Grace and Heath were sitting in bed reading when Grace's phone showed a notification from Duncan.

She smiled. "Heath, he finally emailed me back."

She opened it, and Heath read over her shoulder. Their faces dropped as they read.

Hello, Mr. and Mrs. Stewart. I am very sorry it has taken me so long to get back to you. I needed to finish sorting things out before I emailed you back. I regret to inform you that Vanessa will not be coming home at this time. It seems that some prisons throughout India have decided to protest the government's decision to send the missionaries back to their hometowns and have kept some as hostages until further notice. Unfortunately, Vanessa is one of them. I am so sorry. My team is keeping on this so we can give you as many updates as possible on when they will finally release these prisoners. Duncan Miller

Grace and Heath looked at each other, mortified, and teared up.

"Oh, Heath! I knew something was off; I just knew it," Grace exclaimed, hugging him.

Heath sighed heavily after a few minutes and started to get out of bed. He had been worried too, but he knew that if he had let his wife know, she would have been even more concerned, so he had kept it to himself. "I should go tell Brody."

Grace gasped and pulled him back onto the bed. "Don't you dare tell him now. He is already stressed about seeing his parents. We don't need to make things worse for him with this news. We don't want to ruin his birthday either. Let's wait until after he gets home; it won't change anything by telling him now anyway."

Heath sighed again. "Yeah, you're right. Or maybe God's favor will have her being released before he even gets home."

Grace hugged and kissed him. "We can pray for that. Anything is possible." They sat in bed and prayed for a whole hour before finally going to sleep.

The next day Heath and Grace broke the news to Kate and Daniel and made sure they knew not to tell anyone else about it, especially not Brody. They reluctantly agreed.

"When will they release her?" Daniel asked after some time, wiping his eyes.

"I don't know. Duncan said he is going to keep on this situation. We just need to pray for her and the others during this time, that they will stay safe," Grace told him, choking up.

Kate sighed. "Oh, my poor friend…in jail. Why is she in jail? What happened? Do you think she was in jail when we talked to her on New Year's?"

Daniel hugged her as she wept. "She did seem a little out of sorts. My guess is yes." Kate nodded in agreement, wiping away tears.

Brody came home on the twenty-third of March, and Grace was more anxious than anyone else. They all knew the terrible news and had had time to process it, but Brody was still clueless. She prayed for God's favor on the conversation and for the chocolate chip muffins she had made for Brody to hopefully smooth the blow, although she knew it wouldn't. How could it? The whole family had been a wreck since hearing the news. She knew Brody would be too.

Brody walked into the house with a grin and hugged Grace. "Hey, Grace, I missed you guys."

"Hey, kiddo, we missed you too," Grace said softly. Brody could tell something was up, and it was confirmed when she handed him the chocolate chip muffins and told him she had made them especially for him.

"What's wrong?" he asked.

She laughed uncomfortably. "Nothing, kiddo. I made them for your birthday."

He frowned. "I don't think so. You look like you have something to tell me."

She sighed heavily and told him everything Duncan had told them.

Brody's shoulders slumped, and he got teary eyed. "What happened? I thought the missionaries were being taken out of there. Do you think she has been in jail since we saw her in the video chat?"

"I don't know, but that is what we all suspect. I'm sorry, kiddo. I know you were excited to see her, but it looks like we all have to use this time to wait and pray for God's favor on her," Grace said, choking up.

"How long have you known about this?"

She sighed again, choking up. "Heath and I found out the night we celebrated your birthday. I didn't want you to know until after you got home. I knew you were upset already about seeing your parents."

Brody hugged her, trying to hold it together. "Why don't we pray for Vanessa and the other prisoners right now before I go upstairs to unpack?" Brody suggested.

Grace smiled warmly and held his trembling hands. They took turns saying heartfelt prayers for the missionaries, crying as they did. After they were done, they hugged, and Brody went to his room. Instead of packing, he laid on his bed and wept bitterly into his pillow.

Chapter Twenty-One

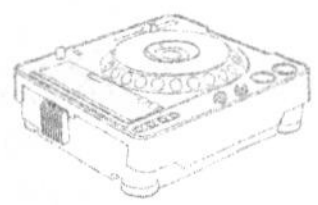

EASTER SUNDAY CAME WITH excitement for Brody. He was in charge of the whole audio production team for the Easter service.

The family still hadn't heard a word about the situation with Vanessa. It was starting to eat at Grace the most. She and Vanessa were always so close, and not knowing what was going on with her baby girl was breaking her heart. The family tried their best to keep her mind off of things, taking her to movies, walks on the beach, and out to eat, but deep inside, no matter what she was feeling on the surface, her heart was sad.

As the next few weeks went by, the family stayed focused on their jobs. Brody was glad that he had something productive to do to keep his mind off of worrying about Vanessa and when she would finally be released. He put every fiber of his being into his work at the diner, doing it for the glory of God and also because the harder he worked, the more he realized he didn't notice the pain he was in.

Brody came home from work, exhausted. "Hey, Brody, how was work?" Grace asked while washing the dishes.

Brody walked over to her, taking a deep breath. "It was more exhausting than usual."

Grace chuckled. "Oh goodness, I am sorry to hear that. Heath's taking a shower. He should be down in a few minutes, and then we wanted to talk to you about something."

"Uh oh," Brody said with a playful snicker.

Heath walked downstairs, and they sat at the table, drinking some bedtime tea together. After a few minutes, Heath cleared his throat and smiled. "So Grace and I have been talking for a while now, and we think you are ready to get your own place, if you feel ready."

"Really? You think I'm ready?" Brody asked.

"Of course! You haven't had a drink in almost eight months. You have been faithfully going to your meetings, you have been involved in the church and working daily on your relationship with Christ, and now you have a job too. We think you are ready for this, but do you feel you are ready?" Grace asked.

"I have been going back and forth on the idea since you were on your vacation. I think that when Vanessa comes back, it wouldn't be right for me to still be living here since we plan to date. I have already been checking out a place not far from the studio. It went on the market last month. I talked to the real estate agent the other day and was going to bring it up to you soon, but since you brought it up first, it must be God's timing. I would like to buy the house. I already have the offer drawn up but just haven't told my realtor to send it over yet," Brody confessed, finishing his tea.

"Then you should do it. You have our blessing," Heath said with a bittersweet smile, knowing he would miss having Brody at the house.

"Okay, I will have my realtor send it over tomorrow," Brody said excitedly. Heath and Grace looked sad, so he got up and hugged them both. "You have no idea how much it means to me that you took me in like you did. You didn't have to, but I am glad you did. You are like parents to me, and I will always cherish the time we had here together. Thank you for helping me get to this place in my life." Brody kissed Grace on the cheek and shook hands with Heath.

Grace started to shed some tears. "Life won't be the same without you here, kiddo."

"That's very true. It won't be easy being empty-nesters again," Heath told him, sipping his tea.

Brody smiled, trying to hold back his own emotions as he sat back down. "I will still come and bug you guys often. Don't worry." They laughed.

Brody called his realtor first thing in the morning, and by noon, the owner had agreed to it. Brody was thrilled and couldn't wait to show the family, so he suggested they have family dinner at his place. He would bring home some food for them from the diner. Brody was able to get out of work early, so he spent time getting the electricity on in the house before dinner and then walked the house to take inventory of what he wanted to renovate. While walking around the house, he grinned at the possibilities. He even thought about the idea of having a family with Vanessa in this house, which made him chuckle, but he tried not to dwell on it, at least for now. *Let's make it past the first date and then think about that, Brody,* he told himself.

The family met at his new place close to six-thirty in the evening. Brody greeted them outside to show them around the cozy yard. Daniel was very impressed by the front and back yards; he was already seeing possibilities of how to upgrade the yards and immediately started telling Brody about it as they all walked inside for the indoor tour. Brody showed them the two bedrooms, the kitchen, and then the living room, where they sat on the floor to eat since there was no furniture yet.

"Brody, your house is wonderful," Grace said happily.

"Yeah, this place has major potential," Kate remarked.

"What do you mean by that?" Brody asked.

Daniel snickered. "It means she plans to help you decorate."

"Sure! I wouldn't know the first thing about doing that anyway," Brody said, not really sure if it was the right call or not since Daniel was emphatically shaking his head mouthing the word "no."

"So I got an email from Duncan not too long before we came here," Grace said with a grin, which led the family to believe she would give them good news this time. "He said the government is finally sending the missionaries home!" Grace exclaimed.

"Really? That's awesome! When?" Kate asked excitedly.

"The first week in June," Grace answered.

"That's three weeks from now!" Kate added.

"That is wonderful news, Mom," Daniel chimed in, hugging her with a glimmer in his eye.

Brody nodded in agreement, his heart fluttering with excitement. "Now I really need to work hard on getting this place fixed up so Vanessa can see it completed."

"Thank you, guys, for coming over to chat with me. I have to finish painting one more room, and then I am ready to decorate. Kate has been chomping at the bit waiting for me to get finished with the renovations. She is very excited to help me decorate, Grace too; they can't stop talking about the furniture they want to get me. It kind of has me worried," Brody told them as he chuckled.

"Do you need any help painting?" Chad asked.

"Sure, I would like that. Thanks," Brody answered.

Chad and Matty grabbed roller brushes and started painting. "So what's on your mind, Brody?" Chad asked while painting.

"Well, I was thinking the other day how awesome it might be to have a worship night once a month in our group. Singing praises to God is very freeing and encouraging for me, and I just thought maybe it could be a good way for those who still feel bound to find a way to release things to Christ. Is that something we could even do? Am I overstepping my boundaries by suggesting it?" Brody asked.

Chad and Matty looked at each other as they painted and smiled before looking back at Brody. "You aren't overstepping at all. In fact, this is a perfect segue into something Chad and I have been praying about recently," Matty started. Brody looked at them, intrigued, as they stopped painting.

"Chad is moving at the end of this month. He got offered a nice job closer to his ailing parents in Michigan," Matty explained.

Brody frowned. "You're going to be missed at the meetings, Chad."

"Thanks, Brody. I need someone to take my place, and Matty and I think you would be a good fit. After all, you are the only one who is still in the group from the day we started it. You have been faithful in coming and have shown progress in your sobriety too. You are also showing leadership skills, not just in this case with the worship night idea but in our group meetings. You are good at getting the conversation back on topic and making everyone feel comfortable and welcome too," Chad explained.

Brody chuckled in disbelief. "I don't think I could ever take your place, Chad. You're a great leader. Could I have some time to pray about it?"

"Yeah, of course. I don't need an answer today, but I will need a definite answer before the twenty-third, just in case you decline the offer, so I have a few days before my last group meeting to find a replacement," Chad responded.

Brody nodded slowly, his mind racing now as they continued painting.

"So only a week and a half left before Vanessa comes home, huh? I bet you're excited," Matty said with a grin.

Brody blushed unexpectedly as he nodded. "Yes, I can't wait to hold her again. I've been dreaming of it for months now."

The next morning, Brody came downstairs looking like a zombie. Heath chuckled, sipping his coffee. "Hey, Brody, what's wrong? You look exhausted. Did you stay up all night working on your place?" Heath poured a cup of coffee for Brody.

"No, I finished painting in the afternoon. Chad and Matty helped me out. After, that I spent the day at my studio just mixing. Nothing substantial—I was just playing around." Brody hesitated before speaking again and walked up to the kitchen counter. "I don't know how to say it, but something bizarre happened to me last night while I was sleeping. It left me feeling a little apprehensive, so I didn't sleep well after that."

Heath handed Brody the cup of coffee, which he took happily. "Why don't you tell me what happened, and I'll see if I can help you through it," Heath suggested.

Brody nodded slowly and recalled the event. "I was dead asleep one minute, and then suddenly I was awakened by a loud crash. I sat up quickly, turned the light on, and looked around. I didn't see anything, so I shut the light off and laid back down. I thought maybe I had just imagined it. I was sure if you two had heard something, you would have been up to check on the noise too."

Heath nodded his head. "Yeah, but we didn't hear anything last night."

"After lying back down, I felt a presence in the room. I couldn't see anything, but I felt it. It made me feel frozen with fear, like I was in a scary movie. I tensed up. I didn't want the presence to stay there, but I was too scared to move or speak to it. I closed my eyes and felt the nearness of something or someone. I didn't dare open my eyes or take my hands out of my blankets at that point." Brody shuddered.

"After a few minutes, I heard my name being called in a sinister whisper. I wanted to open my eyes, but I was too afraid. I closed my eyes tighter and prayed quickly for whatever was there to be gone. Then I heard another voice whisper my name, but this one was kinder. I could feel the negative presence go away immediately as the calm voice spoke my name a second time. The bad feeling was gone completely at that point, and I opened my eyes finally. I didn't see anything; I was completely alone." Brody looked at Heath, concerned. "What does this mean? Was I dreaming? Am I cursed? Has this happened to you before?"

Heath nodded vehemently. "Oh yeah, I know *all* too well what you're talking about. I have dealt with this before and still do sometimes. Brody, I think it was another spiritual attack."

"Seriously? Another one? I thought I was done with those after I kicked my alcohol habit and my past to the curb," Brody said nervously.

"We are never finished having our faith tested, Brody,

remember? I told you that. When one attack method fails for him, he will just find another way to attack you. He is trying to keep you in fear now for some reason.? Do you know why? What happened recently?" Heath asked.

Brody sighed. "Yesterday Chad and Matty asked me to take Chad's place as a coleader of our recovery group. He is moving away at the end of the month. I told them I would pray about it, but by the time I got back here, I already felt God telling me to take the position. I planned to tell them today that I will do it."

Heath's eyes lit up. "What a great opportunity for you, and now we know why Satan is messing with you."

"He's trying to scare me into not taking the position, right?" Brody asked.

Heath nodded. "That's right. We are all in a spiritual battle. The enemy attacks us with his fearful presence, but we have the Word of God and the Holy Spirit inside of us to help us fend him off. God doesn't give us a spirit of fear; fear comes from the devil. So whenever you feel fearful, that is *not* God. That peaceful voice you heard after praying was God calling to you—I'm sure of it."

"I can't believe I heard God's voice. That's so cool. So I can expect these types of spiritual attacks to happen to me often then?" Brody asked.

"I don't know if these specific types of attacks will happen often. I guess that depends on how often you let the devil win these attacks. Next time you feel fear, just call out Jesus's name. The demons flee at the very mention of his name," Heath encouraged Brody.

"I think if Satan is trying to scare me from this opportunity, it must mean God really wants me to do it and Satan sees me as a threat, right?" Brody asked next, smiling.

"As long as you plan to go hard after God's calling on your life, the devil will try to deter you from it. Satan won't mess with you unless you're a threat to him, so if spiritual attacks weren't happening to you, I should say you should be more worried about that; that might mean you are not following God's path for your life. Read Ephesians 6:10–18. It will give you the best weapons to fight the devil off," Heath replied.

"Will you tell me about some times you had spiritual attacks?" Brody asked next.

"Sure, let's get some breakfast, and I'll regale you with some," Heath responded.

Chapter Twenty-Two

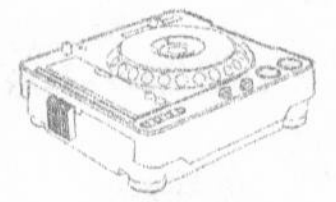

It was now the last Sunday morning in May, six days before Vanessa was scheduled to be home. Brody was beaming from ear to ear all morning at church and could barely contain his overwhelming excitement or his nerves. He wanted to see her so badly, but he was also nervous to finally date her. He had dreamed about it and played out their official first date as a couple in his mind so many times, and each time it left him with butterflies and a grin. He tried to stay focused on the sermon as much as possible since he was in charge of the audio team again, but boy, was it hard.

After church, Grace said she wasn't feeling well and that she wanted to go home instead of to the diner like they usually did after church. Heath took her home, and Daniel insisted they have lunch at the house together instead. After a light lunch, Grace laid on the couch while Heath rubbed her feet.

There was a knock at the door not long after that. Daniel ran to the door to answer it and saw two men standing there, one in his fifties and the other an Indian man maybe in his early thirties.

"Hello, is this the Stewart residence?" the older man asked.

Daniel nodded and invited him inside.

"My name is Duncan Miller. I'm in charge of the Southeast Asian branch of the ministry Vanessa serves with," Duncan said as he and the mysterious man followed Daniel into the living room where the family was sitting and watching TV. Heath turned off the TV, and Brody, Kate, and Heath walked over and shook hands with Duncan.

"Hello, Duncan. Nice to see you in person again. It's been a while. Why are you here?" Heath asked with a furrowed brow.

Duncan was about to introduce the guest and answer Heath's question when Grace stood up and looked at the mystery man gravely. "You are here to tell us that something happened to Vanessa, aren't you?"

The others looked at her with surprise and then turned their gaze to the mysterious man. He didn't speak but simply hung his head.

Grace sighed heavily and sat up on the couch as tears started forming. "Last night I had a dream about her, and it left me uneasy. Now I understand why." Grace turned to look at Heath. He was not sure what was going on. She stood to her feet and put her arm around his waist, crying and trembling.

Duncan started to speak solemnly. "This is Ronit. He was the last one to see Vanessa alive."

"Alive? You mean she's dead?" Kate blurted out. Duncan nodded sadly. Kate started to cry and nuzzled her head into Daniel's chest. He, too, started to weep.

"I'm sorry. I don't understand. So you are telling me that my baby girl was killed?" Heath choked out the question. Duncan shed a few tears and nodded. Heath held Grace tightly, and they wept loudly.

Duncan and Ronit hung their heads as the family started to cry, all except for Brody. He wanted to cry, but he wasn't able to at the moment. It was like someone was keeping him from showing emotion. As he huddled with the family and grieved with them, his face was stoic, but on the inside, he was screaming in pain. *All my dreams for our future!*

After a few minutes, Duncan spoke again. "Ronit can explain what happened to her."

All eyes turned to the young Indian man dressed in a white shirt and jeans. He looked sad and nervous as he started to speak in English. "She was imprisoned with seventy other foreign missionaries throughout her region. This was back in October," Ronit started.

All eyes turned to Duncan. "Why didn't you mention this information to us, Duncan?" Heath asked angrily.

"Vanessa never wanted her name mentioned in the list of prisoners," Duncan admitted.

"She didn't want to alarm you all," Ronit piped up again. The family turned back to look at Ronit.

"What happened? Why was she imprisoned? Did she do something wrong?" Daniel asked with concern.

Ronit shook his head. "No, she and the others were only imprisoned because they were believers. Christianity isn't allowed in India anymore."

Daniel hung his head and hugged Kate, wanting to say something to this man that wouldn't have been very friendly, but he refrained.

"When all the other prisoners were told to leave the country, the government held on to ten prisoners from each jail in India so that they could serve as a warning to future missionaries to stay away. Vanessa was one of the prisoners chosen to stay behind where I served as a jailer, in the southeast of India. About a month ago, the government decided that these missionaries needed to be executed as a final testament to the seriousness of their demands. The government lied to the Americans in order to dissuade suspicions."

Grace burst out in a wail as Ronit reluctantly continued, "She and all the others were killed a week ago, shot to death," Ronit explained, sounding very disturbed by the statement.

Heath and Grace cried out again, holding each other until Grace pulled away from him and pushed Duncan. "Why did you allow her to go back when she was here safe in the States last year? You must have known by then that it was hostile. She was in tears the day she left and said something bad was happening back in India and she needed to leave. Did you call her and tell her something about it?" Grace asked angrily.

Duncan nodded. "Yes, I called to inform her that it might not be safe for her to go back and she should just stay where she was until further notice."

The family looked at him, taken aback, especially Brody.

"You told her what?" Heath asked in almost a whisper.

Duncan continued. "I told her she needed to stay here. She asked me what was going on, so I told her in detail. She almost begged me to get her on a flight that night, saying she *needed* to go back. I didn't make her leave; I wanted her to stay, but you know Vanessa. She is a headstrong girl, and she loves people greatly."

Grace collapsed to the floor at his feet. "I know. I'm sorry for accusing you. I should have known she would have left no matter what. She loved what she did."

Everyone rallied around Grace on the floor and hugged her tightly. The family cried, but still Brody was emotionless. He couldn't figure out why he wasn't able to cry. He had cried for smaller things than this in the past. Why was it so hard now to grieve for the love he had just lost?

"Did you kill my sister?" Daniel asked, standing to his feet abruptly and squaring off in front of Ronit.

"I was supposed to," Ronit said, standing firm just in case Daniel tried to throw a punch.

Daniel furrowed his brow. "What do you mean, were *supposed* to?"

Ronit looked at the family and then at Duncan before speaking. "Ever since Vanessa came to my jail, she was the nicest person to be around. I took to her, not only because she was pretty but because she was nice to me, even in her situation. She would tell me about this Jesus person who made her go to jail. The more I talked to her, the more I felt different around her. Well, we formed a bond as friends, which wasn't a good thing for me as the jailer, so I had to keep it secret. The day I found out about the execution plans, I told her about it. She said she had a feeling it was coming; she said her God was preparing her." Ronit looked at the family. They were hanging on his every word.

"I told her I would plan her escape. She asked if I could take the others, but I told her it was too risky to try to rescue them all. I said I could only take one, and I chose her because she was my friend. She just smiled that smile she always did and said she couldn't leave everyone behind. She said it wouldn't be right; they were her family. She told me she wouldn't go," Ronit explained, frustrated.

He sighed heavily and then continued, "I kept trying to convince her to leave with me, but she wouldn't. I begged her for weeks leading up to the execution. The day of the execution, I was supposed to take the missionaries to the yard where we were to execute them. I and another guard led them out toward the yard. I made sure Vanessa was the last one in the line and that I was the one guarding the back of the line."

Ronit paused and looked away, distressed, and then looked back at the family. "I made a rash decision that changed the course of our lives. I grabbed her hand and covered her mouth as I led her down a small hallway and out of the jail unseen since all of the guards were outside waiting for the execution. She was upset with me at first, but I told her I had to. I told her someone with her inner beauty couldn't be killed like this."

Grace started to cry more, and at this point, Ronit looked like he wanted to cry as well, but he didn't. He continued, "She finally agreed to follow me, but she was still upset with me. I knew someone who worked as a pilot, so I asked him to take her away. He agreed and said to hurry; he had already heard over the radio that a prisoner in our area had gone missing, and they were looking for us. By the time we got to the airfield, there was a small group of police standing there with guns. There we stood, hands in the air, guns pointing at us. 'You should be killed along with her for treason,' the main officer said. I knew he was right, but I didn't care at this point. She was my friend, and I cared about her and didn't want to see her dead. I was about to speak. but Vanessa spoke up first." Ronit started to tear up now.

"She told the guards that she was happy to die for Christ, but she asked if she could have a few moments to talk to me alone first. They agreed. She turned to me and thanked me for risking my life for her. She also told me that Jesus loved me very much and saw the sacrifice I had made for one of his children. She told me Jesus wanted me to know that He had to die a brutal death too so that one day I could have the chance to become one of his children." Ronit wiped his eyes and watched as the family kept weeping uncontrollably.

"She turned to the police and said, 'If I allow you to take my life, will you please let Ronit be allowed to live?' The firing squad was surprised by her request, but I think I was more surprised that they agreed. She turned to me, hugged me, and whispered, 'Find God so I know you will be okay and I can see you again someday.'"

Ronit looked at the family sadly. "She was shot after that, and they told me to get on the plane and leave forever. If I came back, I would have the same fate as her."

The room was silent except for some sniffling coming from everyone but Brody, who hadn't shown any emotion other than disgust when Ronit was sharing his story.

Suddenly Daniel growled, "She gave up her life for yours?" He lunged at Ronit and pounded his chest, weeping loudly.

Ronit stood there and responded, "I love Jesus now because of her sacrifice!" Daniel stopped hitting him and looked at him pathetically.

Ronit looked at the family, hopeful. "Because of her talking to me all these months and her witness to me, I now know Jesus like she did, and I understand why she did what she did. I am sorry you lost your child, sister, and girlfriend." He looked at Brody and lingered. Brody swallowed a lump in his throat but still didn't show emotion, even though he was truly broken inside.

Ronit continued, "I have been reading the Bible every day since I got to America, and I prayed that God would give me courage to tell you my story, even though I knew it would hurt you all so much. Your Vanessa was a great woman, full of love for God. I know my life doesn't mean much to you right now, but I hope in time you will see that her sacrifice was worth it in God's eyes. I believe you all know, deep in your hearts, that Vanessa would have agreed."

The family was taken aback by his boldness and candor, but they knew he was right. The room was silent for a while.

Finally Heath walked up to Ronit, and with much sadness, he hugged him, choking up. "Welcome to the family of faith, Ronit." He turned to look at the family. "Vanessa would have made this decision a thousand times over if it meant someone would come to Christ. It's what she lived for." The family nodded in agreement as they hugged Ronit one by one. Everyone, including Duncan and Ronit, wept together—all except Brody, who was still without emotion.

After a few minutes, Duncan prayed for the family and then spoke. "Our ministry is planning on holding a ceremony for all the fallen missionaries. The bodies will be released to us soon, thanks to Ronit and some connections he still has there. I will call you as soon as I have the details. The whole family is welcome to come." Duncan looked specifically at Brody and Kate.

Heath shook hands with Duncan, thanked him for everything, and watched as the two men started toward the door. Ronit was about to exit the house when he saw Brody standing behind the family, looking very solemn. He walked up to Brody and took his head in his hands gently, much to Brody's surprise and slight discomfort. Ronit stared at Brody for a few seconds before he spoke with a genuine smile.

"Vanessa loved you a lot, Brody. She talked about and prayed for you often. At first it annoyed me how much she prayed for you, but after a while, I admired the devotion. I asked her about you the day after you two talked on the video chat. She told me your whole story. You have been through a lot of pain, and you have overcome. I can see losing Vanessa will impact you greatly, as it should; you two shared a bond, and it's obvious even to me. Do not give up on God through this. She wouldn't want you to. I am sorry for your loss," Ronit said with such compassion that Brody almost felt like breaking down right there.

He swallowed the lump in his throat, willing himself not

to start crying, and nodded. Ronit smiled sadly, let him go, and left the house with Duncan. All eyes turned to Brody as he stood there motionless and holding in his emotions that were screaming to escape now.

Heath called Pastor Brian and tried to get through the call without bursting into tears but to no avail. Pastor Brian and his wife, Jill, came over right away to pray over the family. He brought some others from the church with him too. Heath explained everything to the pastor and the others. He told them about Ronit and his testimony too.

After a time of prayer, the room was filled with worship, heavy sobs, and deep sorrow mixed with peace and encouragement knowing Vanessa was with her creator and that she had made her life count while she was here on Earth.

Brody kept his distance from everyone else, standing against a wall and staring at everyone in frustration as his anger seethed. His heart started pounding loudly, and his ears rang suddenly as the weight of the news and what Ronit had said to him finally hit him like a tidal wave.

He started to hyperventilate as he looked down at the family, broken on the floor and huddled together with church members singing loudly and weeping. He felt a tightness in his chest as he held back tears and clenched his fists so tightly his knuckles were white. He raced out the door unnoticed.

After two hours, the sadness was still present like a wet blanket, but their spirits were a little calmer knowing Vanessa was in a better place now.

"Thank you all for coming," Heath said, hugging people as they started to leave.

Pastor Brian looked around the room as he was about to leave and furrowed his brow. "Where is Brody?"

"I don't know. He was here when we started praying. Did he say he was leaving?" Daniel asked, wiping his eyes with a tissue. No one had an answer.

"He was very quiet the whole time. I don't think he knows how to process this news yet," Matty commented.

"Oh my goodness, you don't think he went to drink his pain away, do you?" Kate asked, worried.

"I don't think so. He was doing well with his sobriety. Maybe he just needed to process his grief alone," Heath suggested, trying to stay positive.

"Should we try to find him?" Pastor Brian offered. Heath nodded and was about to rally a team together when Matty's phone rang. He answered it and motioned for everyone to stay put. They looked at him intently.

"Okay, Brody, I will be right there," Matty said. He put his phone in his pocket and started toward the door.

"Where is he? Is he okay?" Grace asked frantically.

Matty looked at the family. "All he said was that he needed help. I've gotta hurry. I will keep you updated." He ran out the door and drove away. Pastor Brian gathered everyone together to pray for Brody.

Matty knocked on Brody's half-open front door and walked in. He called out for Brody a couple times before he heard screaming and loud sobs coming from one of the bedrooms. He walked quickly and heard the sounds get louder as he approached the first room. He opened the door, turned on the light, and saw Brody curled up in the fetal position, weeping and occasionally screaming out in emotional pain.

Matty frowned when he saw a bottle of alcohol next to Brody and blood on his knuckles. Matty looked around the room and saw various holes in the wall that indicated Brody had been punching them in anger. Matty sighed and knelt down next to him. "Hey, Brody."

"It hurts so much!" Brody screamed out in agonizing sadness. Matty frowned and picked up the bottle next to Brody. He noticed it was never opened and smiled in relief.

"I was going to drink that because all I want to do is forget this nightmare. I didn't drink it, though, because I thought of Vanessa," Brody started, sitting up, "She would be devastated to hear I was no longer sober. I couldn't do that to her, even if she is gone...." He started wailing again, rocking back and forth. "Why is she gone? I thought God was giving us a second chance."

Matty patted Brody on the back. "I understand your frustration. It's never easy losing a loved one."

Brody groaned. "What do you know, Matty? No offense, but I don't think you know what it's like to lose someone you care deeply about."

Matty looked away briefly and then spoke. "I haven't told anyone except for my family about this, because I'm ashamed by it, but I think you need to hear it."

Brody looked up at Matty with sad but inquisitive eyes. Matty sighed heavily. "I lost my cousin when we were eight years old. We were camping one summer with our families. We snuck out of our cabin around midnight so we could play in the creek behind my house. We liked being out there at night to catch night creatures, but our parents didn't want us out there because it was dangerous. Well, I dared him to jump from one side of the creek to the other. We had done that before, so it shouldn't have been difficult, but in the dark, he couldn't see what he was doing and slipped on a rock. He smacked the side of his head into a boulder and died instantly. I was scared they would be angry if they knew I dared him to do it, so I just said we were walking and he slipped. That secret ate at me for years before I finally confessed it to my family while I was going through my steps to recovery. It was one reason I drank and did drugs—so I could mask the guilt I felt."

Matty turned to look at Brody and wiped away a few tears.

Brody frowned. "I'm sorry, Matty. I shouldn't have said what I did. I am just in so much pain. I saw a future with her, and I know she felt the same about me," Brody said pathetically.

Matty sighed. "I'm sorry, Brody. This sucks; I know it does." They stayed silent for a little while.

"I guess I'm not ready to be your co-leader, huh?" Brody asked sadly after collecting himself.

"Why do you say that?" Matty asked in response.

"Because I tried to drink again," Brody told him.

"You think you are the only one who gets tempted by their past addictions? You didn't do it. That is what counts, and what makes you a great leader is that you realized what you were about to do wasn't right and called someone to help. That was a wise move, Brody. I think you are even more ready to be my second in command now," Matty told him with a smile.

Brody smiled sadly and then burst into tears again. "I'm happy Vanessa gets to be with God and isn't suffering anymore in this world, but I want her back, Matty. I want her back! I miss her so much!" Matty hugged Brody and let him cry it out for a while.

"He's back!" Jill shouted, seeing Matty's car pulling into the driveway.

Daniel and Kate greeted Matty at the door and then grabbed Brody and hugged him tightly, crying and thanking God he was safe. "Please don't run off like that again. If you need to grieve, we are here for you," Daniel told him, choking up.

Brody nodded and looked at Pastor Brian. They shook hands.

"I'm glad you're okay," Pastor Brian said, patting Brody on the shoulder as he and his wife left.

Matty hugged Brody. "I understand if you want to hold off co-leading until next week; just let me know. I can always go solo for one week." Brody nodded, getting choked up again. Matty turned to the family to give them his condolences once more, and then he left too.

Brody followed Kate and Daniel into the living room, swallowing a lump in his throat as he stood in front of the couch, looking at the Stewarts. Their heads were hanging, and they were both still crying. Brody knelt down and touched them both on the shoulders. "I am so sorry I ran off…."

Grace looked up first, her eyes heavy with tears. She sniffed loudly and then lunged forward and wrapped her arms around Brody, knocking him backward as they embraced.

"Please don't ever do that again, Brody. I couldn't take it if I lost another one of my children!" Grace spoke with such passion and hurt.

Brody started crying immediately. He had never realized they saw him as one of their children, although they treated him as one often. He never felt it in his heart of hearts until that moment. They sat up, and then Heath knelt down to hug him too, followed by Kate and Daniel.

Brody went to his room that night and laid on his bed, staring up at the blinding light on his ceiling fan. His senses were dulled by the pain he was in, so he didn't care about the intense light. He sighed heavily as his phone rang. His sister was calling—horrible timing. He thought about ignoring the phone call, but he remembered his mom and dad were moving in with her this last week, and he had told her to call him once they were safe at her house. He reluctantly answered the phone and tried to sound upbeat so she wouldn't ask questions.

"Did they make it to Colorado safely?" Brody asked, lackluster. Regina started to talk his ear off about everything and how their mom liked the weather difference but not their father. Brody tried to keep it together, but he could feel his sadness starting to come back. He bit his lip, hoping he could finish this conversation before he started to cry again.

His sister went silent suddenly. "What's wrong, Brody?"

"Nothing. I'm okay," Brody choked out.

"I know that's not true. Talk to me," Regina said sternly but lovingly too. Brody started weeping as Regina called the family together so Brody could explain what had happened.

Once he was finished, his sister and mom begged Brody to come out to Colorado to see them, insisting he needed a break from his troubles. He wasn't sure what they had in mind to help him, but he was sure he wasn't ready for it. He told them he would think about it later on, but right now he wanted to stay close to her family and let God help him heal through his pain.

After much debating about the issue, they finally accepted his decision, and he hung up. Brody groaned loudly, putting the pillow over his head before screaming, crying, and punching the bed with a fist until he fell asleep hours later. The Stewarts heard everything, and their hearts broke for Brody as well as for themselves.

Chapter Twenty-Three

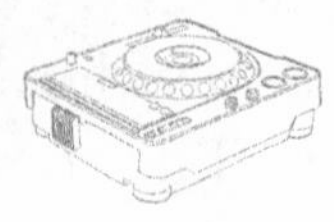

THE NEXT DAY GRACE received another email from Duncan, and she reluctantly read it.

> *I wanted to let you know the ceremony will be two days from now, on Wednesday, at 10 in the morning. I have attached the family's plane tickets and hotel arrangements in this email too. I have you arriving first thing in the morning. A shuttle will take you to the hotel so you can freshen up before the ceremony. The hotel is only for one night. I assumed you wouldn't want to stay around here too long. Also, we are paying for any burial expenses you may have for Vanessa, so please keep that in mind when you make arrangements.*

Grace winced at the words. The idea that Vanessa was gone still stung, no matter how glad she was that Vanessa was with her Creator.

Grace called the family together for a family breakfast so they could discuss what was supposed to happen in two days.

The family ate silently until Heath reluctantly spoke. "So the ceremony for the fallen missionaries is Wednesday. After that, we can take her body home." Heath choked up and shook his head slowly, signaling to his wife that he couldn't continue.

Grace sadly took up the torch. "There is a ticket and accommodations for all of us. Do you want to go or not? No pressure either way. I understand this isn't going to be easy for any of us." No one spoke right away.

"I want to be there," Daniel said finally.

Kate nodded. "Me too."

Brody was hesitant to say yes. He had just told his boss he needed some time off right now to process things because he wasn't able to function. How could he function at a ceremony for the deceased woman he loved? However, he knew he would regret not going, so he decided to go too.

"Okay then, the flight is at seven in the morning on Wednesday. Maybe you and Kate should stay here with us so you don't have to be up too early," Grace suggested, looking at Daniel. He nodded slowly, and they all ate in silence.

On Wednesday, the family was taken to the ceremony. They were hesitant to walk toward the huge church where the ceremony was being held. They saw many other grieving people walking inside, however, so they finally did the same. They were greeted with a rose and a flyer with information about the ceremony proceedings. The family was ushered to the left side of the room and sat next to another family that was in tears. They shared what had happened to their son, and the Stewarts shared what had happened to Vanessa. The ceremony started not long after they gave their condolences.

The founder of the ministry spoke first, and then the mission team leaders from all parts of India spoke, including

Duncan. Lastly, Ronit and some others who were impacted by these missionaries' sacrifices spoke. The ceremony was beautiful, haunting, and painful too. When the speakers were finished, all the names and pictures of the fallen missionaries were shown on a big screen. Brody and the family wept loudly when they saw Vanessa's picture, the same as everyone else there seeing their own missionary.

After that, a worship team came up to sing praises to God. Brody was passionate about it this time after hearing the stories of how people were impacted by this situation. He knew that what had happened to these missionaries was bigger than him and his own personal feelings, as painful as they might be.

When the ceremony was finished, the families were told to stay behind so they could receive their missionaries. Heath wasn't looking forward to this part of the ceremony because that would solidify the fact that she was gone.

The family waited in the auditorium for an hour before Duncan and Ronit came by and shook their hands. "Thank you for waiting. I am sorry for the delay. I needed to keep you all longer than everyone else because I have something very special to send you all home with, aside from Vanessa of course." Duncan said, motioning for Ronit to hand them the manila envelope.

Heath took it from his hands with a confused look. "What's this?"

"The week before the execution was to happen, Vanessa handed me letters for each of you," Ronit said. "She made me promise I would find a way to give them to you all."

Grace started to weep again. "Oh, sweet girl, always looking out for our hearts."

Ronit nodded in agreement. "She loved you all very much." The family smiled.

"Thank you, Ronit, for being a friend to her," Grace said, shaking his hand. Ronit smiled softly.

"Have a safe trip back home. Again, I am sorry for your loss. Working with Vanessa was one of the highlights of my career. She was truly special," Duncan said, shaking everyone's hands as they exited the auditorium.

The ride to the hotel was a bit livelier as the family talked about the letters and when they planned to read them. Kate said she couldn't wait any longer to know what Vanessa had said to her. Daniel and Grace agreed with her and also decided to read their letters back at the hotel. Heath said he would wait until morning because he was tired and wasn't ready for that yet. Brody was apprehensive to open the letter at all if he was being honest. He worried something she had said might ruin whatever happy memories he had of her. He decided to wait until he got home to read the letter.

The family was in much better spirits now after reading their letters from Vanessa, which gave Brody hope for his unread letter. Dropping his luggage onto the bedroom floor, he grabbed the letter and pressed it against his chest before opening it.

Brody,

I should have stayed in New Hampshire with you when Duncan told me to instead of coming back to India. This is what we both agree should be said right now because we both know it's the truth. I was scared of what could happen between us, so I let my head-strong nature get the best of me, and well, here we are. I think that is why I had to write your letter last—because it is the most painful one for me to write. As much as we both know I should have stayed, I think we can both agree my leaving turned out to be good for you. I don't think life for you would have turned out as amazing as it has if I had stayed.

Brody sighed heavily as he kept reading.

As I sit here in my cell with several other believers, they are singing praises to our Creator and thanking him for the lives they have enjoyed—but not me. See, as much as I know it was a good thing that I left, it was only a good thing for you, in my opinion. You are a Christian now, which is so great and fills my heart with much delight. But me? I am in prison instead of being with you. I am angry and weeping over the life with you that I will never get to have.

Brody started to weep.

You know I was never someone who thought about having a family someday. It was never on my mind. Even as a teen, I wasn't into boys much. I remember when I was sixteen, Kate and I made a list of qualities we wanted in a future mate. It was so hard for me to write. I had to outsource my list to God. I prayed for him to give me a list of qualities that would work for me, should I ever marry someone. The next morning a small list came to mind, so I wrote them down and showed Kate."

Brody wiped his eyes and continued reading.

No one ever met those characteristics in a way where I could see myself pursuing them, not even here in

> *India. Then I met you, and things between us escalated quickly. I wondered why, so I dug up that list and reread the qualities. I noticed you were checking off all the boxes on it, except the biggest and most important one: being a believer.*

Brody smiled and wiped away more tears as he continued reading.

> *This is why I had a hard time giving my heart to you completely. I knew at the time it was not right for us to be together, but the more I got to know you, the more I could see myself with you, and it scared me. I prayed every night for you to find Christ before I fell in love with you, but each day I was growing in my affection for you. The day I told you I would stay and date you, I was conflicted in my decision. I really wanted to stay, I wanted to see where we could go together, but at the same time, I kept seeing the last box on my list not being checked off. The guilt got to me, and well, you can see what I did with it: I ran away.*

Brody's eyes rested on that phrase, and he grimaced. It reminded him of what he had done by first coming to New Hampshire.

> *I am very pleased to see that you took my advice and pursued God. Please don't give up on that now that I am gone.*

Brody started to weep again.

> *Brody, I am so proud of who you have become, and although I may not be there to see what God will do in and through you in the future, he has been kind to me by giving me dreams of what he plans to do with your life, I am very excited for your journey. Now I need you to do me a favor: Don't give up on life. I want you to live with an open heart toward God's calling on your life and toward loving someone again. As I write this, I am crying bitter tears because I don't want to lose you. What keeps me going is knowing one day we will see each other again in heaven. Sorry this was so long. I had so much to say to you. I love you very much, Brody, more than you will ever know, and I will always be praying for you in heaven. God bless you. Vanessa*

Brody hugged the letter to his chest again, weeping silently for a long while.

After a few minutes, his tears turned from bitter to sad but peaceful. He kissed the letter, folded it, and placed it in his Bible. "Thank you, God, for letting me know Vanessa, even for the short amount of time it was. She truly impacted my heart for a lifetime. I am angry you took her from me before we got a chance to be together officially, but I am glad she gets to be with you now and isn't suffering here on Earth anymore. I will miss her greatly, but I am glad you are here with me now. Vanessa, if you are listening right now, I love you too, very much," Brody said, staring at the ceiling and blowing a kiss.

He sat at the desk with his journal and wrote his feelings down, tears dropping onto the pages. Once he finished his journal entry, he looked at it with an intrigued look as he noticed it seemed a lot like song lyrics. He grabbed the journal and went downstairs. He saw Heath and Grace sitting on the couch. He hugged them tightly and told them that he was off to the studio to write some music. Brody left quickly.

Chapter Twenty-Four

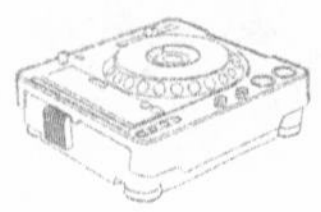

AFTER THEY CAME HOME from the ceremony in Texas, the family decided to have a memorial service for Vanessa at the church the following Saturday. The family had buried Vanessa already the day before, but they wanted the church to have a place to mourn and share their inspiring stories of Vanessa. Brody had been working hard to make sure his song was ready for the service; after all, the ballad was called "A Song for Vanessa." Everyone was impressed because they didn't think he had such range to be able to do a slow song nor did anyone know he could play the guitar.

After the service, many people came up to him and told him how the song had impacted them. This gave Brody the idea of sharing the song with the world, so at the luncheon the Stewarts put on at their house, he asked the family for their blessing to upload the song. Naturally, the family was pleased with the idea and gave him their blessing.

Before Heath went to sleep for the night, he received a call from Duncan. He wanted to let the family know that the August issue of their missionary magazine was going to be dedicated to the missionaries who lost their lives in India recently, and they wanted to do a feature on Vanessa and her life.

Heath wasn't sure he wanted their pain to be broadcast like this, at least not while the wound was so fresh, but after Grace explained the significance of Vanessa's testimony and how it could impact lives, he decided to trust God to use this to help the family through the grieving process, and he gave Duncan their blessing.

The family decided June 7 would be a good date for everyone to do the interview with Duncan.

During the next several days before the interview, Brody fought off intense pleading from his mom to come visit the family. Brody still wasn't sure he wanted to go see them; his heart ached too much, and they weren't exactly the supportive type of parents. Plus he hadn't finished his house, and the interview was coming up. He felt these were all valid reasons to pass on this trip for now, so he told them he would be able to make a trip out there as soon as he did the interview and finished decorating his house. His mother admitted defeat and accepted his answer.

Brody sighed heavily after getting off the phone with his mom for the tenth time in the last three days. He started back into the furniture store. *Lord, I can't do this. I can't pretend I am doing okay, because I am not. Losing Vanessa is the worst thing that could ever have happened to me, and now, to make it worse, my mom wants me to visit her. If you want me to go visit, please strengthen me for that visit. This is a painful time in my life, and I am vulnerable. I don't want to get into an argument with anyone about anything, nor do I want them to try to entice me into anything I will regret later.* Brody prayed as he walked back over to Grace and Kate, who were looking at couches for his house.

"How did it go?" Kate asked.

Brody groaned. "She is relentless. I told her I would visit after I finish the interview and finish my house."

Grace hugged him with a solemn face. She could clearly see he wasn't happy about the decision. "I know you are frustrated about this, but I also know your family will be very happy to see you."

He just shrugged.

"So which couch?" Kate asked, pointing to three different ones, trying to break the tension.

The day after the interview, Brody and the women finished buying all the furniture for his house. After making the plans to visit his family, Brody wasn't in much of a hurry to get his house finished so quickly. He was annoyed that they were. He asked Kate why the rush, and she finally admitted that being busy was the best way for her to keep her mind off losing her best friend.

Brody understood. He wished he could find a way to deflect his pain, but everywhere he turned in Hampton Beach made him think of Vanessa. Every time he closed his eyes to sleep, he would see Vanessa's smiling face and start weeping.

"Thanks for all the help today, Kate," Brody said, waving to Kate as she left. He turned to Grace and frowned. "Thanks for your help too. I really wish you hadn't rushed me through the process though. Now I have to go see my family."

Grace sighed. "Sweetie, I know you don't want to see them, but God has a plan for this visit. Try to lean into it, and if I can give you some more advice, coming from a mom who just lost her chi–" She started to choke up but collected herself the best she could and finished her statement. "As a mom who just lost her child, I have realized that life is precious, and you never know when someone's time is up. Try to make the most of your time with them."

Brody paused before answering. "Thank you for the advice Grace. I will try to follow it." The moment was becoming too heavy for him, so he tried to lighten it up a little. "Now that my furniture is here, you will finally be able to kick me out," Brody joked.

She smirked. "We aren't itching to get rid of you, Brody. I wouldn't mind if you stayed longer, especially after everything that has happened." Brody just smiled sadly and walked Grace out to her car.

Brody opened the car door for Grace. "Are you heading back to the house now too?" Grace asked.

Brody shook his head. "No, I'm heading to the studio now."

Grace looked at him, intrigued. "What is this, song number two?"

"Yeah, I have been struggling with different emotions since I read Vanessa's letter, and I guess it is giving me fuel for my lyrical fire," Brody said.

Grace hugged him. "I understand the mixed emotions. This whole situation feels like a bad dream I can't seem to wake up from, no matter how hard I try."

Brody watched as Grace got into the car. "You aren't curious at all to know what she said to me? Kate and even Daniel and Heath wanted to know, but you haven't asked me anything. Why?"

Grace looked up at him. "I know I can be curious at times—it's where Vanessa got it from—but I also know my boundaries. I don't need to know. It was between the two of you and I respect that privacy, but if you want to tell me yourself, you are more than welcome to."

Brody waved to her as she started her car.

Grace looked in the rearview mirror and saw him getting into his car. She smiled sadly as she remembered what Vanessa had said to her in her letter.

Mom,

I know you already know how much Brody and I liked each other, and I am sorry you will never get to see your daughter marry the love of her life. Please never give up treating Brody like a son-in-law, even if he finds someone new to love, because I believe strongly that we would have been married one day had out time together not come to a tragic end.

Grace started to weep as she drove home.

Brody spent the rest of the night at his studio working hard on a great melody that fit perfectly with the passionate lyrics he had come up with for his song. Once his neck started to hurt and his eyes got heavy with sleep, he decided to call it a night, but unfortunately for him, it wasn't night anymore; it was five o'clock in the morning. He yawned and stretched as he closed down everything in his studio and headed back to the Stewart's house.

He walked into the house and saw Grace sitting at her desk reading the Bible. He walked over to her and kissed her cheek. It was wet with tears, so he handed her the box of tissues on the dining room table and hugged her while she dabbed her eyes with a tissue.

"Are you just getting home from the studio? How did it go? Is the song finished?" she asked in a soft tone.

Brody groaned. "I wish. I hit a roadblock."

"What kind of roadblock?" she asked.

"I tried singing the song myself, but it didn't feel right. I don't know...maybe I'm not meant to sing this song. But I feel God wants me to sing it, so I'm confused," Brody told her.

"Maybe someone is supposed to sing with you," Grace suggested.

"Like a duet?" Brody asked in a tone that suggested he thought the idea was awkward.

Grace chuckled. "Well, you don't have to use the word duet—I know it sounds romantic—but yeah, maybe that is what you are supposed to do with the song...a collaboration."

Brody mulled over the idea for a few seconds before shrugging. "Yeah, I think that could be an idea. I'm going to sleep now and see how I feel about it when I wake up. Thanks, Grace," Brody said, walking up the stairs.

Brody slept for six hours before he heard someone opening a door downstairs. He shot awake and looked around bewildered before finally getting up and heading to the bathroom to splash water on his face. As he left the bathroom, he saw Heath coming up the stairs with a stoic look on his face.

"Hey, Brody, how's it going? Grace told me you were up all night working on song number two," Heath said in a melancholy tone. He hadn't been himself since he lost Vanessa, and out of everyone, he was the one acting most out of character. He didn't sing in the mornings while getting dressed, he didn't smile or joke much, and he cried randomly. This upset Brody to see his mentor so heartbroken. He often prayed for him to be comforted.

"Heath, can I ask you something?" Brody asked hesitantly. Heath nodded. "I want to know if you would sing a song with me," Brody suggested shyly.

Heath's eyes lit up slightly. "Seriously? You want me to sing a song with you? I don't know. I haven't sung techno music before."

"It's not a techno song. I wrote a rock song," Brody said with excited eyes.

Heath looked at Brody and chuckled in disbelief. "A rock song, huh? May I see the lyrics?"

"Sure. I'll get my notebook." Brody went back into his room, and Heath followed him. Brody was relieved to see a little glimpse of the old Heath. It warmed his heart.

They sat on the bed as Heath read over the lyrics, and then Brody played the melody for him. By the end, Heath was smiling for the first time since he had read his letter from Vanessa. "I love the beat. I would love to sing this song with you."

"Yes!" Brody exclaimed.

Heath stood up to leave the room. "So now that you seem to have your writing mojo again, are you going to be releasing a whole album with these songs on it?"

Brody shrugged. "I don't know. I've thought about it, but I don't know if I feel led to do so yet."

"Just be in prayer about it," Heath suggested as he left.

"Are you finally finished with your mystery space? Can I see it now?" Kate asked, trying to peek into the bedroom as Brody shut the door quickly behind him.

"Yeah, it's finished. I'll have you all come over for dinner tonight, and I will show you the room then, as a family," Brody told her.

"Good. I can't wait to see it. I've been waiting forever," Kate said as they headed to the living room. "When do you leave for your parents' house?" Kate asked.

"I'm leaving tomorrow," Brody said, lackluster.

Kate hugged him. "Are you at all excited to see your family?"

Brody shrugged. "Not really. I am still grieving Vanessa, and it's not easy being a Christian around them. I am anxious about the trip."

"I understand. Keep praying for your parents, and be Jesus to them. It won't always be easy, but in time, they will see that you are different, and they will be changed too. Who knows, maybe while you share the situation with Vanessa, it might plant a seed inside them."

Brody shrugged again. "Maybe. I plan to send them a copy of the magazine when it's available, so if my visit doesn't do anything for them spiritually, maybe that will."

Brody had just finished pulling out the lasagna from the oven when his doorbell rang and everyone entered.

"Okay, I'm dying to see the room. Let's go!" Kate said, dragging Brody by the arm. Everyone followed Kate. Brody opened the door and turned on the light. They went inside and gasped, looking around them. Kate and Grace got teary eyed. Brody looked around with a peaceful look on his face.

The room was painted in a light green, his favorite color, and had a bookshelf on one side with books he had accumulated over the last year, along with his bible and notebooks. On the walls were Bible verses stenciled in black paint. On one wall, near his black leather chair and end table, there was a Bible verse written in red stencil; it was bigger than all the others: "James 4:17 – Remember, it is a sin to know what you ought to do and then not do it." Heath read the verse out loud. They looked at Brody with smiles. "Why do you have this verse colored different?" Heath asked, choking up.

Brody got shy all of a sudden. "This is my and Vanessa's

life verse." Brody blushed uncontrollably as the girls smiled sadly at him.

"The room is great, Brody. Now that your house is finished on the inside, I would like to work on your landscaping before winter comes. I see a koi pond in your future. Vanessa loved koi ponds, and I think it could be a good tribute to her," Daniel said, putting his arm around Brody as they started toward the kitchen for dinner.

Chapter Twenty-Five

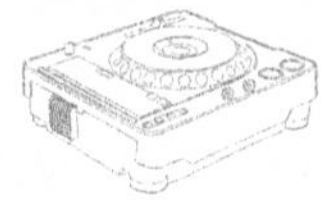

BRODY CAME BACK FROM his trip a week later. It had definitely been a healing visit for him and his family. He finally confronted his parents about the hang-ups he had toward them from the past, and they asked him for forgiveness, not realizing they had hurt him so much. He also talked about Vanessa and told them about the magazine interview he had done.

The best part of the trip was when his father said he was proud of Brody for not drinking anymore. He admired his willpower and courage to change. That made the whole trip worthwhile for Brody.

Once he returned home, Brody went back to work and also moved into his new house. He had a hard time the first week of July being alone in his home since he hadn't lived alone in a long time, but by the second week, he was feeling more at peace with it and, like Grace, had found the solitude to be great.

Now that Brody was back, he and Heath started to work on their collaboration whenever they weren't at work. They worked hard for a week and a half before finally feeling ready to record something.

"Do you feel ready for this final recording?" Brody asked, not sounding convinced himself. Heath nodded. "Don't worry. I'll make sure we're satisfied with the recording before we call it a day," Brody said, trying to calm his own nerves.

Heath snickered. "Why are you so nervous about this one? You have recorded many songs in your time, and so have I."

"Yeah, I know, but I have never recorded with someone as famous as you. I want to make sure it's perfect so when people who are fans of your old band hear you sing in this, they'll be proud of what we created," Brody admitted.

Heath snickered. "The song will bless who it is meant to bless. This is an anthem for people who have been battling addiction and want to be set free, so let's sing the song with passion and raw emotion. This song will be great."

Brody took a deep breath and let it out slowly as he nodded.

"Let's pray before we start," Heath suggested.

Once they finished the final recording, they cheered and hugged; they couldn't wait to share it with Daniel, Kate, and Grace. Since it was family dinner tonight, they decided that was the best time to share the song. Heath and Brody ate quickly and then sat everyone down on the couch to listen.

"This is amazing! You guys did an awesome job," Kate exclaimed.

"Wow, I would have never guessed you had it in you, Brody. You never cease to amaze me with your talent," Grace said, kissing his cheek before kissing Heath on the cheek too. "And as for you, Heath, I am so proud of you. I never tire of hearing your voice."

"What's the name of the song?" Daniel asked.

"'Darkest Before the Dawn,'" Brody answered.

"I love the name! Seriously, you have a great talent for making music," Kate added. "You and Heath did an amazing job singing together. I could feel the pain and the hope; you did a great job. You should upload it soon so others can hear it and be impacted."

"Yes, I'm going to upload it now," Brody said, getting up to grab his laptop from his bag while the family sat on the couch and watched TV.

Over the next several weeks, reviews, interviews, and comments came flooding in from everywhere for his latest song as well as his song for Vanessa. He saw many positive reviews from fans about his new song, but he also saw a few haters. Podcasters wanted to interview him about his two most recent songs and what led him to write them. He also received a couple phone calls, one from a well-known Christian magazine and then another magazine, a secular one, that was writing an article about artists who reinvented themselves successfully. He felt privileged to be able to give God the glory each time he got to speak out in some way.

All this attention he was getting from his music, even the bad press, was encouraging and really got him thinking about his future in the music business. He decided to focus his prayer time on getting direction in this area of his life. He had his own ideas about what he wanted to do with his music career, but he wanted to make sure he lined up with God's will.

"The magazine is here!" Grace exclaimed, coming in the house with the mail.

Heath jumped off the couch and raced to her side. "Open it," he said excitedly.

"Shouldn't we wait for the kids?" Grace suggested.

Heath snorted. "You mean Thursday? I can't wait that long. I've been excited to read it since we did the interview."

Grace kissed his cheek. "No, we don't have to wait until family dinner. I will call and see if the kids can come over here for dinner tonight, and we can read it together then." Grace walked away, putting the mail on the counter.

"I guess I can wait until tonight," Heath said with a sigh.

Brody showed up at the house as everyone was sitting down at the table. "Sorry for being late. I needed to get gas in my car after work," Brody said, sitting down next to Kate.

"So where is this magazine?" Heath asked after he finished praying for the meal. Grace grabbed the envelope from the counter and handed it to Heath. "It's heavy...must be a big issue," Heath commented.

"Or there is a copy for each of us," Daniel suggested. Heath opened the envelope and pulled out five copies. Daniel grinned. "I was right."

They ate silently while they all read to themselves.

"This was amazing! Many people will be encouraged by this issue, I can tell," Kate said after some time, putting her magazine down to finish eating. Everyone nodded in agreement.

"I need to send a copy to my parents; I think they will like this," Brody said, closing his copy and tucking it away on his lap.

"You can take mine. Heath and I don't need two," Grace suggested, handing Brody her copy.

He took it with a smile. "Thanks, Grace."

The next morning, Brody and Daniel walked into the Stewart's house wearing backpacks, shorts, hiking boots, and t-shirts.

"Good morning, kids. Excited for your hike?" Grace asked, sipping her coffee on the couch.

"Yeah, it should be fun, but today is supposed to be really hot, so we need to go now. Where's Dad?" Daniel asked.

"He's almost ready," Grace said simply. "Make sure you grab the lunches I prepared for you." Daniel and Brody headed into the kitchen and grabbed the brown paper bag lunches, each marked with their name on it.

"Thanks, Mom," Daniel said, kissing his mom on the head. He looked at his watch and grunted. "Dad, come on. We're burning daylight," Daniel shouted impatiently.

Brody chortled. "Burning daylight? It's barely seven in the morning. I think we have plenty of daylight left."

Daniel shrugged with a smirk.

"I'm coming. Sorry, I couldn't find my other boot," Heath said, jogging down the stairs. Daniel handed his father his backpack, and they started toward the door.

The guys had been hiking for a few hours when they found a nice place to stop for a break and a snack. There was a trickling stream nearby that they stuck their feet in and cooled off. It was mostly quiet where they stood, aside from the birds chirping and some bugs buzzing around. The guys finished their granola bars and got their bandanas wet to wipe off their foreheads.

"I have some big news," Daniel said, after some time. Heath and Brody turned to look at him, intrigued. "I'm going to propose to Kate at your birthday party, Dad, so she won't suspect it's coming," Daniel confided proudly.

"Congratulations," Heath and Brody said in unison, eyes widened.

"On my special day, huh? Yeah, she sure won't be expecting that," Heath remarked.

"Is that okay, Dad? Would you rather I wait? I can wait if you want," Daniel suggested nervously.

Heath chuckled and shook his head. "No, of course not. I don't mind. I think it's sweet."

"I'm really nervous about it," Daniel confessed, "but I feel it's time. After what happened to Vanessa, I realize that life is short, and I should live it to the full while I can."

"Well, this is awesome news, Daniel. Kate will be thrilled. Congratulations again," Brody piped up.

"We should keep moving so we can make it up the mountain before it gets too hot," Heath suggested as they packed up their things, cleaned off their feet, and put their shoes back on.

They arrived home just as Grace was setting the table with a nice meal she had prepared for them: chicken enchiladas, rice, and beans. They went straight to the table, sweaty, smelly, and dirty. Grace chuckled and sat down to pray over the food before they started digging in.

"So how was the hike?" Grace asked, trying not to breathe in the stench of sweat.

"Great. We had a lot of fun, and I think I speak for us all when I say we are exhausted," Heath said with a chuckle while shoving food into his mouth.

"Guess what, Mom," Daniel said with a mouthful of food.

"What?" she asked.

"I'm going to propose to Kate on Dad's birthday," Daniel said with a toothy grin.

Grace squealed with delight and hugged him. "It's about time!" They laughed, and then Grace sighed. "Oh, your sister would have loved to hear this news. She always wanted her and Kate to be sisters for real."

Daniel grinned. "I told her already." They looked at him

quizzically. "When we did our video chat months ago, I told Vanessa I wanted to propose to Kate but needed the financial security first. I told her to pray that a huge client would fall in my lap; then I would know it was time. She told me she would pray that I would take a step of faith without needing the financial safety net first. Well, a month ago I started thinking about that conversation she and I had and decided to take her advice and exercise my faith. I bought the ring and had it sized for Kate and decided to propose at Dad's party. After I took those steps, then the huge contract came. Praise God for his faithfulness to her prayers for me," Daniel explained happily.

"Your sister was a remarkable intercessor," Heath said proudly. Daniel nodded in agreement.

The morning after Heath's party, Brody went to the beach for an early morning stroll; it was so early the sun hadn't even come out yet. He didn't mind though; he hadn't really slept well last night anyway. He didn't think that Heath's party would affect him as strongly as it did, but before the party even started, Brody was flooded with memories of last summer, when he and Vanessa had gone to the party together. He could even see, in his mind's eye, what she had worn that night and how beautiful she had looked.

Once he got to their house, the pain only increased as he and the family went outside so Daniel could give his father the two gifts from him. He had made him a fire pit and benches and also a statue that caused Heath to burst into tears immediately. It was a statue of Vanessa as a child being tossed in the air by her father, and she had a huge smile on her face.

Heath explained what the significance of this was. "When Vanessa was a little girl, she always loved it when I would toss her into the air. She would squeal and say her tummy tickled. It has always been one of my fondest memories of her."

Hearing this broke Brody's heart further, almost making him want to leave the party before it had even started. After Daniel proposed to Kate in front of the guests, it was all Brody could do to not rush out of the house screaming in agony that he would never have that chance with Vanessa.

He kicked up sand as he walked, like a toddler throwing a temper tantrum. He looked out at the ocean and then at the boardwalk and up at the sky, trying to focus on anything but his thoughts, which weren't anything but negative at the moment.

He stopped at the spot where he and Vanessa had their heart to heart and sat on the sand, his head resting on his knees as he started to weep, mourning what he had lost and also what he would never have. As the sun started to come up, he looked out at the ocean. "Why did you have to take her, God?"

"I ask myself that question often too," a soft voice piped up from behind him, shocking Brody. He turned around quickly and sighed with relief when he saw Kate standing there. She, too, looked like she had been crying. Brody frowned and motioned for her to sit next to him.

"I have been up for hours crying. All I wanted to do was celebrate this awesome news with my best friend and talk wedding plans, and I can't." Kate started to wail and leaned her head on Brody's shoulder.

He sat there motionless, crying too.

"I miss her so much. I have dreams about her almost every night," Kate added.

"You too, huh? I thought I was the only one who dreamed about her. I can't imagine the pain you are in. You two were close for such a long time. I barely knew her, and I'm torn up."

"You two shared a bond that I have never seen her have with anyone, Brody. She has helped many people detox, but I think helping you was the toughest case on her emotionally. She was vulnerable with you, and she allowed you to be vulnerable with her too. Vulnerability can strengthen any bond, no matter how short the time. Plus, Vanessa was a very remarkable girl. I am not surprised you fell for her so easily," Kate encouraged him.

Brody smiled sadly. "I'm just surprised she fell for me too."

Kate laid her head on his shoulder again. "Brody, you are a great catch. Don't sell yourself short."

Brody smiled. "Thanks for being my biggest fan, Kate. Congratulations on the engagement. I really am happy for you two." Kate kissed his cheek, and they sat there quietly staring at the ocean for a while before parting ways.

Chapter Twenty-Six

BRODY SAT PENSIVELY IN a chair in his prayer room. He was reading his Bible, singing praises, and praying. After a few minutes, he heard the buzzing from his phone on the bookshelf. He tried to ignore it, but it kept buzzing so he checked to see who it was. The caller ID was blocked. He declined the call and was about to sit back down in his chair when he heard a loud knock at his front door. He stood up and ran to the door to answer it.

"What are you doing here, Michael?" Brody asked, surprised.

Michael chuckled and shook hands with Brody. "What? You aren't thrilled to see your best friend? I'm glad you finally answered the door. I've been knocking for a while now; I even called you. I was beginning to think I had the wrong house or that I should call my Uber to come back."

"I'm sorry. I was in my room. Come inside. I was thinking of making lunch. You want something to eat?" Brody asked, ushering his old friend inside.

"You cook now? I remember we used to always eat fast food whenever we toured together because we were both useless in a kitchen," Michael said, dropping his bag on the floor.

"Yeah, I have learned to make my own food recently," Brody answered. Michael sat down on a barstool and watched as Brody made turkey sandwiches. Brody cleared his throat. "Shouldn't you be in Texas right now for that annual Labor Day thing you do?"

"That was last weekend, man," Michael reminded him. "Oh, yeah, you're right," Brody said, handing Michael a sandwich.

Michael chortled. "This is your idea of cooking for yourself?"

Brody smirked. "It's better than fast food."

Michael nodded in agreement and started to eat.

"What brings you here to see me, Michael? We haven't talked since you told me I was an idiot for giving up my life's work for some religion," Brody asked him while making his sandwich.

Michael sighed heavily. "Well, it looks like maybe I was the real idiot, not you." Brody looked up with a quizzical brow.

Michael frowned suddenly. "Amber kicked me out, man. She said she was tired of being with someone who wouldn't commit to her after so many years together. She also said she is tired of me smoking pot and acting like a fool. She told me if I come back, I better not be smoking anymore and I better have a ring for her."

"I'm sorry to hear that, Michael. What can I do to help? I don't have pot, so I hope you aren't looking for any from me," Brody responded boldly.

Michael shook his head. "No, of course not. I know you haven't smoked for a long time. No, I'm here because I need a place to crash for a while."

Brody snickered, taking a bite of his sandwich. "Why me? I know you have a lot of friends in New York you could live with. Why did you come all the way out here to see me?"

Michael looked at Brody hesitantly. "I've been following your life since you quit the business." Brody was taken aback as Michael continued with a sigh. "At first I did it because I was hoping to see you fail miserably and so I could make jokes and entice you to come back to your senses, but the more I saw your new posts and listened to your new songs—great music by the way—I could tell you had truly changed and that you would never come back, not in the same way you left."

Brody stared at Michael intently, assuming he had more to say. "I also listened to every podcast and read every single thing that was written about you. I basically stalked you," he added. Brody couldn't believe his ears.

Michael was eight years older than Brody, so he was like an older brother, not just his mentor and best friend. Michael was also a very intelligent man. He knows four languages and loved reading everything and anything he could get his hands on. He taught himself everything he knew about the DJ business when he was still in high school and became one of the most successful DJs within a year of being in the business. Brody had been honored when someone of his intelligence and abilities wanted to take him under his wing and teach him how to be the best.

Michael was also the most adamant, out of everyone from Brody's past, that he was making a big mistake walking away from his career the way he did, and he made it known to Brody almost every day for the first three months after he left. To hear him now having regrets for thinking that way was inconceivable.

Michael continued, "Last month, while I was flying home

from a show in Paris, I flipped through a magazine that was left by the previous passenger. I hadn't heard of the magazine before, but you know I love reading, so I read it anyway. Turned out to be a magazine about your Vanessa, and you were featured in it. I am sorry for your loss, man. I can't imagine losing a loved one like that."

Brody smiled sadly. "Thanks. Losing Vanessa was a tough period of my life, but I will see her in heaven one day. I hold on to that thought whenever I get sad. May I ask you a question? You and Amber have been together for a while, and you still haven't asked her to marry you. Why not? I thought you loved her."

"I do love her. I just don't see why she needs a ring and a legal document to make my love legit to her. We've been together for six years. Isn't that good enough for her?" Michael protested.

Brody chuckled. "You are a fool, Michael. She wants to know that you love only her and will only love her for the rest of your lives. Marriage is a long-term commitment between a man and woman that shows you will stay devoted to that person through thick and thin. That's what she wants from you—to know that you want to commit to her for life."

Michael snorted. "When did you get to be sentimental like that?" Brody just chuckled. "I didn't think of it that way," Michael continued. "Aw man, I screwed up. What if she finds someone else? I don't want to lose her, Brody," Michael said with sad eyes.

"I don't think she will find someone else. She told you to come back with a ring or don't come back at all; that means she isn't done with you yet. She is just giving you a chance to get your act together first," Brody reassured him.

Michael finished his sandwich. "Well, I wanna get it

together, and that is why I came here to see you. I see that you have your act together and thought you could introduce me to this God of yours who helped you so he can help me too."

Brody grinned from ear to ear and chuckled. "Well, you sure picked the best day to come here then. Today is my weekly Bible study with my spiritual mentor, Heath, and his son, Daniel. You can join us," Brody responded.

"Oh, I don't want to impose," Michael objected.

"It's not going to be an imposition. He will be thrilled to have you join us; trust me. Daniel just started to join us for these Bible studies a few months back; his schedule finally cleared up enough. It's not until tonight though, so if you're up to it right now, I would love to show you my studio," Brody suggested.

Michael nodded. "Yes, I'd like that very much, and I also want to hear your whole story. I'm sure it wasn't all in that magazine, right?"

Brody nodded. "That's true. I didn't go in depth about everything. Come on. I can share the whole thing with you on our drive to the studio," Brody said, grabbing his keys and heading out the door with Michael.

Brody unlocked the doors to his SUV, and Michael chuckled. "Where's your motorcycle? I was looking forward to riding it while I was in town."

They got into the car, and Brody laughed. "I gave it to Chuck."

Michael laughed loudly. "Of course you did. That guy was always trying to take it from you."

Brody drove away and began to share his full testimony.

"Wow, Brody, your life is so different now, and your story is incredible. I can't imagine detoxing like you did. I think I would have given up. You're stronger than I am," Michael commented as he got out of the car.

Brody opened the door to his studio and turned on the

lights. "God gave me the ability to stay strong. I wanted sobriety, but there was no way I was getting it without his help."

Michael looked at Brody with a huge grin and chuckled. "Good for you, Brody. I'm proud of you for breaking away from the herd and starting your own life."

Michael walked around the studio in awe and excitement. He started to fiddle with the soundboard and turned on some random beats that fit together well; he was always good at coming up with an epic sound on the fly. He started to record it on his phone and then started to beatbox to the melody too. After watching Michael for a few seconds, Brody started in with some random lyrics he had just come up with, something he was never able to do before. The beat had inspired him.

Michael shut the recording off after a few minutes and looked at Brody, impressed. "Brody, my man, you got more skills than I knew about. I didn't know you were such a lyricist. I can't even come up with lyrics on the spot that have such fire, and I've been doing this for a very long time."

Brody smiled. "After Vanessa died, I don't know...something happened inside me, and my spirit came alive for Christ. I started having an easier time writing music. I write from my heart now."

"It shows. Those were sweet lyrics. I want to use this recording for my next album if you're down with that," Michael suggested.

Brody nodded. "That would be amazing!"

"Awesome. And don't worry—I'll give you a cut of the profits. So is making music your full-time job now, like before?" Michael asked.

"No, it's not my job. I just wanted to make a studio because I love making music," Brody responded.

"I see. So what do you do for a job now?" Michael asked next.

"I work as a waiter at a diner," Brody said with a smirk.

Michael burst into laughter. "It must be hard to do menial things like that after being such a big star."

Brody chuckled. "I like the work. It's fun, and I get to share my story with people sometimes too. I also serve at my church in the audio production team, and I co-lead a recovery group there too."

Michael chuckled in disbelief. "Wait...no way. *You* help run a recovery group? You...who used to drink like a fish? That's crazy awesome. It gives me hope." Michael turned to fiddle with the buttons on the soundboard again. "I haven't been smoking pot as often as I did when you saw me last, but I still haven't kicked the habit. Maybe I should check out your group sometime."

"We meet Fridays at seven. If you're still in town, you are welcome to come with me," Brody offered, smiling now. "So we still have some time to kill. Should we go look at rings now?"

"Why do we need to do that?" Michael asked with a nervous chuckle.

"You know why," Brody said.

Michael turned around and swallowed a lump in his throat as he faced the soundboard again. "Yeah, maybe we can do that, but first let's record another song." He set up the music, turned on the record button on his phone, and started his beatboxing. Brody sat down in a chair next to him and started to come up with lyrics that roasted Michael for his cold feet. Michael laughed loudly.

After a half an hour of looking at rings, Michael finally found the perfect one and purchased it. He was both excited and nervous about the idea of marriage, but after thinking about how excited Amber would be, he calmed down some and couldn't wait to give her the ring. He knew he needed to fix his other issues first before he came home to her.

As he and Brody walked back to the car, Brody couldn't help but feel a sense of melancholy once more knowing he would never get this chance at happiness with Vanessa.

"What's wrong Brody? Did I get the wrong ring?" Michael asked, concerned.

Brody shook his head. "No, the ring you got Amber is great; she'll love it. That's not my problem. Vanessa's brother is getting married, and you are about to get engaged..."

"And you are feeling bummed because of what happened to Vanessa, right?" Michael asked with a frown.

Brody nodded. "Yeah, it's a wound I haven't been able to fully heal from yet. I don't know if I ever will. I can't see myself with anyone else but her. I really loved her."

Michael patted him on the back. "Sorry, dude. I can't begin to relate to what you are going through, although this distance between Amber and me has been unbearable—and it's only been a day."

Brody willed himself to perk up. "Time to get out of my funk. Let's go home and eat something before we go to the Bible study."

Chapter Twenty-Seven

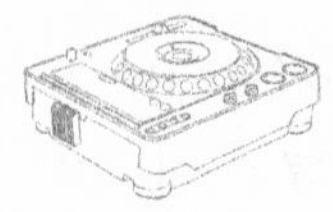

Brody pulled his car into the driveway behind Heath's car. He and Michael got out and walked up to the house. "So this is Vanessa's parents' house?" Michael asked. Brody nodded as they walked inside.

Grace and Kate were standing by the table, getting their Bibles and notebooks, when the guys walked inside. "Hey, Brody, how are you?" Grace asked, hugging him. "Who is this?"

"My name is Michael. I'm an old friend of Brody's," Michael said, shaking hands with Grace.

"I'm Grace. It's nice to meet you Michael,"

Kate laughed in disbelief. "You're DJ Michael Peterson!"

Michael looked at her with a chuckle. "Yeah, that's me, but you can call me Michael.

Brody smiled. "This is Kate. She's a big fan of techno."

"Nice to meet you, Kate," he said, shaking her hand.

Heath started down the stairs just then and hugged Brody. "Hey, Brody, who is this you have with you?"

Brody smiled. "This is Michael. He's an old friend."

Heath shook Michael's hand. "Nice to meet you."

The girls excused themselves and left for their Bible study, and Heath turned to look at Michael. "So what brings you to town, Michael?"

"I'm down on my luck right now and looking for whatever it was that helped Brody get out of his hole. He said tonight is a Bible study. I'm here to join, I guess, if that is alright." Michael said.

"Yeah, it's totally fine if you join. Sorry you won't get to meet Daniel, my son, tonight; he got asked to do a job for a friend," Heath told him, motioning for them to follow him to the couch.

"I noticed there were a few platinum albums on the wall over there. What are they for?" Michael asked.

"You don't recognize me, huh?" Heath chuckled.

Michael looked embarrassed. "Should I recognize you?"

"Only if you listened to rock in the late eighties and early nineties."

Brody piped up, "This is Heath Stewart. He was the guitarist for Jealous Creatures. Remember, I told you about them when we first met."

Michael's eyes lit up once he recalled the memory. "Oh yeah, you mentioned that your father was a huge fan of them. That's pretty cool that you know someone from the group now. Sorry I didn't recognize you; I only listened to rap and techno."

"Don't apologize. Those were the old days. I'm happy being incognito now." He cleared his throat. "Michael, let me find you a Bible so you can follow along with what we are reading," Heath suggested.

"Do you have a notebook or paper I can write on too? I'm a notetaker," Michael said.

Heath came back with a Bible, notebook, and pen. They turned in their Bibles to Psalm 51. Heath asked Brody to read, and Michael listened intently to his friend.

"Okay, it sounds like this person, David, was very upset. What was he upset about?" Michael asked after Brody finished reading.

"He was upset with his sin," Heath explained. "See, David was a king. He was also called a man after God's own heart. He had sinned, and it was a really big one, so in this chapter, he was repenting from what he had done wrong against God and was asking for forgiveness and mercy from God."

"What did he do wrong?" Michael asked next.

Heath smiled. "He committed adultery with the wife of someone from his troops, and when she became pregnant, he had the husband killed after his plan to cover up his incident didn't work out. He then married the dead man's wife."

Michael laughed awkwardly. "Wow, I have done some pretty shady things in my life but nothing like that. Geez."

"The Bible is very clear: None of us are exempt from the wrath of God. We have all fallen short and sinned to the point where we need to repent and seek forgiveness and mercy from God. This is found in Romans 3:23. That is where asking Jesus into our hearts comes into play. See, in this psalm, David was repenting from his many sins and realizing his need for a savior. He called out to him for mercy and received it," Heath explained at length.

"What is repenting?" Michael asked after some time.

"Repentance means to turn away from something you are doing wrong. Simply put, if you ask Jesus into your heart, you turn away from the sins in your life that keep you from being close to him. Do you know what sins are?" Heath asked.

Michael nodded. "Yeah, I have read the Ten Commandments before. I know I have done some of those, and I am sure there are more I don't know about that I have also done."

"Those things keep you from God. That is why we needed

a savior, and that is why God sent his only son, Jesus, to die on the cross for us. He was the perfect, sinless sacrifice needed to keep right standing between us and God, and because of his death on the cross and his resurrection three days later, we now have eternal life if we accept his free gift," Heath answered.

Michael winced. "I think I have many things to repent from. So how do I go about asking Jesus to forgive me and get on my way to healing? I want to be better than I am now, and I want to get right with my girlfriend too," Michael said matter-of-factly.

Brody looked at him, concerned. "You know that God isn't a quick fix, right? It will take work and determination on your part to make a relationship with God work. It's like your relationship with Amber; it will take hard work, but it will be worth it if you put the work in. The connection you will have with God is awesome, unlike any other connection."

Michael nodded slowly, as if he were processing what was being said.

"Also, walking with God isn't easy. It's a daily struggle between doing what is right and what is easy. Your flesh will want one thing, but your spirit will want something else; it's a battle. You might have to give up some things in your life—a career, people, family, fame, who knows. A life lived for Christ is one of sacrifice," Heath added.

Michael chuckled, looking at Brody, "Did you know all this before you became a believer?"

"Yeah, Heath didn't sugarcoat anything for me, and I am glad he didn't," Brody told him.

Michael looked at the guys and smiled. "I have always been an avid reader. I have read parts of the Bible before, so I know about Jesus and his sacrifice. I have also read about the fall of man and some other random things in my time. I have the head knowledge, but I want to know him personally now. I believe what the Bible said about him and who he personally claimed to be too. I've read a lot of books and studied many things and haven't seen any contradictions in the Bible. And seeing Brody sober and completely different from when I saw him last, I can only say it is because there is a God. Okay, I'm in. I don't care about hard work. I love a challenge. I want to give my life to God and learn all I can about him. I also want him to help me get over my addiction to pot, forgive me for every sin I have ever done, and help me make things right with Amber, no matter how long it takes."

Brody smiled. "I have always loved your passion for learning. In this case, it has already given you a foundation that I didn't have before I came to Christ."

Heath patted Michael on the shoulder. "I love your enthusiasm. Okay then, let me read another verse that might help you understand how to pray and ask Jesus into your heart. Let's turn to Romans 10:9–10."

Michael smirked. "No need. I've read that before too."

Heath grinned and nodded. "Okay, go ahead and start praying then, Michael."

Michael closed his eyes and dove right into his prayer. "God, I need your help. My girl doesn't want me because I am messed up, and if I am being very honest, I don't like how I have been lately either. Brody's change has inspired me, and I figured maybe I could have that too. I am ready to change. I'm forty-one years old, too old to waste my life anymore. If you will have me, I am sure I will be able to be a good addition to your kingdom. I hope I don't sound boastful. I accept that Jesus is the son of God and that you died for all the evil things I have done and continue to do. I thank you for being able to rise from the dead and making it possible for me to come to you now for help. Please accept my repentance and accept me as your child. Amen."

The guys hugged and congratulated Michael. Just then the girls came in the house, and Michael ran over to them to tell them the good news.

"Thanks for inviting me tonight. That was a really awesome night. I feel different already," Michael said, grinning.

"You're welcome. I'm glad you are now my brother in Christ. God is so good," Brody said, getting choked up. He cleared his throat. "Heath told me this before, and I want to tell you now: This high you feel at the moment won't last, so don't chase it; chase after Christ instead. Our feelings will come and go, but God is always constant," Brody told him.

Michael nodded. "I understand. Thanks for the tip."

Brody pulled into his driveway. "You know you will get backlash for this decision, just like I did. Make sure you are strong through it."

Michael sighed. "Yeah, that is the stuff that scares me. I know how I acted toward you, and I know you probably went through it from all different angles. I'm a veteran in the business as well, so if I start acting different, even if I don't leave altogether like you did, people will notice. I'm trying to mentally prepare myself for whatever is going to happen in my future. But I meant what I said. I'm ready to do the hard stuff to make this relationship with Christ work."

They got out of the car and walked into the house. "Glad to hear it. If you need help or guidance, I'm here for you," Brody assured him.

"Thanks, dude," Michael said, patting Brody on the shoulder. Michael picked up his things and followed Brody toward the bedrooms.

"You can sleep in here, and I will sleep in the spare room," Brody suggested.

"Nah, man, I can't take your bedroom. I can sleep in the spare room," Michael protested.

"It's okay. I don't have a bed in the spare room; it isn't set up for company yet. I would feel bad having you sleep on the floor," Brody explained.

"I have slept on floors before, Brody. I don't mind," Michael said, walking into the room. He turned on the light, and gasped, "Wow!" Michael exclaimed, surveying the room.

"Yeah, this is my prayer closet," Brody said proudly.

"Nice. I am gonna have to get me one of these. Why is this one in verse in red and the others aren't?" Michael asked.

"This was my and Vanessa's life verse," Brody answered.

Michael smiled and nudged Brody. "You ol' softy." He dropped his bag on the ground. "I think I will be happy in this room. I see a lot of books I can read right now. You know I can't sleep at night anymore...been in the business too long."

Brody nodded. "Yeah, it was hard for me to get back into normal sleeping hours too. I will bring you a blanket and a pillow just in case you get tired."

Brody came back into the room with a blanket and pillow, laid them on the floor, and then observed Michael. He was skimming through some books on the bookshelf. Brody chuckled. "Good night, Michael. Happy reading." Michael waved but didn't look up from the book in his hands.

Chapter Twenty-Eight

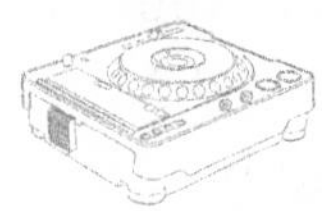

THE NEXT MORNING, BRODY woke up early and made breakfast for himself and Michael. After an hour, Michael came into the kitchen dressed nicely, clean shaven, and with his hair combed. He saw Brody putting a plate of food on the table for him. "This looks so good. Thanks, Brody. I hope it's as good as it tastes," Michael joked, sitting down.

Brody chuckled. "Well, you didn't die after eating the turkey sandwich, so I guess I'm not that bad of a cook. Why are you so put together this morning?"

"I'm planning to ask Amber to marry me today. Will you come back with me?" Michael asked excitedly.

Brody grinned. "Sure, I would love to go back with you. I would like to see Amber again; it's been a long time. So how do you feel about this decision?"

Michael sighed. "I'm super nervous."

"Don't be nervous. You know she loves you," Brody reassured him.

After they finished eating, Brody went to his room to get dressed and then came out into the living room to find Michael on the couch reading a book.

Michael paused and looked up at Brody. "Can I take this book home with me? I can send it back when I am finished."

Brody smiled and looked at the devotional that Michael was reading. It was a book for newlywed men. Brody chuckled and wondered why he even had the book, but then he remembered that when the church found out he was needing books for his library, they started giving him anything and everything. This must have been one of those.

"You can take it. I don't think I will ever have a need for it," Brody said as he followed Michael toward the door. Michael stuffed the book and his Bible into his bag and hoisted it onto his back as they started out the door.

Brody pulled his car into the driveway leading to the big mansion where Michael and Amber lived. Brody always enjoyed coming over to visit Michael. His house was full of exciting things to do, from the trampoline, arcade, spa, and pool to the bowling alley in the basement. There was never a dull moment at Michael's house.

"I have so many memories of being here," Brody mused as they got out of the car.

"I'm sorry if they aren't good memories."

"Everything that happened in my life was for a reason and is now being used for God's purpose in my life. I can't wait to see Amber's face when you pop the question," Brody said as they started toward the front door.

Just as Michael was about to open the door, Amber, a slender thirty-year-old woman threw open the door. Her eyes lit up as she wrapped her arms around Brody and laughed with excitement. "Brody! So good to see you again! What are you doing here with this lowlife?" She pointed to Michael with a scowl.

"Aw, baby, don't be like that. I love you, and I have some great news," Michael said with a smile.

Amber folded her arms and stared at him with narrow eyes. "Oh yeah? So that means you are drug free then?"

"I haven't had anything since we went to that party Sunday, and I will continue to stay drug free too—but that's not what I was talking about," Michael explained, barely containing his excitement. Amber was intrigued and let them follow her into the house.

Michael dropped his bag on the couch and searched through his bag until he found what he was looking for. Amber stood next to Brody with her arms folded and a scowl still on her beautiful face. Michael grinned from ear to ear as he turned around and knelt down in front of her, opening the little jewelry box to show her a huge engagement ring.

She gasped and started to cry, her eyes wide with anticipation. "Is this for me?"

"Of course. I love you, Amber, and the last few days made me realize just how much I need you in my life. I want to spend the rest of my life with you. Please marry me," Michael said, getting choked up.

Brody looked on with pride in his eyes and a little pain too. Again he was caught watching someone else get their happily ever after while his was lying dead and buried six feet in the ground. He tried to contain his frustrations and be in the moment for his friend; he knew this was a big thing for him to do, and he wanted to show as much support as he could. He silently prayed for God to give him strength.

Amber looked at Brody seriously. "What do you think? Should I marry him?"

Brody chuckled as he looked at Michael, "Why don't you tell her the best news, Michael? I'm sure it will help her say yes."

Michael nodded happily and stood up to hold Amber's hands, putting the ring back in his pocket. He stared at her with an intense gaze, and she grinned uncontrollably.

"I am a Christian now, baby. That means I will become a better man after some hard work. I have been reading the Bible ever since I made that commitment last night, and I just got a book about being a good husband so you know I can make a commitment to you too. Please say you will marry me. I don't want anyone else but you, and I don't want drugs either. I will go to rehab if you want—whatever you want. Just say you will marry me." Michael spoke with pleading eyes.

Amber laughed in disbelief, tears forming in her eyes. She looked at Brody, wide eyed. "You know, I think all the months he spent stalking your life has slowly been changing him." She turned to Michael and smiled. "I would have never expected you to find Jesus, but I am sure glad you did. I can already see you are different. The old Michael wouldn't be caught dead begging a woman to be with him. Of course I will marry you. I only love you. Now let me have that fantastic ring, and you two can tell me how this transformation happened to my future hubby. Brody, I want to hear all about your life as well," Amber said, hugging Michael then giving him a kiss as he put the ring on her finger.

The trio spent the next hour talking about the last few days as well as Brody's life and heartache. Amber was in awe and disbelief as Michael told her his transformation story. At the end of it, she looked at Brody. "It's amazing! This Jesus has changed him in a matter of days. I would have never thought it possible. I have been trying to do it for years!"

She turned toward Michael and took hold of his hand. "Whatever you have, I want it too—right now."

Michael and Brody were both in tears as Michael

proceeded to tell Amber about Jesus Christ, what he did for her on the cross, and how he defeated death so she could have eternal life. He quoted a few scriptures too that he had read many times throughout the night. After that, he helped her pray a prayer to accept Christ into her heart. The room was then filled with happy tears and hugging.

"God is so good! I would have never thought in a million years I would be here to witness my best friend coming to Christ and, not only that, him choosing to marry the love of his life and also leading her to become a Christian too. God never ceases to amaze me," Brody said, wiping his eyes.

Michael shook his hand. "Thank you, Brody. I owe this all to you and the seeds you planted in me when you walked away like you did. You didn't know it until now, but as Amber mentioned, that really did change my life."

"I am glad I was able to help you that way. Okay, I'm going to head home. I love you guys. I am so happy for you both!" Brody said before giving Michael and Amber a hug.

Michael chuckled and held onto Brody. "Nah, man, you can't leave yet. I asked you here for a reason. I need you to be here to support me."

Brody furrowed his brow. "I thought I just did that."

"Yeah, you did for the proposal, but what about the wedding? I need a best man, right?" Michael said, glancing at him before turning to Amber. He took hold of her hands. "I feel strongly that God wants us to just get married now. We have been playing house long enough, don't you agree?"

Michael looked at Amber with intent, and she smiled. "You know I agree with that. It's why I lit this fire under you. I don't want to wait another second to become your wife."

Brody chuckled awkwardly. "You guys gonna just go to the courthouse or something?"

Amber gasped. "That is a great idea, Brody! Let's go now." She grabbed the guys and rushed out of the house and to her car.

They walked into the courthouse and went to the clerk's office. "We need a marriage license now please," Amber said excitedly.

The clerk behind the counter chuckled and handed them the paperwork. Michael filled out his portion, and then Amber filled out her part. Brody sat in a chair, agonizing about how he would try to keep cool during the ceremony. His heart ached being here, but he was also very happy for his friends; he didn't want to be a damper on their special day. He willed himself to forget his pain, at least until he got back home.

They paid for their license and asked if there was someone available to officiate now. The clerk walked away to ask someone a few questions.

Amber looked down at her clothes and gasped. "I'm in jeans and a t-shirt! I can't get married like this!"

Michael chuckled and kissed her cheek. "You always look beautiful, Amber."

She grimaced. "You're dressed so nice though."

"That's because he looks like a beach bum when he's dressed in his usual attire," Brody piped up with a chuckle.

Michael smirked. "True. That's why I shaved the scruffy beard too. Baby, you look fine, but if you want to wait and change, we can do that too."

She shook her head. "No, I will be okay. I said I didn't want to wait any longer to be your wife, and I meant it."

Brody got back home from New York late. He was exhausted, not just mentally and emotionally but physically too. After the ceremony, they had insisted on taking Brody to dinner, and then they went bowling together before Brody left. On his way home, he was beside himself, crying happy tears for everything that had happened recently with Michael and Amber but also crying sad tears, still mourning what would never be for him. By the time he got to his house, all he wanted to do was go to sleep, but his phone started ringing. It was an out-of-state number. He reluctantly answered it.

"Hi, Brody. My name is Bill Hamill. I am the pastor and director for the Way Addiction Center out in Boise, Idaho. I wanted to know if you would be willing to come out and speak at our center for our weekly church service. My eldest son, William, just finished his last year of college and came back home to join the center as a counselor. He has always been a huge fan of your music. When you decided to release new music as a Christian, he was curious to listen to it. He said it's amazing and that your story is even more amazing."

Brody laid on his back and listened as Bill continued. "He has encouraged me to find a way to get in touch with you so you could share your testimony with our rehab center. So what do you say? I know this is very last minute, and I do not mind paying your airfare. You are welcome to stay at our home as our guest, if you want to; otherwise, I can book you a hotel. This would mean a lot to my son, and I am sure our addicts will be encouraged by your story too. If you could come Friday, I can introduce you to the family and show you around Boise before Sunday," Bill finished.

Brody was speechless for a few seconds, mostly because he was tired and trying to process everything. Finally, he smiled. "I would be honored to do this. I have never done a public speaking event, so this will be interesting for me. And I would like to meet William very much. Any fan who stuck with me during my musical transition has a very special place in my heart. I will message you back when I can leave. Friday evenings I am usually co-leading my addiction group out here, and I haven't missed a day since I started going to it. I want to make sure my co-leader will be okay without me for one meeting," Brody replied.

"Wow, what a dedicated person you are, Brody. That will be very encouraging for people here to know about. Let me know what you choose. If you want to catch a flight after your group, that is fine too. This number I called from is my cell, so you can call or text me here when you have an answer. Thank you again. William will be thrilled, and I am excited to meet you too. Goodbye for now," Bill said as he hung up.

Brody chuckled to himself as he laid on his bed and texted Matty to let him know what had happened.

Brody drove to the Stewart's house for family dinner and planned to tell them the exciting news. He saw Daniel and Kate getting out of their car at the same time, so he waved to them.

"Hey, Brody, where's your friend?" Kate asked as they walked into the house.

"He went back home yesterday morning. I'm assuming he and Amber are on their honeymoon now," Brody said.

Kate gasped. "His what? I didn't know he was engaged."

"He just got engaged yesterday," Brody told her as they walked toward the kitchen.

Daniel chuckled. "And they are already married? Did they get married in the same day?" Brody nodded. "Oh wow, they sure move fast," Daniel said as his parents greeted them and had them sit down for dinner.

"We have some news," Kate said excitedly as she put food on her plate. "Daniel and I are getting married in December!"

"That's wonderful! What day?" Grace asked.

"The twenty-second," Daniel said proudly.

Grace sighed. "Aw, the day after your birthday...that's so sweet. We need to start planning then. It's only a few months away." Grace started making a list on her phone with Kate.

Brody could feel that nagging sadness creeping up as he again had his wound ripped open. He tried to smile. "Congratulations, guys. I'm glad you were able to come up with a date."

There was a momentary pause and then Brody spoke once more, hoping that sharing his news would get the focus off of the lovey-lovey stuff again. "So something exciting happened to me last night before bed."

"Oh yeah?" Heath asked. The ladies stopped what they were doing and turned to look at Brody.

"Someone from an addiction center in Idaho called and wants me to share my testimony at their Sunday service this weekend. I leave tomorrow afternoon," Brody said.

"That's wonderful, Brody. What a great opportunity!" Grace exclaimed.

"That's awesome! Good for you, Brody. I'm sure you'll encourage many hearts," Kate chimed in.

"Yeah, good job, Brody," Daniel added, patting him on the back.

Heath started to get teary eyed as he smiled at Brody. "Vanessa would be so proud of you right now, and I am so proud of you too."

Brody started to get choked up, so he deflected with a joke. "Well, my news isn't as exciting as a wedding."

"No, yours is better," Daniel said with a chuckle.

"Well, since we are starting to talk about news, the worship team at church wants to make a worship album," Heath told them. Everyone smiled.

"Really?" Brody asked.

"Yeah, it's been on my mind for a while now, and when I talked to the worship team about it, they thought it was a great idea. What do you all think?" Heath asked.

"Do it!" they said in unison.

"All right then, Brody, you want to produce it for us?" Heath asked with a smile.

Brody looked genuinely stunned by the offer; he had never thought about producing music for someone other than himself. "Yes, that would be awesome!"

"Great, I will talk to the team about when they are able to start, and then we can see if it fits with your schedule," Heath said.

"This is so awesome! I can't wait to hear it," Kate exclaimed.

Chapter Twenty-Nine

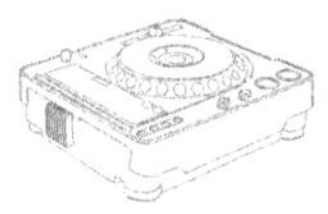

BRODY STEPPED OUTSIDE THE airport doors and saw a man about fifty-two years old, a woman who was probably the same age, and a preteen standing near a beat-up truck. The man was holding a sign that read *Brody Maddox*.

"Hi, Brody. I'm Bill. Nice to meet you in person. This is my youngest son, Max, and my wife, Claire," Bill said, shaking Brody's hand. Brody waved to everyone as they piled into the truck.

"Sorry William wasn't here. He had to work today at the center, but he will be home around three o'clock," Bill said as he drove away.

"How was your flight?" Claire asked from the back seat.

"It was great. I managed to nap the whole time," Brody told them.

"So I told the residents at the addiction center about your upcoming visit. To say that everyone is excited to hear you speak would be an understatement," Bill said with a grin.

"That sounds great, but I am nervous. I have never done something like this before," Brody confessed.

"Yeah, but aren't you a world-famous DJ? I'm sure you've

performed in lots of different places and in front of lots of people," Max chimed in, not looking up from his cell phone game he was playing.

"That's true, but this is different. My music is usually doing the talking for me," Brody explained.

"I'm sure you will do great," Claire encouraged him.

They pulled into a long driveway leading to a farmhouse. Brody was impressed by its size. They got out of the truck, and Bill took Brody on a tour of the farm while Max and his mother went inside to make lunch.

"Thank you again for doing this. Some of the people at our center have really been struggling with their addictions lately, and William really felt that you coming and speaking life to them could be just what they need from God to help them find true freedom. You are the first guest speaker we have had, you know," Bill said, leaning against a fence and watching his horses graze.

Brody laughed nervously.

"No pressure, huh?" Bill smiled. "Just be yourself, be honest, and let God lead."

William burst into the house a little after three with a huge grin and wide eyes. "Where is he?" His mom chuckled and pointed to the backyard, where Max and Brody were jumping on the trampoline. William raced to the backyard like a child.

"Hey, William, how was work?" his father asked, hugging him as he started back toward the house from the chicken coop.

William looked past him as he answered, "I'm great, Dad. Work was good. I think my group made a breakthrough today."

Bill chuckled and motioned for his son to go see Brody, and William jogged toward the trampoline. Brody saw William approaching and got off, huffing, puffing, and sweating.

"DJ Maddox in the flesh—such an honor!" William exclaimed, shaking his hand vehemently.

Brody tried to catch his breath before speaking. "Actually, I'm the one who's honored. It's wonderful to meet a true fan who stuck by me even through my tough times and transition. I'm very grateful to you, William, really."

William chuckled. "Thanks. I am so glad you are going to speak at the center. The morale there has been low, and I think this is just the pick-me-up they need to get back on track. Would you please sign the posters I have in my room?"

Brody nodded. "Yeah, sure, I would be glad to." He turned to look at Max. "Thanks for the workout, Max. I think I will be sore for days." Max laughed at Brody and kept bouncing higher and higher as William and Brody walked to the house.

William opened the door to his bedroom, and Brody was instantly transported to his former life. He chuckled in disbelief. "Wow, you have every poster from every festival I was ever at since the beginning of my career."

"Yeah, I collected them. I wasn't old enough to go to many of them, but I still listened to your music. It really got me through tough times in high school and college. I did manage to go to four concerts of yours when I was in college though," William told him as he handed Brody a sharpie.

Brody started toward the first poster and signed it, looking at it with a smile and remembering how nervous he was at this event. It was his first big break, the one that launched his career. As he traveled through time signing his posters, he smiled fondly, got choked up, and chuckled too at some of the memories.

As he signed the last one, he looked at William. "This was the last concert I did before I ran away to Hampton Beach. So many memories..." He handed William the pen.

"What happened there?" William asked.

Brody sighed. "It wasn't the show necessarily. It was a culmination of emotions being stifled that made me run away that day."

"I went through depression as a teenager," William replied. "I didn't have friends, so I was alone a lot. People made fun of me because I believed in Jesus. I didn't eat for a while because of the depression and lost a lot of weight. My parents were worried about me, so they took me to a Christian counselor. By senior year I was feeling better, and that is when I knew I wanted to be a counselor myself. I chose addiction counseling because I know it is a real need in the world today," William explained.

Brody smiled. "Thank you for confiding in me about your situation. I'm glad you are in a good place now. Depression is truly something scary that sometimes gets pushed under the radar." William nodded in agreement as they headed into the living room.

Brody spent Saturday helping the family with their farm chores, and then Sunday everyone piled into Bill's truck and headed to the addiction center. Brody felt his stomach churning with nerves as they pulled into the parking lot and got out of the car. He had spent many hours the night before praying for God's wisdom on what to say today, but as much as he felt confident that God wanted him to just share his life story, he was still nervous.

They walked inside and were greeted by some of the staff. Bill showed Brody to the small auditorium, where the addicts were currently waiting for him. Clare, Max, William, and Brody sat down in the back of the room. Everyone sang a few worship songs first, and then Bill started to introduce their guest. Brody walked onto the stage holding his Bible and grinning.

After Brody was finished speaking, he received a standing ovation and was approached by several addicts who wanted to encourage him with how he had impacted their lives. Some announced they were finally ready for lasting change, while others were still not there yet. Brody also took the time to pray with them. He was encouraged in his faith by the time he left the auditorium.

Brody flew back Monday morning and went straight home to take a nap before his shift at the diner that evening. He was exhausted but still on fire about what had happened over the weekend. He couldn't believe the rush of emotions that had come over him while he spoke. He loved it and was excited for another opportunity to speak. Two hours into his nap, someone knocked at his front door. He reluctantly got up and saw Michael and Amber standing there.

"Hey guys, what are you doing here? I thought for sure you would be on a honeymoon or something," Brody said, yawning.

"Yeah, we are going on a honeymoon in a few days, but we had some things to do first. Did we wake you?" Michael asked.

"I just got home from the airport not long ago. I was napping before my shift at the diner," Brody told them.

"Oh, I'm sorry we woke you. Where were you traveling from?" Amber asked, hugging Brody.

"I was in Idaho, at an addiction center. I was sharing my testimony there." Brody told them, yawning again.

Michael smiled. "My man, a motivational speaker now. Awesome!" Brody snickered. "So we came by to tell you some news, but we can always go to your work and tell you then. Text me the address where you work, and we will meet up with you then. Go get some sleep," Michael said, watching Brody yawning again.

Brody nodded. "Okay, I will. See you guys." They left, and Brody barely made it to his bed before falling asleep again.

Brody was busy cleaning a couple tables when Amber and Michael showed up. They waved to him and sat in a nearby booth.

"Hey, guys, I'm going to take my break soon. Did you want to order before I do that?" Brody asked.

"I will just take a plate of fries please." Amber said.

"May I have a grilled cheese?" Michael asked.

Brody nodded and headed behind the counter to tell the cook the order, and then he clocked out. He sat down at their table. "So what's up, guys?"

"We're moving here. We have been talking and praying about the idea, and we both feel like God wants us here. We aren't sure why yet, but we want to be obedient," Michael explained excitedly.

"We looked at a few houses today and put in an offer on one we really liked. We're waiting to hear back if they accepted it," Amber added.

Just then the cook rang a bell to let them know their order was ready. Brody got up and grabbed the three plates off the counter and took them back to the table with him. Brody grinned. "This is great news! I'm excited to have you two so close."

"I want to go to your addiction group too. When is it again?" Michael asked, taking a bite of his sandwich.

"Fridays at seven," Brody answered.

"Awesome. I haven't wanted to smoke anything since Amber kicked me out, but I will go at least once to see what you do there," Michael told him.

"Well, I would be happy to have you join us, even if it is only one time," Brody said. They ate silently for a few minutes.

"What is it like working in a diner, Brody? I can't imagine working a normal job after having the career you did," Amber said with a smile.

Brody chuckled. "It wasn't easy at first, but I needed to work. I needed something to keep me out of my head while I was grieving for Vanessa. Now I just love working here. It's laidback, and the people I work with are great and flexible too."

"That's great to hear. I'm glad you have something productive to do," Amber said in response.

They finished eating, and then Brody got up to go back to work. "Guys, if you are able to, I am heading over to the Stewart's in an hour. Do you want to meet me there and say hello? I know they would like to see you again, Michael, and they would like to meet you too, Amber. I'm going by to tell them how my trip went."

"Yeah, we will head over there. Just give me the address and what time we should be there," Michael said as they shook hands and left the diner.

Brody pulled into the Stewart's driveway, and Michael pulled in right after. They walked up to the house. "Hey, Brody. Hello again, Michael," Kate said, hugging Brody.

"Hi, Kate, let me introduce you to my wife. This is Amber." Michael introduced the girls. They shook hands just as Daniel was coming toward them. "Former supermodel Amber Friedrich? Way to go, Michael!" Daniel chimed in, shaking their hands. "Sorry, we haven't met yet. I'm Daniel."

Michael smiled. "Oh, you're Vanessa's brother, right? Nice to meet you. And yes, I did get lucky to land such a wonderful girl." Amber blushed.

They started toward the living room where Heath was sitting on the couch next to Grace, engrossed in a cooking show.

"Oh, Brody is here, dear," Grace said, turning the TV off. They stood up and hugged Brody, shook hands with Michael, and introduced themselves to Amber.

"You wouldn't happen to be Heath Stewart from Jealous Creatures, would you?" Amber asked.

Heath chuckled. "Yes, I am."

Amber giggled. "My mom was a huge fan. In fact, you were her favorite band member."

"Well, thank you for the compliment," Heath said.

Toward the end of the night, Brody, Heath, and Michael were sitting together chatting on the couch. Daniel had headed home, and Grace had gone to sleep. Kate and Amber were chatting about many different things, from careers to childhood and their faith.

"We should get a mani-pedi together after I move here," Amber suggested excitedly.

Kate's eyes widened. "Yes, that would be fun. I have never done that before."

"You and Vanessa never did that together?" Amber asked. Kate frowned. "I'm sorry. I shouldn't have asked. That was probably insensitive of me," Amber apologized.

"No, it's fine. I love talking about Vanessa. When I think of her, I have happy memories, but one thing I do regret about her passing is that I never did things like that with her. She always wanted me to go to a spa with her, but I am not really into that, so I always put her off until later. I didn't think I would never have the chance to do that with her," Kate explained, choking up.

Amber put her arm around Kate and hugged her tightly. "We will make it a spa day in remembrance of Vanessa."

Kate wiped her eyes. "Sounds good. I can't wait. When are you moving here?" Kate asked.

"I don't know. we need to hear back about the house we put an offer in for. It has been torture for me to wait. It's such a cute house. You want to see pictures?" Amber asked, pulling her phone out.

The next morning Brody received a phone call from Matty asking if they could meet up for breakfast to discuss something. Brody tried the whole ride to figure out what on earth he wanted to talk about. He walked into the small cafe and saw Matty sitting at a table near the window. He waved and walked over.

"Hey, Brody, have a seat," Matty said. Brody sat down nervously. "I wanted to talk to you about the recovery group," Matty started.

Brody chuckled. "Have I been doing a good job of co-leading? Am I getting fired?"

Matty smiled. "You have been doing a phenomenal job. That is why I wanted to talk to you. I want you to take over for me as the leader of the group. I already talked it over with Pastor Brian, and he thinks it's a great idea too."

"You're leaving the group? Why?" Brody asked, confused.

"My wife and I feel God calling us to go back to our hometown of Chicago and start a group out there," Matty explained.

Brody looked sad. "Oh, I see. It's a good reason for leaving, I suppose. When am I supposed to take over?"

"First meeting in October."

Brody's eyes widened. "Seriously? Wow..."

Matty touched Brody's shoulder. "I know this is

overwhelming, but you can do it. I believe I am leaving this group in great hands. I have been praying for a long time that God would bring me a good replacement when my time is up here, and yesterday I felt God telling me it was time to tell you to take over."

Brody smirked. "Yesterday, huh?"

Matty nodded. "Yeah. Why?"

Brody snickered. "Yesterday was my one-year anniversary of being a believer."

Matty smiled; "Then it is very fitting."

Brody nodded. "Well, I will sure miss you. So will everyone in the group. I think I already know who would be good to help me with co-leading."

Matty smiled. "You are going to say Anne, right?" Brody nodded. "I agree. She would be perfect. I will run it by Pastor Brian and then call Anne to tell her the news," Matty told him.

They shook hands before Matty left, Brody's heart racing and his head swimming with anxious thoughts as he went to order something to eat.

Chapter Thirty

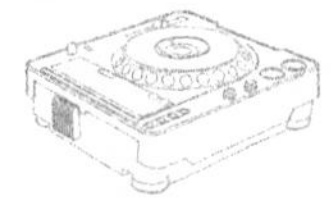

BRODY WENT HOME AFTER his meeting with Matty and sat on his couch to pray through his anxious feelings. As soon as he started to pray, there was a knock at his door.

He opened it and saw Michael and Amber standing there with smiles. "We got the house!"

Brody chuckled. "Congratulations, guys!"

"Come with us. We want to show you the place!" Michael said, grabbing Brody and ushering him out the door and to his car.

They pulled up to a two-story house with wood siding and white trim. They got out of the car and stared at the house. The yard was filled with various types of flowers.

"Don't you just love it!" Amber exclaimed.

"It looks great! I am so happy for you guys. When will you move in?" Brody asked.

"We need to go fill out all the paperwork now and get the keys, and then we can head home to pack up the house," Michael said.

Brody frowned. "What about your honeymoon?"

"We pushed it back. We wanted to move in first, so we are

going to pack everything and then have movers do the rest. We will come home from our honeymoon and just have to unpack," Amber explained.

Brody turned to look at the house again and chuckled before punching Michael in the shoulder playfully. "Amber is turning you into a proper family man, huh?"

Amber giggled, and Michael snickered. "Yeah, it's pretty crazy, right? Who would have guessed I would have the white picket fence life?"

"Not me, that's for sure." Amber chimed in, kissing his cheek. Michael kissed her back.

"That's how I know there is a God," Brody joked.

"That's funny, but on a serious note, God really is good giving me a second chance at life," Michael started, taking Amber's hand in his and squeezing it. "I couldn't be happier. God really is a miracle worker. I am glad he chose to work in my life. He truly is my savior."

"Well, I am very happy for you two in this new chapter of your life, and I am glad that we are going to be living so close to each other too," Brody said as they got back in the car.

Brody parked his car in the empty church parking lot and sighed heavily, nervously drumming his fingers on the steering wheel and staring at the church building. His thoughts were all over the place. He wondered how the group would fare now that Matty was gone. The group seemed receptive of the new leaders, but he wondered if the people would stick around and trust their recovery to Brody and Anne.

He was startled out of his thoughts by someone knocking on his driver's side window. He turned and saw Anne standing there with a smile, waving at him. He got out of the car and waved. "Hey, Anne."

"Hey, Brody," Anne said, sounding as nervous as Brody felt.

"You're nervous too, huh?" Brody asked. She simply nodded, and he took her hands in his. "Maybe we should pray before we go set up." Anne nodded in agreement. They closed their eyes and both said a prayer.

After praying, they went into the building and set up for the group. People started to come in shortly after. Michael was one of the last ones to arrive before the meeting started. Brody waved as Michael sat down next to Anne.

Once it was seven, Brody quieted the room down and started the group. "Good evening, everyone. I am so glad you chose to come. That is a big step. Why don't we do introductions now; I see a few new faces here. Go ahead and tell us your name, what your addiction is, and how long you have been sober. If you aren't sober yet, that is okay too. This is a safe space. Everything said here is confidential, just between the group," Brody said, clearing his throat. "I will start. My name is Brody, and I was an alcoholic. I have been sober for a year. Praise God!"

Next it was Anne's turn. She took a deep breath and then spoke in her soft voice. "My name is Anne, and I'm recovering from a food addiction. I weighed two hundred pounds a couple years ago, and for a woman of my petite size, that was very unhealthy. After having my daughter, I knew I needed to get healthy, so I joined and gym and lost sixty pounds." Everyone cheered.

Michael was next. He looked nervous to speak, which Brody thought was funny since he had never known Michael to be shy about anything.

"Hi, I'm Michael. I'm an old friend of Brody's. I just became a believer not too long ago. I have an addiction to pot, although I haven't had any desire to have it since I became a believer." Everyone clapped for Michael.

Once everyone else was done introducing themselves, Brody spoke again. "Thank you all for your honesty. As I said earlier, this is a place that is meant to be a safe space. Okay, let's pray and then start today's lesson on letting go of past hurts."

"That is an amazing group, and you and Anne did a great job running it," Michael encouraged as he and Brody walked out the door.

Brody locked the building and shrugged. "Yeah, it went better than I expected."

"I think a few of our friends back home could benefit from this addiction group, right?" Michael asked after some time.

Brody snickered. "Yeah, I agree, but as Vanessa used to tell me, they have to want it for themselves. We can't make them change."

"Very true. I guess we need to pray for them. It will happen in time. Maybe the three of us can take a trip to New York soon and start witnessing to them. What do you think?" Michael asked, a glimmer in his eyes.

Brody chuckled and nodded. "Yeah, that could be a great idea. So how was the honeymoon? I hope you didn't have to cut it short to be here for tonight's group."

"Nah, it's all good. Amber had made plans with Kate today anyway, something about a spa trip."

Brody chuckled. "I didn't think Kate was into things like that. I'm glad they are getting along though." Michael nodded in agreement. "Are you all moved in? Did you need help unpacking? I'm off work tomorrow. I don't mind helping if you need it," Brody offered.

"Sure, that would be great. We have too much junk to unpack," Michael said with a chuckle.

The rest of October was frustrating for Brody. Kate was now in full bride mode, and all she did was talk about wedding stuff. As part of the wedding party, he was already dealing with more romantic things than he wanted to. The more involved he got with the planning, the more his heart hurt and his angst grew. His annoyed feelings were escalated when Heath mentioned that they had to push back the start date for working on the worship album project because a few members had gotten sick.

Brody was counting on that project to keep his mind busy. Instead, he chose to grab a few extra shifts at work to fill that void. When he wasn't working, he was in his studio, mixing. He wasn't creating any new music; he was just trying to keep his mind busy. He wanted this wedding to be over so he could move on from all the romance; then maybe his heart would finally stop aching.

By November, Brody was over the wedding stuff and decided to spend Thanksgiving with his family in Colorado. Going on this trip proved to be a good move. It gave him a chance to tell his parents about Michael and Amber, which they couldn't believe, and it also gave him a chance to share how he got to preach at an addiction center, which impressed even them. When he came back in December, he was feeling a little more relaxed, which was a good thing because he needed to put his groomsman hat back on.

The evening after Brody got home from his trip, Michael and Amber had him over for dinner. Brody knocked on the door, and Amber opened it quickly. She hugged him and walked him inside. "How was your trip?" she asked as Michael came downstairs.

"It was really good. I needed it. My folks say hello to you

two," Brody added as he sat down at the kitchen table with Michael and Amber. Michael said a prayer, and then they started to eat.

"I have some news," Brody started, a huge grin on his face. His friends waited in anticipation. "I think I'm going to turn my studio into a music production company. It's something I have been thinking about for months now. I've been praying about it constantly too, and I finally felt God telling me something about it during this last trip. I think he is saying it's time," Brody said excitedly.

Michael and Amber looked at each other awkwardly. "Oh yeah?" Amber inquired softly.

"Yeah. So what do you guys think?" Brody asked.

Amber slurped up a spaghetti noodle and looked at Michael. He looked apprehensive as he opened his mouth. Brody furrowed his brow. "What's going on? I thought you would be happy for me. You have always been supportive of my music. What's changed?"

Michael looked at Amber gravely.

"I guess this is the time you have been praying for, Michael. Tell him," Amber said sadly.

Michael sighed heavily. "Yeah, okay."

Brody looked at his friends completely confused and disheartened.

Michael looked up at Brody. "I wanted to buy the studio from you." Brody looked surprised as Michael continued. "Since the day I asked God into my heart, I felt God wanted me to do something new with my career, but I wasn't quite sure what or of the timing. Well, while we were on our honeymoon, I felt God telling me it was time. Amber and I prayed hard about it, and a few days ago, I felt God tell me that I was supposed to ask you for your studio."

Brody was taken aback. "You're telling me God wants you to steal my studio out from under me?"

Michael chuckled awkwardly. "I wouldn't put it that way. I was going to turn it into a music production studio."

Brody gasped. "That's what I just said I wanted to do with it! You can't steal my idea!"

Michael looked at Amber and then back at Brody. "I'm not stealing any ideas, Brody. I'm just following God's calling on my life. I have been praying and reading the Bible, seeking God's will for my life, and I strongly feel this is what he wants from me," Michael explained.

"So what do you feel he is telling you to do with your production company?" Brody asked in a rude tone.

"I'm going to start making spoken word and also will still make techno but for Jesus this time. I want to witness to people about Christ, and this is a perfect way to do it. I want to give people a place to come where they can share their craft and witness to people," Michael said passionately.

Amber looked at him admiringly while Brody sat there brooding.

The room was quiet for some time as Brody processed what he wanted to say. He felt anger, frustration, hurt, and bitterness. Finally he pounded his fist on the table, shocking his friends as he glared at them. "Why couldn't God give me this dream? Why did he give it to you? You're older, and before long, you will to too old to do this stuff! I should be the one to give God glory in this way. I was the one who introduced you to Christ, and I am the one who suffered when I lost Vanessa! Don't you think I deserve this?" Brody started to tear up.

Michael grimaced. "Brody, do you hear what you are saying right now? Does any of it sound like something God would be proud of? You say you want to do something for his glory, but you are trying to say you are better than me because you came to Christ first and suffered more than I have. Is that how Jesus talks? I have read the gospels, and I am sure he says the first shall be last and the last shall be first. You don't sound very humble right now."

Brody's eyes flared. "How dare you say that! I have been praying for God to use me, and he hasn't! And you have been a believer for two minutes, and he uses you to steal my studio that I put my heart and soul into! How is this fair?"

Amber gasped. "How can you say he isn't using you? You are leading an addiction group—that's a big deal! You are pretty much following in Vanessa's footsteps, which I am sure she is very proud of you for. If you can't see that what you do every Friday is a big part of God's kingdom, then you are just blind."

Brody didn't respond.

"I agree. This doesn't seem fair or make sense to me either. You and I both love music so much. It would make sense for us to go into business together, which is something I prayed about a lot too, but God strongly said it has to be *only* me doing this project," Michael told him.

Brody chortled and leaned back in his chair, folding his arms and scowling.

Michael was frustrated now but kept his composure. "Brody, I told you that I have been doing nothing but seeking God since I became a believer. I have laid down my life and given God control of every part. I mean, just look at me. I'm running the risk of losing my best friend over this, but I don't care when I think about losing God if I choose you over him. Have you truly been seeking God's will for your life, or have you been trying to get him to bend to your will?"

The room went silent again. Brody sat in his chair,

brooding again, but this time it was because he knew that Michael was right in calling him out—but he wasn't going to let him know that.

He glared at Michael. "What did God tell you specifically when you asked about me being a part of the project?"

Michael looked at Amber. She smiled softly and motioned for him to tell Brody. Michael looked at him and said with all seriousness, "He won't need it anymore."

Brody's eyes widened in disbelief. "What does that mean? Am I supposed to die? What kind of statement is that?" He jumped to his feet. "You know what? Fine! If God wants to take me home to him, then okay! At least I will be with Vanessa. I don't think I could live in a world where music is not a part of my life!" Brody raced out the door, slamming it shut.

Amber hugged Michael as he started to cry.

Brody rapped at the door to the Stewart's house, and Grace answered the door. "Brody, oh my goodness, have you been crying? What's wrong? Come inside. I'll get Heath." She rushed upstairs, and she and Heath came down quickly. Heath motioned for Brody to sit on the couch.

"Why is God doing this to me? What have I done to deserve such harsh treatment?" Brody asked angrily. Heath was about to respond, but Brody spoke again. "Michael wants to take the studio from me. He said he heard from God that he is supposed to start his own production company."

"Maybe you can do it together," Grace piped up.

Brody wiped his eyes and shook his head vehemently before speaking scornfully. "No, we can't. He heard from God that it was supposed to be only him. I asked why, and he said God told him specifically that I wouldn't need it anymore. What does that even mean?"

Brody wiped more tears from his eyes. "I'm not ready to die, Heath! As much as I would like to see Vanessa again, I am not done here on this earth; I can feel it. So why is he doing this to me?"

Grace wrapped her arms around Brody and started to pray silently while the men talked.

"Slow down, Brody. I know how that phrase sounds, but it doesn't have to mean you are going to die. It could just mean that you are finished with that chapter of your life and moving on to something else," Heath suggested.

"Like what? I'm just a musician who serves at church. What else do I have to offer the world if I can't make music anymore?" Brody growled.

"Who said you can't make music anymore?" Heath asked.

"God—he is taking it away from me. He wants me to sell my studio," Brody whined.

"That doesn't mean you can't make music anymore. God hasn't taken away your talent to make music, has he? He is just telling you it is no longer the big piece of your life. He has other plans for you," Heath encouraged.

"What does he want me to do? He won't tell me anything," Brody shouted in so much frustration that the Stewarts could tell this had been bothering him for a very long time.

"You have to ask yourself a very important question, Brody. If you are getting this worked up over a studio, who were you making music for, yourself or God? If you are making music for God, then you won't feel dependent on having a studio. You will know that you can write lyrics anywhere. The studio was just a vessel where you felt more comfortable. You can praise God anywhere, Brody," Grace said.

Brody didn't speak for a long time. Finally, he sighed heavily. "You're right. I'm acting foolish. I'm sorry, guys. I'm just so frustrated. Michael hasn't been a believer for a long time and God already tells him in great detail what he wants him to do through him, but I have been a believer for a year and feel useless for the kingdom."

Grace gasped unexpectedly and stared at Brody with a motherly look. "Brody Maddox, bite your tongue!"

The guys were taken aback. She had never used his last name before, or if she did, it wasn't to scold him.

She continued, "Nothing done for the kingdom of God is useless! That is a lie from the pit of hell, so don't listen to it! You do such amazing work in that addiction group, and you are now the leader. What do you mean you aren't being used for God's kingdom? Your vision is narrow. You have only been thinking about music because that is where *you* want to be called to, but I think God is taking you in a completely different direction. Instead of kicking and screaming over it like a little child, just say yes to it."

She looked at Brody and started to get teary eyed as she touched his face softly. "I was a successful dance instructor with my own dance studio when I met Heath. Once we got married and had kids, I felt God calling me to sell the studio and raise my children. I fought it for a year, and then I finally surrendered and did what he asked. I felt so much better, and being a stay-at-home mom was so rewarding for me. When the kids went to school, I started to work where I work now. Sometimes our plans for our life change, and we need to accept that and work with God to better our lives. He is making you an offer right now, sweetie. Take it and watch what he does with your obedience."

Brody wrapped his arms around her and hugged her tightly, crying on her shoulder for a long time. Heath smiled, proud of his wife for sharing a very vulnerable part of her life. "I love you guys. Thank you," Brody said after some time through his tears.

Brody left the Stewart's house feeling like an awful friend for the way he had attacked Michael. He wanted desperately to go and apologize to him, but he couldn't face him right now, not tonight. He knew he needed to approach God at his throne first and make things right with him before he could make things right with anyone else.

He went to his prayer closet, turned the lights off, and mourned what he had thought his life would be. After some time, he changed tacks, got on his knees, and asked God to forgive him for how he had acted today and for trying to get God to bend to his own will rather than the other way around. After he finished making amends with God, he held his hands out, palms facing up, and really surrendered to God's will—completely this time.

Chapter Thirty-One

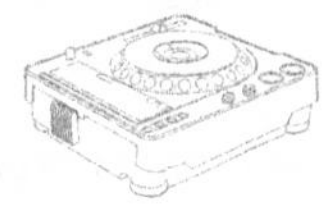

BRODY COULD BARELY SLEEP that night. All he wanted to do was make things right with Michael. Once the sun came up, he shot out of bed and raced over there. He knocked on the door and waited impatiently for someone to open the door. After several minutes, Michael opened it. As soon as he saw Michael's tired face, Brody reached out and hugged him tightly.

"I am so sorry for how I acted yesterday. I was awful to you and so full of pride. Please forgive me. I'm in a better place now."

Michael chuckled as he ushered Brody into the house. The guys sat at the kitchen table and started to talk.

"I will give you the studio—no charge," Brody told him after a while.

"No, man, I can't take it from you. That wouldn't be right," Michael protested respectfully.

Brody's eyes lit up. "It won't be completely free to you; I have a request. In exchange for the studio, I would like two things: One, make sure that you produce the worship album for Heath as your first project, and two, I want you to be my producer for any future music I make."

Michael grinned and shook hands with Brody. "Deal."

Brody smiled. It was bittersweet for him to hand over the keys to the studio to Michael as he left, but he felt good knowing he was being obedient.

From that point on, Michael started the process of starting his business. It tore Brody's heart out watching the changes happening, so he focused more on his relationship with Christ, working, and pouring his whole heart into serving on the audio production team on Sundays and the addiction group he led on Fridays. He also was reluctantly involved in wedding planning, which was thankfully almost finished since the wedding was coming up in a matter of weeks.

The studio was finished two days before Daniel's bachelor party, and Michael texted Brody and told him he wanted his opinion. Brody was excited and a little sad to oblige his friend's request. He pulled up to the studio and saw a sign had been put up: *Second Chances Music Production Company.* Brody smiled warmly; he loved the name.

He got out of the car and saw Michael standing there, grinning from ear to ear. "Hi, Brody. Come in, and I'll show you around," Michael said, ushering Brody inside. Brody looked around, and much to his delight, the place hadn't changed much inside, except Michael's music accolades and some credentials on the walls. He had also put up a big metal cross, and a Matthew 28:18–20 was written on the wall next to it: *Jesus came and told his disciples, I have been given all authority in heaven and on earth. Therefore, go and make disciples of all nations, baptizing them in the name of the*

Father, and the Son and the Holy Spirit. Teach these new disciples to obey all the commands I have given you. And be sure of this: I am with you always, even to the end of the age.

Brody smiled warmly. He didn't feel as saddened by this visit as he had anticipated; in fact, he felt a sense of freedom knowing this place was in good hands now. Seeing this verse confirmed it.

"What do you think? Is the name a good one? I sure hope so. I'm already getting the trademark on it," Michael asked finally.

Brody patted him on the shoulder. "It's a great name...very inspiring. How did you come up with it?"

"I was in the middle of a Bible study I was doing one night, and it hit me. I was given a second chance at living...why not give the same thing to someone else? I want everyone who comes here to know that God is in this place and can give anyone a second chance. Do you think you feel that when you are in here?"

Brody looked around once more and then looked at Michael teary eyed. "Yes, I think you achieved your goal. This is why God wanted you to have the studio and not me; I understand now. I wanted it so bad, but I didn't have my *why* for setting it up, not like you do. God picked the right man for this job, and I couldn't be happier that I get a front row seat to see you doing this."

"Thanks, Brody. That means so much to me...really. I appreciate your support," Michael said, choking up.

They started out the door. "So I talked to Heath yesterday. The worship team is coming by this week to start working on the album. Did you want to sit in on it with me so we can work together?" Michael asked.

Brody chuckled and opened his car door. "Nope.

Remember, you told me that God said I wasn't supposed to be involved at all, and I believe that is a good call. I am fine watching you do it alone. Good luck. I'm sure it will be great." Michael nodded and got into his car.

"Can you believe it? Your wedding is only a few days away. How are you feeling?" Brody asked as he drove himself and Daniel to the bachelor party.

Daniel sighed, "I'm excited but also anxious. Not about marrying her. Kate keeps saying she hopes nothing goes wrong, and now she has me thinking worst-case scenarios."

Brody chuckled. "I'm sure everything will be okay, but even if it isn't, we will make it the greatest day for you two."

"Did I get a chance to tell you where I'm taking Kate for the honeymoon? I can't remember who I've told already," Daniel said with a chuckle as Brody pulled into a parking lot.

"Yeah, you said you're going to Switzerland, right?" Brody recalled, turning the car off and getting out.

Daniel nodded. "Yeah, two weeks in Switzerland will be amazing. I could use the time off. I've been working like crazy to save up for this trip. I'm sorry. I bet this romantic junk is bothering you again, huh?"

Brody smiled slightly. "No, it's not bothering me. I have spent the last several days reevaluating myself, and I realized I was placing things that mattered to me on a higher pedestal than God—my love for Vanessa being one of those things. I have repented for that, and now I'm not affected like I was before. Don't get me wrong. It still hurts like heck whenever I think about how we don't get to share life together, but it doesn't consume me anymore."

"That's good to hear. I hated seeing you so torn up over

losing my sister," he said as they approached the other guys waiting for them in front of the paintball arena.

The wedding was beautiful and flawless. After the ceremony, everyone headed to the reception. There was plenty of dancing, laughter, and funny best man and maid of honor speeches. They cut the cake, and Kate threw her bouquet.

After a few hours, Daniel and Kate made their way to all the guests and said their goodbyes. Brody helped Heath and Grace clean up until Michael and Amber stopped him to say their goodbyes before heading home.

Pastor Brian approached Brody on his way toward the door. "Hey, Brody, can you please come by my office tomorrow? I need to talk to you about something important."

"Sure. Am I in trouble?" Brody asked with a chuckle.

Pastor Brian belly laughed, which, for some reason, didn't reassure Brody. "Everything's fine. Just meet me at my office at nine tomorrow morning if that works for you," he responded.

Brody nodded and swallowed a lump in his throat as he went back to work, mulling over all the different things that Pastor Brian could want to talk to him about.

The next morning, Brody pulled into the church parking lot and took a deep breath as he stepped out of the car. He approached the church offices, his heart pounding. He knocked at Pastor Brian's door after some hesitation and waited anxiously.

"Hey, Brody. Have a seat," Pastor Brian said as he opened the door. Brody sat down quietly in a chair across from his desk, and Pastor Brian looked at him with a grin. "Why do you look so tense? This is a good meeting. Don't worry."

Brody sighed with relief, and Pastor Brian continued, "I have been observing you for the past two months since you took over the addiction group."

Brody swallowed a lump in his throat.

Pastor Brian said, "I have enjoyed seeing the new ideas you implemented into the group, like the worship night once a month and the outreach idea you want to do every three months. You have some good leadership ideas, Brody."

"Thanks, sir. That means a lot to me. I am always trying to give God my best," Brody said.

Pastor Brian smiled warmly. "I know, and that is why I believe God wants you to be the addiction ministry pastor here."

Brody looked genuinely surprised by the suggestion. "The what?"

"Ever since Matty took over being the leader of the addiction group, I have thought about having an addiction ministry pastor. I prayed about it with Matty and alone too—often. I was thinking he could do it, but then he hit me with the bombshell that he was moving away, so I assumed God was pointing me in another direction. I kept praying, and your name popped into my head. I was prayerful about it and observed you. I agree with God's choice, and I think you would be great in the job."

Brody couldn't believe his ears. "Me? Really?"

Pastor Brian smirked. "Of course. Why not you? You have been free from alcohol for a year, and you have shown wonderful leadership, as I said, not only in the group but also every Sunday as you serve on the audio production team. You have also shown me in your everyday life that God comes first. As you just said, you want to give God your best in everything you do. I know you will do the very best job you can, for God's glory."

Brody's thoughts were running wild. Out of all the scenarios he had come up with for what Pastor Brian wanted to talk about, him becoming a pastor wasn't one of them.

"What would be the job description for an addiction ministry pastor?" Brody asked finally.

Pastor Brian cleared his throat. "As the addiction pastor, I would expect you to oversee everything in your department, which, right now, only means your group and the leadership team you have in charge of it. I was also chatting with Sheila in our counseling department, and she thinks it would be a great idea if you were to get a degree in addiction counseling so you could take that caseload from her."

Brody chuckled in disbelief. "Me doing addiction counseling?"

Pastor Brian nodded. "Sheila said she would have you do your hands-on training with her, and there are many online schools that you could look into for the schooling. The process takes years, so it's not like you would start counseling right this second. As lead pastor, Amy and I do marriage counseling, and Sheila does family counseling. It would be good if our addiction pastor could do addiction counseling specifically."

Brody chuckled anxiously but didn't speak.

"I know you are hesitant, but I feel strongly God is calling you to this position, Brody," Pastor Brian assured him.

Brody ran his hands through his hair and looked away momentarily. "I am okay leading a small group, but I don't think I could lead like this, like you do. It seems like it is too much responsibility for me. I don't think I'm ready."

"God doesn't call the equipped, Brody, but he equips those he calls into action. He is calling you into action, and he won't leave you high and dry," Pastor Brian reassured him. Brody was quiet for a while, thinking.

"So what do you say? Are you ready to step into this role?" Pastor Brian asked after some time.

Brody ran his hands through his hair again and swallowed

a lump in his throat. "Can I have a day to think and pray about it?"

"Of course. I know this is a lot for you to process. Get back to me on Sunday. I would like to let the congregation know about this decision before January since that is when I want you to start. It would be good for you to enroll in an online school as soon as possible too," Pastor Brian said, shaking hands with Brody as if he had already accepted the position. "Don't let fear or the idea that you aren't ready keep you from something great God wants to do in and through you, Brody. We will talk later."

Brody left Pastor Brian's office and walked over to Heath's office. He knocked on the door and waited for him to answer. Heath opened the door with a smile. "Hey, Brody. So how did it go?"

"Did you know what he wanted to talk to me about?" Brody asked, coming into the office.

"No. What did he want to talk about?"

Brody slumped into a chair. "He wants me to be the addiction ministry pastor. Can you believe that? How could someone like me become a pastor of anything?" Brody said in wonder.

"Brody, don't forget the story of Saul becoming Paul. If God can redeem him, don't you think he can redeem you?" Heath asked seriously. Brody shrugged.

"Don't disqualify yourself because of your past—that is the very reason I can see you being the pastor of this particular ministry. You have come such a long way, Brody. You have a great testimony of deliverance and healing. Why wouldn't you make a great pastor? Your heart and passion for God and helping people is evident in everything you do," Heath encouraged him.

Brody smiled. "I'm nervous about the idea though. It sounds

like a lot of responsibility. He wants me to learn to do addiction counseling too. I can't be a counselor."

"Vanessa thought the same thing when she first started her training. I will tell you what I told her: God will hold you and help you through. If he has placed this in your heart, he won't let you go." Heath told him. Brody could feel himself choking up as he smiled.

"It is a lot of responsibility being a pastor, but that is why you get people to surround you who are like-minded and will see your vision too; then it becomes a little easier to handle the load. It's a lot of work, but it's fun work because it's for the Lord."

"I just don't know how to wrap my head around all this. I never thought of going to college for a degree nor did I ever imagine I would become a pastor," Brody confessed.

Heath smiled. "Brody, if God is calling you to this position, don't you think God will work everything out for you? Your God is big enough, right?"

Brody nodded.

"Okay then. If he is big enough, then why should you worry about it all? He will work everything out for you. just take that step of faith he is asking of you, and trust him for the rest. I never saw myself as a pastor either. When I left the music business, I wanted to stay out of music forever, but here I am, leading worship weekly and making another album. Sometimes God takes us from where we thought he wanted us to places we never thought we would go, but that is the beauty of God. Everything works out for his good to those who love him and are called according to His purpose for them, according to Romans 8:28."

Brody looked at Heath with wide eyes. "I don't want to abandon music. It is still a part of me. I still love creating it, but since I surrendered to God's will and gave Michael my studio, it's like a weight has been lifted off my shoulders."

Heath smiled. "Maybe he was releasing you from a burden that was holding you back from your full potential. You can still make music, but it just isn't your career anymore. And you are finally in a place where you are okay with that. This is how God works. He doesn't just thrust things onto us; he will sow seeds and make them grow until we are finally ready to listen and obey. That is why I love God. He is patient with us."

Brody smiled nervously. "Thanks for the talk, Heath." Brody stood to his feet and left for the beach to think and pray.

The Christmas service was almost over. Heath and the worship team finished their last song as Pastor Brian walked onto the stage with a huge grin. Brody watched him from behind the stage curtain where he was standing and waited until it was time to come on stage, his stomach in knots and his palms sweaty. Pastor Brian started by telling the church about upcoming announcements, and then it was time.

"One last announcement for you all, and then I will let you go so you can celebrate our Savior's birth. Brody, will you come out here please?" Pastor Brian said, watching Brody hesitantly walk onto the stage. Brody stood next to him and smiled nervously. Pastor Brian put his arm around him.

"For all of you who may not know this young man, this is Brody Maddox. He was a world-famous DJ before he came to be a believer and came to our church a little over a year ago. He has been the leader for our addiction group for the past three months. Before that, he was the co-leader and a member of the group. For anyone who knows him, you have seen the change from the first day you met him until now, and for those who don't know him, I encourage you to get to know him and ask him about his story; it is pretty epic. Anyway, I am pleased to announce that starting in January, Brody will become our addiction ministry pastor. Please join me now as we pray for him at the beginning of this new journey and congratulate him too."

Epilogue

Brody looked at his watch and saw that it was time to leave the office for the day. He said goodbye to the church secretary and Cole, the youth pastor, before heading out to his car. Once he got in his car, he sighed heavily, stroking his clean-shaven face before he drove away.

He pulled up to the cemetery and hesitated before exiting his car, grabbing the bouquet of flowers he had in his passenger seat. He held them in his trembling hands as he walked toward the path leading to Vanessa's gravesite. He knelt and laid the flowers down quietly and then touched the tombstone.

"Sorry I haven't come to see you since the day before Daniel and Kate's wedding. Life has been rather busy for me since then. I know, I know…it's a lame excuse," Brody said, chuckling. "So let me fill you in on the last three years. Daniel and Kate bought a house last week, next door to your parents. They plan to start a family soon. Daniel also got a new client, and with this job, it's supposed to give them some financial freedom for a while." Brody cleared his throat.

"Your parents bought a house in Hawaii that we can all use whenever we want. They are spending the winter out there;

they left yesterday actually. They needed this vacation. The worship team released a third album, and they are becoming a big deal on the music scene." Brody smiled warmly.

"So my friends Michael and Amber are doing well too. Amber is four months pregnant, and they got a golden retriever puppy, Freddy. Michael has had a lot of success in his new job too; he has several clients now, not counting our worship team. He has been producing his spoken word in a podcast now too. He has received a lot of praise for that." Brody chuckled, remembering something else.

"Michael, Amber, and I went back home to visit some old friends after the New Year. They couldn't believe the transformation stories we had. They were really impressed, and a few even wanted to know more about Jesus. We took some of them with us to a church there. My former agent, Chuck, came here to visit me last year. He had recently gotten married and it didn't work out, so he was feeling low. He gave his heart to Christ while he was out here and decided to stay. He is currently working for Michael's company as a talent scout."

Brody paused for a while before he spoke again. "I'm sure you want to hear about me now. Well, I haven't been making music...haven't had time lately. I'm a pastor now. I run the addiction ministry at our church—can you believe it? Me? It's been two years, and I am still in awe that I am a pastor. God is so good." Brody looked away briefly and then turned back to the tombstone.

"I added a second story to my house because friends and past acquaintances have been coming by now and then, looking to talk to me or get help detoxing and finding freedom from their pain and suffering. I have realized my calling now. God wants me to help people find the freedom that you introduced me to when you sacrificed your time to help me overcome my addiction. I wanted to create a space in my home for that. So far I have had six friends, not counting Chuck, who have come by to stay with me and detox or just to rest and get clarity. Only one, aside from Chuck, has accepted Christ though, but I rejoice in that. I am sure you are thrilled to hear I am practically following in your footsteps. It's kind of funny to me that our careers are so similar."

Brody paused again, stroked his chin and frowning suddenly. "I still love you, Vanessa. Not a day goes by that I don't think about you. That is why this next thing I have to say is going to be so hard for me to tell you."

He took a deep, labored breath and wiped away a few tears, wringing his hands. "I finally shaved my stubble after all these years. I never shaved before because it made me think of you and how you liked it. Well, I have been shaving it recently because I met someone five months ago. Her name is Nora Madison." Brody wiped the tears from his eyes again.

"It just sort of happened. I wasn't expecting to have feelings for her. In fact, when I did, I felt guilty, like I was cheating on you or something. I prayed and fasted for a month that God would let me know if it was okay to pursue Nora. I felt his blessing, so I finally asked her out. I hope I also have your blessing too, Vanessa, and that my moving on doesn't make you think I don't care about you anymore. You know I do and always will." Brody wiped away some more tears.

"She knows about you. She feels honored to be the first person I have fallen for since you. You are a tough act to follow, in my opinion, but Nora is a pretty great girl. She is a preschool teacher. She loves kids, animals, and the beach, and of course she loves God. She serves in the audio production team at our church; that's how I met her," Brody said with a sad chuckle, feeling again like he was betraying Vanessa.

"I hope I have your blessing, Vanessa. I remember in your letter you told me to stay open to new things, and love was included in that, so I believe you are happy for me now. I have to go. Nora and I are going out on a date in a few hours." He stood to his feet and looked at her tombstone, his lip trembling. "Goodbye, Vanessa. I love you more than you will ever know." Brody blew a kiss, waved, and walked back to his car.

The End

CPSIA information can be obtained
at www.ICGtesting.com
Printed in the USA
BVHW080928010622
638531BV00001B/34

9 780578 348162